A BOY'S GUIDE TO TRACK AND FIELD

Sabrina Broadbent's debut novel, *Descent*, won the WH Smith Raw Talent Award. She lives in London and works part-time as an English teacher. *A Boy's Guide to Track and Field* is her second novel.

ALSO BY SABRINA BROADBENT

Descent

SABRINA BROADBENT

A Boy's Guide to Track and Field

VINTAGE BOOKS
London

Published by Vintage 2007

2 4 6 8 10 9 7 5 3 1

First published in Great Britain in 2006 by
Chatto & Windus
Random House, 20 Vauxhall Bridge Road,
London SW1V 2SA

www.vintage-books.co.uk

Addresses for companies within The Random House Group Limited
can be found at: www.randomhouse.co.uk/offices.htm

The Random House Group Limited Reg. No. 954009

A CIP catalogue record for this book
is available from the British Library

ISBN 9780099464532

The Random House Group Limited makes every effort to ensure that
the papers used in its books are made from trees that have been
legally sourced from well-managed and credibly certified forests. Our
paper procurement policy can be found at:
www.randomhouse.co.uk/paper.htm

Mixed Sources
Product group from well-managed
forests and other controlled sources
www.fsc.org Cert no. TT-COC-2139
© 1996 Forest Stewardship Council
FSC

Typeset by SX Composing DTP, Rayleigh, Essex
Printed in the UK by CPI Bookmarque, Croydon, CR0 4TD

For Ruth and Anna

'Mind the gap'
The London Underground

Walthamstow Central

LEM WOKE WITH a sudden snort. Eyes tight against the day, he closed his mouth and swallowed. The change in his domestic circumstances was recent enough to require him to check his bearings on waking. He noted the fungal fug of the duvet and the cool wet patch on the pillow by his lips. He could hear birdsong, not traffic, and the floor beneath his bed was still. Oh, yes. He was twenty-five and alone in the bed he had grown up in.

As endings go, it had been almost too painless, which is to say that he wasn't lying there feeling sorry for himself. Not at all. On the contrary, he liked the narrow confines of the familiar sagging bed. It made him feel secure and earthed as if he were in a cot, or a coffin. Not that the end with Dawn had made him feel like dying. It wasn't that kind of ending. If anything it was a bit of an anticlimax. He had got home from work just before Christmas and found her taking the baubles and tinsel off the tree. He watched her put them into a Miss Selfridge bag and then add the heart-shaped cushion she had given him on Valentine's Day, while he stood inside the open doorway, the muffled roar of the North Circular the only sound. When a short man with a grey ponytail came out of the bathroom, Dawn looked up and saw Lem. She grimaced, squeezing one eye shut like she did when the bathwater was too hot. 'This is Ian,' she said. Ian had looked at the beige carpet by Lem's foot, said, 'All right?' and then picked up the television and left. Dawn got to her feet, brushing the fluff from her too-tight black cords. 'Don't try and stop me,' she said, and so he moved out of her way saying, 'What about the fish tank?' And that had been that. After she had gone he sat in the bedroom doorway where he could feel the traffic vibrating through his feet and haunches. He watched the tropical fish do their drift and turn and waited for the sensation of missing or loss. No feeling answering either description arrived.

Lem stretched both feet so that they extended beyond the end of the bed. In the cherry tree outside the window, the blackbird was whooping it up like there was no tomorrow, which these days could not be entirely ruled out. Every one hundred and eighty seconds the planes came out of the eastern sky, silencing the bird. They moaned off-key as they followed the Thames upstream: Tower Bridge, the Houses of Parliament, Battersea, Kew. In these summer months the volume of planes increased from one every five minutes to one every three. Each year, according to his father, Todd, the quota rose so that the planes began earlier and earlier. Todd had even commissioned a television documentary about it '*because*,' he said, striding about in his Wandsworth back garden, 'there was never any consultation about quotas and soon, *soon* there will be planes flying all of the time, all through the night'.

The most pressing fact that needed to be established before Lem could open his eyes was whether today was a work day. With difficulty he summoned up the days of the week in his mind's eye, rolling them out like a length of striped cloth: red Wednesday, blue Thursday, green Friday. Today was yellow and a Tuesday which meant that the long haul had only just begun. He kept his eyes shut against the glare of the white blinds. *Blinds* was the word for them, he thought. There had been some perfectly good maroon curtains up at the window when he was growing up, the sort that disguised the hour so you could sleep till midday. His mother, Fay, had taken them down and now they lay folded in a bulky heap in one corner of the room. He took a deep breath and felt the familiar jangle of want and reserve, for his room these days was suffused with the smell of her painting. He could detect the woody oil of linseed, the damp clay scents that oozed from twisted tubes, and pervading everything was the keen edge of white spirit. His bedroom had become Fay's studio as soon as he had left home. That first Christmas he had come back from the snowy wastes of the University of Central Lancashire to find that she had decamped from the garden shed and installed her studio in his room. 'Your bed's still up there, Lemuel,' she had said. 'Don't call me Lemuel,' he had muttered. 'It only makes sense space-wise, Lem,' said Alan, his stepfather. And once, Fay had said, 'You could always sleep in the shed.'

When he was little, he used to stand in the doorway of that shed watching her while she worked among the stacked canvases. Against the doorjamb he had marked his height and put the date, the lines wobbly because writing on wood was tricky and none of Fay's pencils were sharp. She would stand with her back to the light, her mouth a thin line, and he sensed he was trespassing. Her studio was a place she did not wish to share, a private world that he both resented because it took her away from him and longed for because he could see that it was a kind of freedom.

The only painting his father did was the walls of whatever new flat or house he had been exiled to by his marital misdemeanours. Todd would be halfway up a stepladder slapping some optimistic colour onto the wall and say, 'Well, what do you think, Lem? It's called Eggnog.'

The planes were actually arriving less than every three minutes, Lem realised. He counted the seconds until the distant rumble of the next one. 'The crazy thing is,' Todd would boom, standing on his decking staring up at the night sky, 'the crazy thing *is* that most of those planes are carrying mangetout from Zimbloodybabwe, lamb chops from New bloody Zealand and corn-fed chicken from Alabloodybama. 'Tell me,' he shouted, 'tell me if I'm missing the logic in all that somehow.'

Lem turned onto his side, away from the window, and smiled into his pillow. Lying there, his too-long body over-flowing at the edges of his bed, he tried to remember what colour Todd's sitting-room wall was these days, but all that surfaced was a shopping trip with Todd one day, years ago on one of his Sunday visits. They were in B&Q and he had looked up at the metal girders of the roof and felt tiny inside the vast hangar of the building. He could remember the sour plastic of the trolley handle on his tongue, his fists against each cheek as he waited anxiously for the reappearance of Todd's familiar form: a rugby player's body going to fat, short arms and a barrel chest. With rising panic he had straightened up and scanned the aisle for the neatly cut sandy hair and the livid complexion, but saw only exhausted strangers hesitating by shelves of stuff to do-it-yourself with. Todd was gone, was nowhere to be seen, and all at once loss, sudden and intimate, had jumped Lem like a mugger so that the fear escaped from his throat.

Then he saw him, striding down the aisle, tossing a can of paint from one hand to the other and shouting, 'You can't find an assistant for love nor—' and the crack as the tin hit the floor, bounced twice and splattered its contents at Todd's feet. Todd with Hint of Apple streaking his jeans, fingers hitching up the fabric at the tops of his legs, slowly lifting one dripping foot and shouting, 'Oh, you find that funny, do you, Lem? Do you realise how much these jeans cost? They're Ralph bloody Lauren, you know!'

Lem rolled onto his back and kicked the duvet off one leg. He ran his palm downwards over bone and skin: ribs, flank, loin, rump, and he thought of Dean and the butcher's shop, then of Dawn's body asleep now in an unknown bed. He tugged gently at his penis, but it was sleepy or sad or something and lay soft and quiet, curled in its nest of bronze

4

hair. Some mornings he would wake, his groin damp and hot having dreamt of her or him or a stranger, and with a sluice of confused happiness he would recall an image of his body against another, breath in his ear. He let his hand lie cupped between his legs and thought how it had been a while since he'd had one of those dreams.

He could hear Alan downstairs, going through the familiar morning routine. The snap of the letter box as he pulled the newspaper from it; the squeal of the tap before the gush of water into the kettle; some throat clearing, three coughs and then the whistle that said, I do this because I want to, followed by the clink clink of two cups on the counter. The end of this phrase was signalled by the scrape of chair legs on stone and a pause while he read the football pages. Lem thought about going down to join him as he sometimes did, because it wasn't that he didn't like Alan. He knew Alan had tried to be a good stepfather to him, it was just that Lem saw that he did it out of love for Fay, and between Alan and himself there had always been either a false bonhomie or an awkward gutter of disconnection. Still, he might go down and have one of their football conversations. One of the ones where they did a slow waltz around the sports pages of the *Daily Mirror* open on the kitchen table.

He had been a bit of a disappointment to Alan football-wise, he knew that. He had always avoided the scream and shove of the football games at primary school, preferring to sit alone digging up dust with a stick or wandering the perimeter fence until the bell. Sometimes he and Alan had tried though, in the early days when Lem was about eight. Alan would kick a ball around with him in the small back garden at Church Path using the apple tree and the garden fork as goalposts. But the violent smack of the ball against Lem's face or the impossible dance of Alan's tackling feet would make him give up and retreat to the television or the chestnut tree in the churchyard. Too late he had realised that football was the only way he was going to manage to interact with Alan or anyone else while he was growing up. No one, certainly not Fay, had thought to warn him that from the age of five a sexual apartheid came into operation in schools so that if he didn't Boy-it he would be completely alone, a gender refugee.

He had been fifteen when he lay down on this very bed with an ache like hunger and worked out that it had been four years since anyone at all had touched him.

Flexing his toes, he put his hands behind his head and wondered whether the stiffness in his knee and ankle wasn't the beginning of something fluey. A day at home might do him good. The trouble was, a day at home was always tempting because it was a particularly comfortable home. Forty-seven Church Path, Walthamstow, was cosy, full of light and mysteriously scented. He had no idea how such a place was created, and on twenty grand a year he didn't think he was likely to find out although he sensed it was not just about money. Of course, anywhere would have been an improvement on Kinloss Court, the flat on the North Circular that he had abandoned after Dawn left. Towards the end, Dawn's temper had become something he hadn't looked forward to going home to because by then, for reasons Lem never fully understood, Dawn had adopted anger as a lifestyle choice and, at twenty-eight, she was well pissed off with just about everything, it got on her tits big time and at the end of the day, with all due respect, she just wasn't going to take any more from him or anyone else because to be honest, to be perfectly honest, if you didn't respect yourself, well, no one else was going to.

Nevertheless, Dawn had not tried to destroy him when she left, and while he could see that all endings involve an element of the sacrificial, it wasn't as though she had actually wielded the knife in the way that Todd had with Helena, Wife Number 3. Blissfully unaware of the symbolism, as Fay was fond of saying, Todd had given Helena breast and eye surgery for her forty-third birthday. She was still bound and ice-packed the day he drove the au pair to the airport and didn't come back for a week. But then Helena was a nightmare, everyone said so, not just Todd; too rich, too American, too marish, although, as Fay was also fond of saying, she was sure that Todd got the nights and the mares he deserved.

Lem heard Fay and Alan preparing to leave for work. At the slam of the front door he opened his eyes like racing traps and jackknifed himself out of bed. He pulled on the clothes that lay in a heap on the floor – jogging pants, T-shirt, socks – and went down to the kitchen. Opening the fridge, he stared at its contents, lifting slices of salami into his mouth as he did so. It was practically empty these days, he thought, sniffing the open jar of capers while wondering about the pickled herrings. He gave up on the fridge and tried the bread bin where he found half a loaf of Alan's homemade bread. Chewing a piece off one dry end of it, he looked out at the front garden.

The garden was Alan's pride and joy and at this time of year you could see why. It was full of veering bees and darting birds and these summer mornings, the leaves and blooms cast pulsing shadows onto the stone flags of the kitchen floor. The kettle was still warm. He flicked the switch and pulled at a leaf of the potted basil while he waited. Crushing it between his fingers, he held it beneath his nose the way he had seen Alan do a thousand times and, at the release of the sweet heat of it, its burst of memory and promise, his throat tightened and tears brimmed so that he had to blink them away as he poured boiling water over a teabag. He wasn't at all sure he had it in him to go to work today. Perhaps he should spend the morning here, organise his room a bit, then maybe he could go over and paint the kitchen at Kinloss Court. They were never going to get a decent price for that flat unless they did it up. 'In need of some redecoration,' was what the estate agent said. The trouble was, if he did that, he would have to encounter the mess that Steve had made since installing himself there. He knew he couldn't face that either and so he spooned four sugars into his tea, took several scalding gulps, smeared jam over a slab of bread, crammed it into his mouth and took the stairs two at a time to the bathroom.

When he came back down he had on one of Alan's clean shirts that he had found on a hanger on the back of the bathroom door. It was chocolate brown with small lime-green and orange cylinders on it and the funkiness appealed to him – that and the freshly laundered smell of it. He shrugged on Todd's old denim jacket, picked up his backpack full of maths books, opened the front door and slammed it shut behind him.

The slam had a malevolent timbre and a finality about it that made him hesitate on the doorstep before he realised that it was the slam that doors make when they have just locked you out of the house. He let go of the doorknob. It didn't matter, Fay and Alan would be back at some point this evening and if they weren't, there were always the spare keys in the water-butt beneath the wisteria. The water-butt ploy was Fay's idea. Burglars, she claimed, were like cats – lazy, emotionally void and afraid of water. They'd no more put their hand in a water-butt than drop their litter in a litter bin.

Lem left the house, turned right into Church Path and walked towards the town centre to join the wordless procession of commuters heading towards Walthamstow Central. 'Two years,' he said aloud, pulling at privet leaves as he walked. Two years as a main-scale teacher of mathematics, fifteen Tube stops away in south London. It was doing his head in. What had he been thinking of? For one thing, he was beginning to find the noise intolerable. Most of the kids had their voices turned up to high volume, and words gushed from them like blood from a wound; nothing Lem could do would staunch the flow, so that some days he was already hyperventilating by break time. The kids were all right really, that's what the other staff said. But there were days when it didn't seem like that to Lem. As far as he was concerned, at school it was open season on teachers all the year round, at least in his classes it felt like that. Even the last lesson yesterday with the sixth form; he had spent some time explaining Arithmetic in a Finite Field, but every time he turned back to the class from writing on the board, he was sure there was one fewer of them than before. Try as he might, he could never catch them at it and before long the lesson degenerated into a Grandmother's Footsteps farce. He attempted to sum up by dictating the definition from the book – 'While each finite field is itself not infinite, there are an infinite number of different finite fields' – a task which took longer than it should have because the two girls at the back whose names he could never remember kept giggling and asking him, 'Did you say "finite" there or "infinite"?' so that he had to look down and read carefully and repeatedly from the page and, by the time he had finished, he looked up and only Hanif and Sebastian were left. Why Dawn could get so hot under the collar about fox hunting and laboratory guinea pigs and not give a damn about cruelty to teachers was beyond him. Two years. When he thought of people like Devora, who'd been at it for twenty-five, he felt sick. It was like a prison sentence. No one in their right mind would put themselves through that for a lifetime. But Devora liked it. She seemed to have an easier time than most and whenever he asked her what the secret was she just said, 'Talk to them, they're human beings, Lem, like you and me.'

Cheered by the thought of Devora, Lem jogged down the steps to the station and checked the time, 7.35. Out on the platform the southbound train was waiting with its doors open and he leapt into the nearest carriage.

It was that leap that gave him the feeling that something was amiss. He sank into a seat and thought about it. Was it that his wallet had been lifted from his pocket? With high-pitched warning beeps, the doors closed and Lem patted the top pockets of his jacket. No, the wallet was there. The train pulled smoothly away from the platform, entered the tunnel and picked up speed. Was it that he had left his bag containing a set of unmarked maths books on the front doorstep? No, his bulging backpack sat between his feet. He shifted deeper into his seat, stared at the couple standing by the doors who were entwined in a drowsy embrace and then with a prod of alarm he understood. He had forgotten to put any underpants on.

For a panicked moment he considered pulling the emergency stop lever, but that was out of the question. It would mean drawing attention to himself in the most hideous manner and besides, he'd have to walk right up to the conjoined couple by the door, reach above them and invade their hallowed aura of lust. He studied them in snatched surreptitious glances that he disguised with eye rubbing and head scratching. There were some days, like this one, he thought, when his hair seemed to defy gravity and grow upwards like a yard brush. He batted it down as best he could and regretted not checking his face in the mirror before he left. He avoided mirrors, apart from when he shaved, which he managed to keep to alternate weekdays and not at all at weekends.

The lovers looked as though they had dressed hurriedly. She had on a thin summer skirt that fell like liquid over her hips and thighs and a loose sleeveless blouse. With her right arm lifted around the back of her partner's head, the curve of her breast was just visible. The man's hands rested lightly on each of her buttocks, his head inclined towards hers, sometimes kissing, but mostly just staring, drinking in her gaze and secret smile. They swayed to the rhythm of the train like drunken dancers and Lem noticed that it didn't look like she had any underwear on either, but that was par for the course given that she was probably at the beginning of a love affair. Going without knickers was all part of the process. They had probably spontaneously combusted or dissolved the night before, he thought, and while he quite enjoyed going without underwear at weekends, he knew that he could not survive the day in front of Emily, Kemal, Theo, Nokia and Jason like this. The possible consequences were just too horrible to think about.

The train slowed to a halt in the tunnel. Faint whisperings and chatterings leaked from people's ears and he cursed himself for forgetting his iPod yet again. The delay caused people to raise their eyes and look about them, skirting around the engrossed couple. He scanned the adverts on the opposite wall for whiter teeth and better career prospects, he glanced at the Anti-Terrorism Hotline's Do You Know These Men? poster, he studied his fingers and then curled the bitten nails into his palms, he considered his trainers and wondered whether he shouldn't have put on fresh socks. As the waiting continued, the smouldering couple provoked small grimaces of melancholy and shame among the other passengers.

The train began to move again and Lem planned an emergency purchase of underwear. If he got out at Euston he could run up the escalator and buy a pair of boxer shorts from one of the shops on the mainline concourse. If he was quick, he could be back on the Tube in ten minutes and just about arrive at work on time. His eyes flicked to the woman's bottom again and he dropped his gaze to check his crotch. He clasped his hands in a casual way so that they hung loosely between his thighs. That, though, might be drawing attention to the area, so he tried sitting with his knees together instead of wide apart in his customary fashion. Knees together required enormous concentration and muscular strength and he wondered how on earth women managed it. In the end he let his hands rest together in his lap like a couple of landed fish. He thought of Devora's hands, which he had spent a good deal of his time looking at while she talked. She had strong, long hands which were tanned and lined. He thought her oblong nails beautiful and wondered about the silver rings she wore. They were hands that were beginning to show their age, but they looked like they could hold on, come what may.

As the train approached the next station, Lem thought of the early weeks of his relationship with Dawn that first hot summer when they'd been like that couple by the door themselves, like newborn babies discovering the world through their mouths and fingers. He used to like to stroke Dawn's bare shin while they watched the tennis on the television. He could remember his fascination with the precision of each pale hair's direction and the way that it made her leg look rather finny, which provoked in him an irrepressible urge to lick it. At times like those he would get the love-bomb feeling low in his belly and, if he held still and attended to it, it would spread in a warm fan up his body and end just behind his Adam's apple.

He rubbed his face with his hand and thought he could detect the faint aroma of hamster or dishcloth. Perhaps the rest of him smelt that way too, he thought, sitting upright in his seat and running his hands through his hair. He clutched the armrests. He needed to get a grip. He sniffed at his fingers again and thought of Devora who, far from smelling of hamster, smelt like the palm of his mother's hand. Heaven.

2

Blackhorse Road

DEVORA HAD BEEN internet dating for a while now. She told Lem that she had started off by giving her real age, forty-nine, but that she'd had no replies at all to that and so her god-daughter had said, 'Take a few years off, no one will be any the wiser and besides, all women do, Madonna's been forty-two since 2001.' Though no sooner had she said that than Madonna started being forty-six and so she'd started putting forty-three, which her god-daughter had said was quite a sexy age these days – what with Madonna and everything. 'These days,' she said, 'it is a known fact that even women of forty-six still have sex, look at Cherie Blair and anyway it's only a number, men really have no idea.'

Lem watched the couple get back into the rhythm of the train as it left the station, the man leaning back with a lazy smile as the woman's pelvis gently battered his. They started kissing again and he tried to work out when exactly the kissing had stopped with Dawn. It was some time before the actual sex had stopped, he seemed to remember. Devora was big on kissing. It was her favourite thing, she told him, and sadly neglected in these days of targets, league tables, toned bodies and orgasms. Not that she had anything against some of these, she added, it's just they had rather crowded everything else out. Lem had listened for a year in five-, ten- and fifteen-minute instalments to Devora's tale of marital collapse and determined dating. They gravitated towards one another in the staffroom at break and lunchtimes. No preamble was needed, she just picked up where she'd left off, like knitting. He enjoyed listening to Devora. Devora was better than a novel, not that he'd ever read one, but if her stories were anything like the novels his mother read, then he could understand why Fay spent so much time on the sofa with a book.

Devora's stories had begun in earnest a year ago when most of the departments had been given an office rather than a cupboard. The offices had proper desks and swivel chairs, the desks had drawers with locks on them and some teachers even had keys to these locks. Each office had a computer in it as well although the network was inoperable, but there was one day when Lem had managed to get onto the internet and found a lesson plan on Angles, Parallels and Polygons and if the printer had worked he could probably have used it to teach with. There were shelves in the offices where teachers could put books, and some offices, not maths, had a sink. Design and Technology had a fridge. Science had a micro-wave. It was all something of a revolution in terms of working conditions, but as a result the heart had gone out of the staffroom and, despite the fact that Mrs Lusher and her tea trolley still appeared at break times, it had become a ghost staffroom where only the lost and the homeless wandered – new people, supply teachers or those seeking refuge from their departments.

Being history, Devora didn't have a department office and so the staffroom was where she and Lem liked to sit, especially when the atmosphere in the maths office became too oppressive. The oppression there was tangible, like an incubus, and began to feed on you as soon as you walked through the door. It emanated from the new hermetically sealed and impossible-to-open double-glazing that had been installed; it came from the private contractor's new central-heating system, which could not be switched off or even turned down; it came from Ameena, the head of maths, and her unshakeable belief in the Chaos Theory whereby towering stacks of paper and folders accumulated on and in any available space so that the office was not a place of calm and order but an actual 3D interactive model of the toppling education system. When Lem tried to shift some of the piles from his desk, Ameena would announce, 'Don't fight it, everything turns to entropy', and Lem would want to point out that the second law of thermodynamics is a tendency, you can't use it to describe chaotic events, but there would be no point in telling Ameena that. It was not possible to tell Ameena she was wrong. And where maths was concerned, well, they never discussed maths at all. In addition to the lack of oxygen and the mess, nothing was private in the maths office. Quite often, for want of some other place to put them, naughty students were dumped in there and they would swing sullenly on someone's office chair and glower, bad-vibing for all they were worth. Even when the office was clear of miscreants, all conversations had to be held in public, whether they were about cervical smears, phone calls from the bank manager or what exactly was in a person's sandwich that day and why. So most days, until recently, Devora and Lem had gravitated to their spot in the staffroom and once they were settled behind the grotesque, antique cheese plant with their buns and coffees, Devora would take a large bite, brush the crumbs off her hands, lean forward so that Lem had to lean forward too and then she'd begin.

'The first time, I got several messages every day. Most of them sounded so charming, interesting and fascinated to get to know me that I thought, crikey, it can only be a matter of weeks before I'm sending out wedding invites, I'd better finalise the divorce quick. But after a while I realised that internet dating is like supermarket shopping. The sheer abundance appeals to our baser instincts; greed and anxiety. You barge round popping God knows what into your basket and then never get round to eating the stuff because you didn't really want it in the first place. It all looks too good to be true and that's because it is. So after a few false starts I became more selective. I'd limit myself to one or two and concentrate on them.'

Lem chewed and nodded and sipped his searing Nescafé. Devora's hair was auburn that day and seemed shorter than before, blunt-cut just at her jaw. Sexy. He waited until she dropped her eyes to pick up her cup before he took another look at the curved cleft of her breasts framed by the brown V-necked cardigan. Pearly buttons secured it most of the way up except for the top one, which kept coming undone so that Lem saw it wasn't a button at all, but a popper. Every now and then Devora would bury two fingers between her breasts and press hard so that Lem could just hear the pop.

'Well, sometimes the messages in themselves were very exciting. You can shortlist quite effectively just from how they write. Any that talked about what they like about a "lady" I deleted straight away and any that did that ":)" thing. You know what I mean?' She drew a smiley face in the air. Lem looked blank. 'You know, a colon and a bracket. A semicolon and a bracket.' She sketched in the air again and he thought of Dean gesturing at him through the window of the butcher's shop while an elderly customer fumbled with her purse.

'Emoticons,' he said.

'Lexical halitosis, I call it. But anyway, with some of them, the mails were surprisingly good. An explosive mixture of the erotic and the intellectual as well as the just being attended to, you know? I hadn't expected that of emails, but I suppose we've overdosed on images these days, haven't we? We've seen it all. I mean, the other day I was channel surfing during the adverts and I saw an elephant giving birth, a woman having colonic irrigation and someone having their head chopped off. More information than I needed, I can tell you.'

He was watching the pulse in her throat and Devora stopped for a moment so that he looked away and worked out how old she was when he'd been born (twenty-four), and how old she'd be when he was her age (seventy-three), and wondered if perhaps this was the future, very old women with very young men, a sociological necessity caused by the harvesting of so many of the young women by older men such as Todd and Dawn's new man, Ian. Lem didn't think he would mind too much, although that was probably due to what Dawn called his dyslexic libido. Of course, men like Steve, who also taught maths and claimed to need several young women a week, would probably just die out.

'Then there are those with rather a redundancy of imagination and effort who can only manage to get one and a half lines up on the screen and expect you to agree to a date.' She stopped and drank some more coffee. 'Anyway, occasionally the mails fly back and forth very easily, just like talking really, and you agree to meet. You've told each other so much that by the time you get to the point of actually meeting you're both sort of primed and ready to go off.'

She looked at him and he concentrated on holding her gaze the way you are supposed to be able to do with another human, but which he always found almost impossible. Her eyes were moss green, flecked with brown and looking like this was hard, he thought as his mouth dried, because it was looking in, not at, and the conversation in her eyes seemed to be very different from the one coming from her lips, and he wondered if she was aware of the heavy thickening that was happening inside his trousers and then he worried that if the bell went he would not be able to stand up, but would have to wait until she had gone and risk being late for his lesson. But it was Devora who looked away, down at her hands, so that he enjoyed the small victory and studied her face critically. It was a face which, caught unawares, looked tired; the disappointed droop of the eyes and the downward turn of the mouth that would soon become permanent. Animated – which she could be when she talked – she looked quite different, even her skin. How that could be, Lem had no idea. It seemed to be something inside her.

He looked up to see Steve's face framed in one window of the staffroom doors. He was trying to scan the room without entering it and Lem shrank lower behind the foliage. When he looked again, to his relief, the windowpane was empty. Steve, who was on a mission to convert the world to a life of untrammelled sexual excess, owed Mrs Lusher too much tea money to risk coming in very often at break time.

Devora took another slurp of coffee, resting a moment in the comfort of the rising heat from the cup. The slurping was relatively new, Lem suspected. It seemed to be both a consolation and a pretence of not caring, yet was no doubt just one of the irritating things about Devora that helped send her husband in the direction of the younger, non-slurping women who glided in and out of the swishing lift doors at work. That was the worst of it, she had never tired of telling everyone, to have come across them in that way, in a place as public as his office lift. She had just dropped his anniversary present and fled. 'Ding, going down,' Steve had rasped into Lem's ear.

'But,' Devora continued, taking a deep breath in so that her breasts rose, 'the thing is, most of the time, the reality is a crushing disappointment. Most of the time all I could think of was that each one was such a stranger. It felt like arriving in a foreign country and there'd be no solid ground on which to base our conversation, not even "Do you come here often?" because you prayed that the answer to that was no. And somehow the thought of his unknown life billowing out behind him like old net curtains . . . well, in the dark nights of the soul, Lem, that would give me the willies.'

Lem began to laugh, but Devora wasn't smiling.

'You see, when you meet someone in the normal way, it may seem like an accident, but of course the chances of two people actually meeting are tiny and so the fact that they have, well, I'm sure there's some mathematical frisson or synergy or something that, you know, helps give the event a little energy and momentum. I mean talking to a total stranger for an entire evening. Have you any idea how long an evening can be under those circumstances, Lem?'

He shook his head, then nodded emphatically. He wanted to ask her the story behind the silver ring with the amber stone on her right hand. He wanted to kill the man from Orpington who had kissed her in the Little Chef car park.

'No, apart from the occasional one, like Philip, where there was definitely something there at the beginning, I just wonder why I am disturbing my bulblike existence. It is possible to live without love, without sex, you know, Lem. You just fold up and sit still in the cool dark of yourself. In many ways there's much to recommend it. Why allow yourself to be forked up, shaken out in the chilly air and deposited in someone's trug for who knows what kind of replanting . . .?' She swallowed some coffee. 'I'm going to stop that metaphor right now, but you know what I mean. You're in a bit of a bulblike state yourself, aren't you?'

Lem looked at the blind aerial roots of the cheese plant and said, 'I went fishing with Dean again on Sunday—' but he mistimed it and Devora was already back on her own track.

'Usually, I take myself off to the Ladies every fifteen minutes just to get away from them. I sit on the toilet and berate myself for not seeing that this one was a complete car wreck or a terminal bore or an alcoholic and I pray for the evening to be over.'

Lem counted the number of little green squares on Devora's check skirt. They were tiny, apart from where the fabric stretched across the top of her bare legs, where they became elongated into rectangles. There were forty-four across the part just above her knees and thirty-three across her thighs. The clock along the wall ticked one minute further towards the next lesson.

'And then, once in a while you do meet one who you think, well, OK, there might be a possibility here and so you meet up again, ignoring the small warning signs you got the first time you laid eyes on him. The warning signs are nearly always in the eyes, sometimes the voice and just occasionally in the trousers, choice of trousers, I mean, not literally in the trousers, although there too, obviously. The eyes are where you'll find signs of the tectonic shifts that have occurred far below the surface, you know, the emotional violence wreaked by the end of a marriage, the loss of a home, children . . . all that . . .'

The creases on Devora's heavy lids were smeared with rust-coloured shimmer and there were sooty spots where the mascara had dried on the skin not the lashes. Under the eyes the skin was pouchy and concealed with some sort of creamy stuff. Lem wondered about telling her to leave the creamy stuff off.

'It wasn't that I didn't want to see the signs, it was that if they were behaving as if nothing had happened, I began to understand that then there would be trouble. After a while I felt as though my opening gambit should be, Look, have you had your breakdown yet because if not I suggest you go away, have a really thorough and horrible one and then come back and we'll see.'

Her ears were small complicated whorls tipped with silver drops at the lobes, which trembled when she talked. Lem couldn't really understand why Devora should want the men in pieces rather than intact, but he decided not to ask. He wanted to brush some of the crumbs off the edge of her skirt. They touched sometimes, a little – the back of a hand, a palm on an arm – and he always noticed that Devora was hot. Not the way that Steve used the word, but hot hot. It felt as though there was something inside that was coming to the boil.

'But what no one tells you is that if you arrange to meet for a second time, that's as good as agreeing to marry them and if, after that, you don't want to see them again, you get a blizzard of vitriolic texts, emails and phone messages as though you're splitting up after a lifetime together. I don't get it, I really don't.'

Lem opened his mouth to speak, but Devora hurried on.

'Well, I suppose I do actually. They're raging against the black storm of loneliness. Suddenly you are the one who is consigning them to a solitary death, and my lord . . .'

She gulped down the remains of her coffee, mouth wide, throat open, leaving a glistening brown moustache on her upper lip.

'Mind you, that doesn't happen often. Most of the time, I see the look on their faces straight away as I say hello and they turn to look at me. It's soul-destroying, Lem, as a matter of fact. It says, Oh, but you're old.'

Lawrence, the deputy head, who wore a nothing-surprises-me-any-longer expression, pushed his head through the foliage and tapped Devora's shoulder so that she stopped and turned round to listen to him, her skirt riding up her right thigh where the flesh was pale and dimpled. Lawrence murmured something about the police, a court order, the mother on the warpath. Lem watched her hand stroking her throat and remembered resting his head in the reeds by the reservoir while he breathed in the honeyed heat of soil and sweat.

He had come home from that first fishing trip with Dean with his trainers soaked through. 'You ought to get yourself a decent pair of boots', Alan was always telling him. Alan never wore trainers. He wore lace-up boots that shone like conkers and stood in a neat pair by the front door. Inside the house he wore the grey felt slippers that Fay had bought him in Paris. 'Your mother's bit of rough,' Todd had once called Alan, sneering into his glass of wine. Lem had felt bad about not being able to join in, but they both knew Alan did not deserve a sneer. Lem had known it since that day when as a seven-year-old he had watched him lift the bonnet of a car, select a tool, bend inside and work methodically on the mysteries of the internal combustion engine. Alan smelt of oil and yeast and he understood how things worked. Alan could fix things as well as bake bread. As Lem watched Todd drain the rest of his glass he realised he didn't know Todd's smell at all.

The trouble with teaching, thought Lem, eyeing the man with the *Financial Times* to his right, was that he was an impostor. He couldn't fix anything and the teaching just wasn't happening. Like yesterday with Year 10, he was wrong-footed by three questions fired simultaneously from different corners of the room and he answered the one questioner that he should have ignored. Saskia normally slept through his lessons, but yesterday she had lifted her head and watched him as he went off-script and said how numbers are the language of nature, take Fibonacci's rabbits for example, and for that moment the room was still and he thought he had them, he had the whole class.

'Have you ever wondered,' he asked them, 'what rabbits in a field and a buttercup have in common?' He drew a cartoon rabbit on the board. It was looking directly at Jason. Jason's mouth fell open and his leg stopped jiggling. Perhaps it had something of the Watership Downs about it, but Osman and Kemal opened their maths books. 'This is university maths,' he assured them, not knowing whether it was or not, but feeling all at once tender towards them, for they were just children after all. Devora had told him that she knew for a fact that all but Kakeka and Salma in this class had been hit by their parents on a regular basis since they were toddlers. They told her all kinds of things. He wished Dawn or Fay or even Devora could see him now. Enthused, he turned back to the board and scribbled the word 'Fibonacci' and then the date, '1202'. He faced the class again and with a little swagger, announced, 'Fibonacci discovered the secret of the universe nearly a thousand years ago.' Kakeka bit her lip. He pointed at her. 'And we forgot it, Kakeka.' Salma's row and Kemal and Osman copied the name down, Emily searched her bag for a pen. Nokia walked in late and sat down quietly at the nearest table. His eyes skittered over Saskia. She was staring at him. 'Fibonacci wanted to investigate how fast rabbits in a field could breed in ideal circumstances.' He added another rabbit on the board.

Emily said, 'I've got a rabbit.'

Osman said, 'Shut up, man.'

Emily did the figure-of-eight sideways head shake (∞), which Ameena said was really an Asian gesture, and he had wanted to say how it was also the sign for infinity. 'Like, I'm bothered.'

Lem said, 'Rabbits can breed at one month of age. Pregnancy lasts one month. So . . .' he turned to the board and began a rabbit family tree with the Fibonacci series going down alongside it. 'You'd start with an empty field (0), then you put in a pair of newly born rabbits, one male and one female (1). Then one month later you'd still have only one pair, so, 0, 1, 1. Two months later, how many pairs?'

Jason's hand shot up. 'Two!'

'Brilliant, Jason, 0, 1, 1, 2. Two months after that, you'd have . . .'

Jason shouted, 'Three, Sir.'

'Correct, Jason.' He wrote 3. 'Now what Fibonacci wanted to know was how many pairs would there be in a year.' Quickly he scribbled the rabbits and the number sequence: 0, 1, 1, 2, 3, 5, 8, 13, 21 . . . saying, 'You see, it's not difficult because it's a sequence. Add the last two numbers to make the next.' He turned triumphantly to the class. 'What is really very weird though, is that this sequence occurs all the time in nature. A buttercup has five petals. Daisies have thirteen. Lilies have three.' The board was a field of daisies, buttercups and rabbits. Jason was busy drawing. Saskia was looking at Lem.

Kakeka, eyes wide, put her hand up and said, 'It's like in this book I'm reading, *The Da*—'

Saskia said, 'Did you catch any sleep last night, Sir?'

'No,' he said, taken aback. 'No. Why, do I look a bit

rough?' He always fell into the trap of trying to be her friend. She was slippery and clever.

'Yes, you do,' she said. 'And you're talking rubbish. Rabbits have loads of babies, not just two. And anyway, we did this in primary school.'

Then everyone laughed, Haaa, haaa, haaa and the lesson collapsed like a house of cards. He tried to get their attention again, but it was like trying to herd sheep, so he gave up and allowed the noise level to rise until the bell went. After a lesson like that he would stand in the emptied, littered room, his head vibrating, his mind stupid from lack of oxygen, and he would wonder why he didn't just walk out of the school gates and never come back. What good did he really think he was doing here? He might be able to explain a bit of maths to one of them possibly every now and then if they just happened to be interested, but quite frankly trying to inspire the whole class for an hour four times a week was a joke. The more he thought about it, the more absurd it was, the idea that he had some knowledge to impart. He didn't of course. The DfES told him exactly what to teach and how to teach it. He was a delivery boy who delivered the curriculum like a pizza, but without the perk of a Honda 50.

The one job that, to his surprise, he had really liked was in the butcher's shop with Dean that summer of his second year at university. O'Farrell and Son was on a busy street in Dagenham between Clinton Cards and Cancer Research and was run by an old school friend of Alan's. It was one of the last shops in the street to have retained its original tiling and shop front. The first day, Alan had taken him in there and Lem had recoiled from the smell of meat; he feared the possibility of blood, imagined there might be blood of horrific proportions, flooding out from under doors like in The Shining.

Patrick O'Farrell had heavy hands and a large veined face, and he took Alan through to the back for tea, which was when Dean pushed his way through the chain-link curtain and stood in the doorway to the shop. He looked about the same age as Lem, not as tall, but lean and more muscular. He had dark hair cut close to his scalp and his face was pale and freckled. At first Dean just stood there and fixed Lem with a look so that Lem felt his scrotum retract and thought, Oh, shit, he's trouble. Two chains from the doorway hung over Dean's shoulder and dangled down the front of his white apron bib, falling away with a clink as he extended his right hand. 'Lemuel Gulliver?' he said. Lem's hand was damp in his. 'Bit of a mouthful.' 'Gulliver's Travels,' shrugged Lem, blushing. 'My parents thought . . .' But Dean's face crumpled into a crooked-toothed smile. 'Yeah, well, parents,' he said. 'Dean's my middle name. My real name's James.'

He had never met a man quite like Dean before. He was brilliant with a knife and used it like it was an extension of himself. That first day Lem had watched while Dean did the cuts and served the customers. There weren't many because six months earlier Tesco Metro had opened up the road and then Sainsbury's had done the same. Most of the people who came in were old and there was a lot of 'Hello love' and 'Thank you darling' which Lem didn't think he was ever going to get the hang of. Just before closing time, an ancient man with translucent skin shuffled shaking into the shop. He was bent right over, his face towards the sawdust and an empty canvas bag in one hand. It took several painful minutes for him to reach the display cabinet and when he did, he seemed to leave go of whatever force it was that was keeping him upright on the earth and wedged himself in the corner where the cabinet joined the window display. Lem watched, wondering if this was what dead people looked like for there seemed to be no blood flowing inside the man's parchment skin. Suddenly the chain curtain leapt and flew behind him and Dean pushed past, grabbing the wooden chair from behind the counter as he did so and reaching Mr Dooley just in time to lower him onto the seat. He said, 'A nice kidney for you, Mr Dooley?' and lifted the loin of pork from the window cabinet. At the block he let the cleaver's broad blade touch the pliable skin once, lifted it a few inches, then brought it down with one sure blow bisecting the T-bone. Mr Dooley lifted his head then let his chin rest back on his chest. Dean took the paring knife from the rack behind him and nicked at the firm white fat and pale pink flesh with its tip. 'With your kidneys, Lem, you want to be sure not to graze the membrane.' He flipped the meat around and finished off with three quick strokes before offering Lem the shining, perfect curve of kidney in the palm of his hand. 'Now that,' he said, 'is beautiful with shallots and Tabasco', and he laid it on the thin greaseproof paper and wrapped it, one, two, three, then again in the heavier butcher's paper, repeating the folding pattern swiftly. He walked round to where Mr Dooley trembled and shook and put it in his bag for him.

It wasn't just because of Dean that Lem had enjoyed that job. He liked the learning too. He learnt all the names that were up on the poster of the cow behind the counter: brisket, loin, chuck, scrag, rump and hock; and he found he enjoyed the order and geometry of the jobs he was given to do. The feel of a thick slice of steak in his fingers, the surrender of dense flesh to steel, the precision of dicing, each cubed piece bright and exact, ready to be put in its tray. And there had been very little blood.

The first thing Lem had noticed about Dean was that he looked straight into his eyes when he spoke. Those eyes were slate-coloured like the wet roof tiles on the houses across the path outside Lem's bedroom window. At first, Lem used to look away quickly, upwards, down to the right, to the left and back up again; his habitual optical dance. When he was at school he had had to learn to look away before they landed you one. 'What you fuckin' lookin at?' was what eye contact was generally followed up with. After a while, he had forced himself to hold Dean's look and he could still remember the small pop of pleasure that first held gaze had given him.

He looked at the Underground map above the passengers' heads opposite him and followed the green District Line to Dagenham, way out towards Upminster. Miles away to the east in Zone 6. Hell to get to from Walthamstow on the Tube, but as the crow flies, not far. Not far at all. Dagenham. Daecca's homestead, AD 690. Dean's look, Dean's hands, the way he dropped that soft laugh and the Belfast lilt of his voice.

3

Tottenham Hale

THE TRAIN HOWLED and clattered down the final section of tunnel before it began braking hard. Lem looked up at the Tube map, although he didn't have to because he knew exactly where he was. The Victoria Line was inching him closer, stop by stop, to work and Dawn's new home with Ian.

Platform lights fluttered by and Lem ducked his head to check the name of the station. He pulled from his bag the little book of London place names that he had borrowed from Fay's bookshelf. The alphabetisation of things, the bold font of nomenclature and information offered in neat sections upon the page reassured him. Here was a book with answers, not questions, and he felt comforted by the banality and brutality of human history that it revealed. He had read up the etymology of every Tube stop on the map, all two hundred and seventy-five of them along two hundred and fifty-four miles of track. The world record for visiting all of them non-stop stood at eighteen hours, thirty-five minutes and forty-three seconds, while the record for travelling on at least one section of each of the twelve lines (including Waterloo and City) was fifty-six minutes, fifty-one seconds, starting at Shadwell (shallow spring or stream, 1222) and finishing at Charing Cross (turn in the road, 1100). When sometimes he thought of his Tube train as a needle stitching him to the fabric of names and lives and times, he felt a thrill of human connection that he rarely experienced above ground. Perhaps he was turning into a man deranged like the serial killer in that horror movie he watched once with Todd. Coke cans and pizza cartons were stacked by their feet on the Indonesian table in front of the sofa. He must have been about ten and the film was so bad it was funny. *Mind the Gap* it was called. The killer lived in the tunnels and had never seen daylight but preyed on passengers, grabbing them from the deserted ends of platforms with a hand that snatched up from below. When the constabulary finally tracked him down, he was like a wolfman. He couldn't walk and he couldn't speak except to growl, 'Mind the gap.' Todd and Lem had sat with their sides touching and he had wished it was more scary so he could hide his face in Todd's arm. A few years ago, when Todd was living in the pink house in Primrose Hill with Christy, Wife Number 2, he and Todd had an argument about that film, one of those arguments where each made the other laugh by a stubborn refusal to back down. Todd kept saying, 'It wasn't called *Mind the Gap*, it was *Mind the Doors*, you pillock. They don't say "Mind the gap" on many stations any more, only Holborn and the ones built on bends. Portland Place is another. Cracking film though, gap or no gap. It starred Donald Pleasance and Christopher Lee and you were absobloodylutely terrified if I remember rightly.' Todd's face would go completely red when he laughed like that, mainly because he didn't let the laugh out properly, he kept it in down the back of his throat and up his nose so that the roped veins on his neck stood out. 'No, hang on,' Todd had started up again, 'it was called *The Death Line*, not *Mind the Doors*. "Mind the doors" was what the cannibal tribe used to say.' And Lem had given him the finger and smirked so Todd had chucked an orange at Lem's head which hit a vase of flowers instead. 'Oh, Jesus Christ, now look what you've done,' he said and the laughter inside Lem shook nearly the whole of him from his groin to his cheekbones, but he managed to say, 'Mind the gap, Dad', giggling and darting out of reach as

Todd tried to whack him with the newspaper. Then Todd had pointed to the floor by the dining room door and said, 'Are those your mucky footprints on the carpet out there, Lemuel? Never mind the doors, mate, or the bloody gap; Christy is going to roast you alive if she comes back and sees those on her Berber Twist.'

Christy had a smiley face and shiny dark hair that swished when she wore her silk dressing gown. She called him Lemmy and put a hot-water bottle in his bed at night-time and always gave him kisses on the top of his head, which he didn't mind too much because the lipstick didn't show there. She made milkshakes out of chocolate ice cream and bananas, and asked him maths questions like she was genuinely interested. But soon after the wedding she gave up her job in public relations and quadrupled in size, so that before long, on the weekends when Lem came to stay, more often than not, Todd was out and it was just Lem and Christy watching the television together and working their way through a few cylinders of Pringles until Christy phoned for a Chinese. Then Todd went away to Costa Rica to make a reality television show called *Paradise Lost*, where indigenous Indians swapped lifestyles with minor celebrities in Florida for a week, and then Todd moved out and Helena appeared on the scene shortly afterwards.

Lem flicked through the *Dictionary of London Place Names*, bending the spine back in the way that drove Fay mad. Grim's Ditch, Piccadilly, World's End. Committing the information to memory and testing himself on it had helped pass the time on his journeys to work. Thirty-nine weeks of journeys is one hundred and ninety-five days which is roughly three hundred and ninety hours. That's forty-two days spent on the Victoria Line. A knowledge of place names had also proved a useful way of filling the conversational gaps that had opened up between him and Dawn. Before the *Dictionary of London Place Names*, he had spent a long time reading *The Origin of Phrases*,

Sayings, Terms and Clichés, which meant he had an endless supply of amusing facts with which to entertain her concerning the original meanings of sayings such as 'balls to the wall', 'sleep tight' and 'kiss of death'. Humour had worked quite well with Dawn and it was with some excitement that he had spotted the *Dictionary of Jokes* in the local bookshop window and which he had fully intended to buy except that she had left him before he could get round to it.

Conversationally, things had begun to falter soon after they moved into Kinloss Court which, now he came to think about it, had been something of a premature decision. When they first met, there had been plenty to talk about. They had talked about their family, their friends, Dawn's work and his studies. Then they had talked about buying a place and moving in. That had taken up hours of conversation, but no sooner had they closed the front door of Flat 9 than there seemed to be nothing left to say. And not long after that Dawn had announced that she thought he might have a dyslexic libido. He had no idea there was such a thing, but it was reassuring to know that his mysterious lack of desire might have a name. He turned the pages of the book, trying to conceal the cover and the contents from the woman in the apple-green jacket on his left who kept looking. Tottenham Hale. Tottenham. Totta's Homestead, 1086. He bet there was no such thing as a dyslexic libido in those days.

'It's not very difficult, Lem,' Steve had told him one after-noon, standing in the staffroom at school. 'Every single moment, every second, presents an opportunity to score. Every woman is a potential shag.'

With his head down, Lem flinched at each hiss of emphasis in Steve's voice. He took a step back to allow a colleague through, relieved to have an excuse to create some space between them because Steve's very demeanour embarrassed him at times: shoulders thrown back, legs apart, jaw jutted and swathed in the powerful aroma of Lynx, Steve was *FHM* personified, *Zoo*, *Nuts* and *Loaded* all rolled into one. And the sad fact was that, other than Devora and Dean, this man was currently his only friend.

'Nokia, Cassandra, Hugo . . .' Sharon, the head of Year 10, was reciting the names of several students suspended for fighting. '. . . and there is a restraining order on Napoleon's mother, who is not allowed within a one-hundred-metre radius of the premises.'

Lem studied Steve's profile. He had dark eyes, wide-set in a pale face, which, along with the sharp nose and the thin-lipped grin, could give him a sharkish look, especially when he was cruising, like now. 'Her, for instance,' he said in his ventriloquist's murmur, stepping back alongside Lem as Ameena eased her way in front of them to study the noticeboard. 'See the arse on that?'

'That' was their head of department, Ameena Patel. Lem glanced over to where she stood, just in time to see her scratch her bottom with the end of her pen. Steve closed his eyes and exhaled like a steam iron. Ameena put the pen in her ear, gave it a waggle and tugged at the fabric of her trousers, retrieving her pants from the crevice of her bottom. Steve groaned.

Lawrence was making a final announcement about the building contractors. He was almost inaudible amid the repeated flap and slam of the swing doors that punctuated the meetings. '. . . if you teach in Block Seven, your windows will be removed sometime during the week as part of the refurbishment programme.'

A small noise like air seeping from an invisible puncture could be heard. This was the sound of morale falling. Refurbishment had been going on for a year. It was all part of the government's Public Private Partnership, which meant that classrooms weren't going to have draughty windows or leaky ceilings any longer. There were currently more builders than teachers in the school, along with a great deal of drilling and dust. Ameena put her hand up to speak.

'Do we know yet when the thirty computers, twenty

keyboards, ten electric ovens, six fridges and my laptop stolen during the holidays are going to be replaced?'

A collective eyeball rolling, buttock shifting and neck craning occurred as Ameena, small and fearless in navy linen trousers, matching cropped jacket and high heels, folded her arms and waited for the answer while Senior Management looked at each other. Ameena had no qualms about making herself unpopular with her bosses with questions like this, and Lem both admired and feared her for it. It made him want her approval in a way that he understood was a little pathetic.

'I hear what you're saying, Ms Patel,' smiled the head teacher, sliding a 'z' onto the end of Ms so that it sounded absurd and looking at a cube of air just above Ameena's head. 'I think you may rest assured that security is now in hand.' He stretched his neck, releasing his Adam's apple from the punishing grip of his collar and tie. 'Heads of departments do need to return any insurance claims by the end of today, however.' He checked the faces of the two deputy heads standing alongside him. Small nods and pursed lips. 'Moving on . . .'

Since the thefts, Lem had noticed that the builders wore hard hats, identity tags and blue shirts with Skilled Worker badges sewn on the chest. A job as a builder was appealing right now. In addition to the hard hats, the builders seemed to have a lot of specialist equipment that they carried in silver attaché cases and leather holsters on their hips, so that they looked like a cross between James Bond and Clint Eastwood. The other day, one of them had ascended slowly past Lem's classroom window with a leather harness strapped round his groin. Lem was explaining the mystery of prime numbers and had got as far as saying, 'Everything around us can be understood and represented in numbers . . .' when the vision appeared. Luckily, most of the kids had their backs to the windows, seats hard up against the heat-pumping radiators, coats on even though it was June and they were, as a result, fast asleep. The only witnesses were the row of Indian and

Bangladeshi girls who smiled to each other but said nothing, waiting politely for him to retrieve the rest of his sentence.

Lem slid a look over at the passengers opposite him and wondered what it would be like to do a job where you had tools to do it with instead of teaching where the main bit of equipment was yourself. He thought of the last time he had managed to bag a set of books before the others in the department squirrelled them away, and of the time last term when he'd managed to drag the TV and video into the classroom to show a video of Parallels and Polygons. If the plug hadn't been stolen and if the blinds had worked in the room, instead of jerking at acute angles before finally seizing up altogether, that would probably have been quite a good lesson, but instead it was as usual a ragged and tortuous hour in which he had kept shouting, 'Will you just . . .' and, 'Look, if you don't . . .' and Jason had been up to his wanking thing again and he had no idea how to handle that. It was usually best to leave that sort of thing to Saskia and Emily, who – after much whole-class yelling of 'Sir! Sir! Make him stop, Sir!' and a lot of hyena baying and hand wringing from the other boys – had upended the table over the sex offender, resulting in a dramatic and impressive silence.

And yet, thought Lem, counting the frequency of the letter 'e' on the newspaper headlines to his right, it wasn't always, all of the time, like that. No, although he often felt ineffectual, that nothing he could do would engage these young people who had so many more important, difficult and exciting things to think about than Probability, Sampling and Standard Deviation, he was surprised just often enough to keep him doing the job. Like the time last term when he had covered a music lesson and Nokia had sung Billie Holiday's 'Strange Fruit'. Just like that, this large unruly girl, who Lem suddenly understood was not a girl but a woman and a woman who did no one's bidding, stood up in the centre of the room. With her hands splayed down by her sides, eyes closed and chin raised, out of her came a voice of such force and passion that his eyes welled and the boys in the room looked away. The students sat in silence listening to her and when she finished the song, the words of the last line hanging in the air, 'Here is a strange and bitter crop', Lem felt humbled and ashamed. Ashamed of his dislike and fear of her, of his low expectation of her, and ashamed of the terrible history behind her song.

'You should hear her sing "Stormy Weather", Lem. That would really blow your mind,' Devora had told him that lunchtime. 'The girl's got serious talent. She's still a monumental pain in the neck, though. Music is the only GCSE she's likely to get, and as she probably won't turn up for the theory paper . . .' And then she had rushed on with her ideas about how school needed to be radically rethought, how it was madness to be still using a Victorian system and that classrooms had had their day, what with their cramped tables and chairs, they were holding back the march of progress and should all be demolished, they should dump the whole concept of timetables, abandon classrooms and completely reconfigure the concept of secondary education.

He had opened his mouth to join in but she had stopped him, crossing and uncrossing her legs and saying, 'First of all, no, listen, Lem, first of all . . .' Devora's compulsion to speak was almost an affliction, he sometimes thought, and not that different from a lot of the students he taught.

'First,' she went on, 'pay all post-fourteen-year-olds to attend and learn. It's an obvious investment in the future. If they don't attend or don't bother, then their pay is stopped. Second, forget lessons and have a week of very exciting and very practical maths or music or physics or whatever. Stop all this arbitrary sit-down-get-your-books-out, eight different lessons a day baloney.'

He watched her slicing the air with her hands, eyes shining. Perhaps that was why she had so few problems in the classroom. She simply out-talked the lot of them.

'Third, in the afternoons, they should be bussed off to Olympic-quality sports facilities to get out of breath and oxygenate their muscle tissue. Fourth, sack the kitchen staff and the cleaners and teach the kids how to do it properly. And for God's sake, fifth, teach them plumbing and plastering too. I've been waiting for a plumber to call for months.'

'So Steve tells me that you live on a motorway,' Devora said not long after they first met.

'Not an actual motorway. It's the intersection of the A406 and the A1.'

'How many lanes of traffic?'

'Er . . .' Lem pretended to count, although he didn't need to. 'Six.'

She was silent for a while and then said, 'Why?'

'It was cheap.'

'Round here is probably cheaper.'

'Dawn wanted to be near her family. It's not so bad. The people living fifty yards further up have nine lanes of traffic in front of them. We're going to sell it soon.'

'So Dawn is your first proper girlfriend, then?' Devora had a way of reaching right into someone and pulling out intimacies that she would exchange for her own.

'I suppose so. In a way, yes. I mean, not, you know . . .' And she had got some of the story from him, interspersing it with tales of her own life at university and no doubt making hers seem more confusing and bleak than it really was.

It was difficult cranking out the words to describe that time, any time from his past really. He found it almost impossible to present a version of himself that bore any resemblance to reality. Not like Devora, Ameena or Dawn. Even Steve, who may have gone for a cardboard cut-out of himself, but it was at least one that was consistent and recognisable apart from the bizarre lapses into poetry that had been known to escape his lips at times.

'There were a couple of . . .'

'. . . confusing encounters at university?'

'I seemed to keep meeting the wrong people.' He scratched his head and a few flakes spun out into the air between them. 'I was either chatted up by men or . . .' He checked Devora's expression quickly. She was listening, not judging. '. . . or a certain kind of woman—'

'. . . looking for a man they could possess like a pet.'

'Sort of. Once we'd been out a few times . . .'

'. . . things got nasty . . .'

'. . . and then the early morning interrogations would begin . . .'

Devora laughed. 'Oh yes. Those. "Why did you rush off like that?" "What's wrong?" "Have you ever thought about how I might feel about that?" and always,' she shuffled forward on her seat, *always*, "What are you thinking about?"'

Devora's lipsticked lips closed over her teeth in a smirk. How did she know all this? he wondered.

'More or less. I discovered that the only way to escape it all was to be out of it. You know, stoned.'

'Pain relief.' She licked sugar crystals from the ends of each finger. 'Mine was promiscuous sex.'

Lem looked at her foot, which was out of its shoe and up at chair level in front of them tracing circles in the air, painted toenails like pink frosting. He pictured her by the rosy light of his lava lamp, laughing naked on his mustard duvet in Preston. He tried to remember whether he had ever washed that duvet cover in the whole three years he was up there.

'So where did you meet Dawn then? Wasn't it the zoo or something?' She was pulling pieces of paper out of her bag and making quizzical faces.

'On a zebra crossing.'

'What the hell is all this?' She withdrew an impossibly long chain of linked paper clips.

'In Friern Barnet.'

'Want one?' She had found what she was looking for, a tattered looking packet of throat pastilles. He shook his head, then changed his mind and took one.

'It was raining. She almost didn't stop in time. She must have been going quite fast.'

Devora stopped fidgeting and said, 'Do you mean she nearly ran you down on a pedestrian crossing?'

'She was in a bit of a state. She had been visiting her brother, Marvin. You know, in the unit.'

'But what were you doing in Friern Barnet, for God's sake?'

'I'd been for a job interview at the council.'

'My God, Lem. She could have killed you.'

'It felt like she had rescued me. The job was in local government finance. She gave me a lift home and that was it really.'

He couldn't help wondering whether things might have turned out differently for him and Dawn if they'd found a place like Church Path to live, although what he'd really fancied was a houseboat on the canal. They had walked past some one day when they'd taken the towpath south from Camden Town into King's Cross. Little rows of brightly painted boats clustered together in companionable groups. Some had metal buckets with geraniums on their roofs and several had smoke drifting from a chimney. He had got quite excited about the idea of living in one, because he thought it might return them to their first night together on Mersea Island in Essex.

That hot August evening, they'd come out of the pub to find that the night had fallen fast, taking them by surprise, so that it was too late and Dawn was too drunk to drive back to London. He'd told her, 'I know a place', and had taken her hand and felt for once like a man in control. They walked down to the mudflats, the salt air still warm from the day, past the tinkling masts of a hundred dinghies, past the wooden jetties and footpaths on stilts leading out to abandoned houseboats and old hulks that lay half submerged in the rising tide of the estuary. They had sat down on a wooden bench that Lem knew was inscribed with the words 'For Dad who loved it here', and Lem had realised they would never make it to Fay's beach hut at the eastern point of the island. He left Dawn leaning against a wooden post while he clambered onto a small boat that looked like the Ark and was moored at the far end of the longest jetty he could find. He didn't know what was making him more nervous, the idea of spending the night with Dawn or the idea of breaking into a boat. He raised his arms above the doors and windows and ran his fingers along the places where Alan had taught him people always hide their keys. Sure enough, his fingers closed round a tobacco tin and inside was the key to the padlock on the hatch.

Once on the boat, Lem's anxiety disappeared. Dawn was funny and cheerful, staggering in the dark, swearing each time she banged her shins and saying, 'I'm not at all sure those oysters agreed with me, Lem.' Then she'd said, 'Where's the toilet? I'm desperate', but there didn't seem to be one and so she had clambered out of the cabin, pulled down her jeans and stuck her bottom over the side. He could see her now, crouched with her backside globed like a pale moon, a torrent cascading from her into the water below. She had been giggling, giggling and shouting at him to turn round and stop bloody staring, you pervert. He'd thought then that perhaps everything was going to be all right, him and her, this inebriated girl on a boat, her backside hanging over the keel, a syncopated waterfall clattering out of her.

Jammed together in the dark on the narrow bunk with little room for manoeuvre, sex had been brief and uncomplicated and Dawn had fallen asleep while Lem lay awake inside her, feeling the ebb and flow of them on the water, the float of them in the darkness as they lay soldered together, hidden in a stranger's musty blankets. He listened to the groan and creak of the berthing ropes pulling against the swell and imagined them inside the ribs of a giant fish, swallowed together, still and unseen. That night, too happy to sleep, he stayed awake for hours inhaling Dawn's winey breath and feeling the soft lift and fall of her encircling him.

That was almost three years ago now. Dawn had seemed grown-up and fun then and for a while he felt as though he had been rescued from emotional drift. She took control straight away, ordering him to give up skunk and take up drinking instead. It was her idea for him to train as a teacher, because as a maths graduate he could get a Golden Hello of £4,000 if he taught in designated schools. She had even discovered and downloaded the Home Loans for Key Workers application form so that they could buy Kinloss Court.

Yet despite the Hello, living with Dawn had never been exactly golden, not like the way it seemed to be with Fay and Alan. Lem pulled up the collar of Alan's shirt and turned his face into it. He had known in his heart it was never right, because his laundry had smelt all wrong from the moment they moved in together and he had had a longing for the smell of laundry the way Fay did it. He didn't know what had happened with the washing machine he and Dawn had got, but the freshly washed clothes smelt alien and synthetic. Often, as he pulled the shirt over his head in the mornings, an olfactory sadness would envelop him, chased by a fleeting sense that he was in the wrong life. He would stand like that for a minute, trying to collect more clues as to the precise nature of his existential misalignment, until Dawn cuffed him over the head as she passed between the wardrobe and the bedroom door, saying, 'What the hell are you doing in there, Lem?' He would poke his head out through the neck of his shirt like a wary tortoise and see her bending over, one foot pointing into the leg hole of her G-string or shimmying up her skirt with just her bra on and frowning down to do up the button at the side. Most mornings she would have a sartorial crisis in front of the mirror on the landing outside their bedroom. The time would be ticking by, the DJ telling them it was seventeen minutes to the hour and that Hangar Lane was absolutely chocker, and she'd be in and out of skirts and trousers and tops and shoes and tripping up over the tray of cat litter. Lem would hover by the door and say, 'Bye', wondering whether to go and give her a kiss, and she would start swearing at the clothes-covered floor and wail, 'I can't find anything to arsing well wear.' He would usually give her a kiss anyway because Alan always gave Fay one and he suspected that Todd probably hadn't when he used to leave for work, not that he could remember that, although there must be some trace of it somewhere inside him. So he'd kiss Dawn, even though sometimes she'd turn her head away and say, 'Don't. I've got my face on', and carry on stomping amid her hosiery and halter necks. But it was important to leave home and enter the blast of the rush hour secure in the knowledge that he had done the right thing and saying to himself as he headed for the bus stop, Lemuel Gulliver, 23, maths teacher, lives with Dawn Jump, 26, Crown Protection Services. They love each other. That was what he told himself for the first few months because mostly it was true. Towards the end he had to edit the statement a little. And then a lot.

'Your secret's safe with me,' Devora had laughed, leaning towards him one day behind the cheese plant.

'They're just fishing trips,' he had laughed back and the leaves of the cheese plant parted and there was Lawrence, a sheaf of tattered papers in his hand.

'Devora, about Gavin Branscombe's exclusion . . .' He had droned on about a boy in Devora's class who had probably had tens of thousands of pounds worth of local authority money spent on him during his school career, and who had recently threatened a dinner lady with a gun because she insisted he pay for his pizza and chips like everyone else.

'So you're saying Gavin is returning to the school?' Devora

41

said to Lawrence, trying to wind up the conversation. 'I thought he'd been thrown out.'

'His expulsion was overturned. It was only an imitation handgun and not in itself a dangerous weapon. The lunch-time supervisor acted in error.'

'And the theft of all those mobile phones?'

'Mobile phones are not allowed on school premises and, as such, cannot be used as evidence against a student.'

'Great.'

'But the good news is . . . he's been tagged.'

'So I won't be able to lose him, you mean?'

'Precisely. Entitlement and Inclusion is our mantra, remember.'

Devora turned back round again to face Lem. She straight-ened her clothes in irritation, pulling at her skirt and blouse with short sharp movements. A button flew off and bounced by Lem's feet. Devora looked down at the gaping fabric that revealed a crescent of pistachio and black satin.

'Excellent. Now I've got to teach thirty adolescents with my bra showing.'

Lem lifted each giant trainer, trying to locate the button, and imagined Steve's protestations as he did so, 'For God's sake, man, get in there. She's bloody asking for it. You gay or what?'

'Not another one,' Devora was bending down to help him with his searching so that their hair touched. 'Don't they believe in sewing any longer, wherever it is that they manufacture clothes these days?' He handed her the button. 'You could fix that for me, couldn't you, Lem,' and she gave him a wide-eyed smile.

Fay had taught Lem to sew and to knit, but this was a skill that he'd thought best to keep to himself. Although Devora knew, because when he'd gone back to hers for coffee after a parents' evening there'd been a sewing machine out on the kitchen table, an iridescent mound of exotic fabric bunched beside it and all the paraphernalia of dressmaking. He had sat

42

down at the machine while Devora made coffee. On the rare occasions when Lem considered the nature of happiness, it often included the sensation of wool twining around his right forefinger, the look of the stitch as it transformed itself from a loop on a needle into something knotted and held within a larger pattern. The knitting was one of the ways he could keep Fay within his radar when he was a boy. Instead of moving away to do a never-ending series of 'I'm just going to . . .' tasks, she would sit close, leaning over him, watching intently and murmuring small encouragements.

'I'm having one hell of a time trying to do button-holes,' Devora had told him when she saw him feeling the heaped material beside the machine. 'It's for my god-daughter, azure lamé. The fabric I mean, not my god-daughter.' And Devora had laughed and Lem thought then that she was beautiful. Illuminated. 'She's going to St Lucia for her honeymoon, so I thought I'd make her something, seeing as I've had that machine since God knows when and never used it.'

It was simple really. He turned the top dial to button-hole mode, except that if you didn't know it was button-hole mode you'd think it was rectangle mode, then he adjusted the stitch dial, asked for a piece to practise on and a few minutes later there it was, a button-hole. All he had to do was slit the fabric with the fabric slitter that was in the secret compartment that Devora had never discovered. She'd leant towards him, put her arms round him and kissed him when she saw that; not a long kiss, but a kiss just the same. With her parted lips soft against his, Lem felt like he'd been short-circuited. Then there was one of those confused, suspended moments that Steve says should never be allowed to happen. Steve always said, 'It's up to you, Lem, being the bloke, to direct proceedings. You're in charge. It's obvious, you wouldn't let a bird drive your car, would you? Or take a penalty? Course not! Same thing applies to sex. She's expecting you to make the first move.'

But Devora. It was all too confusing, what with her being

forty-nine and knowing about the knitting and everything, and so Lem had stood up too quickly and knocked the table and spilt the coffee she'd put down there, which spread in a brown flood towards the dress and then they were both apologising and looking round for something to mop up the mess, a crimson tide rising up Devora's neck, and Lem felt terribly sorry because he hadn't meant it to be a horrified rejection, but of course that's what she thought it was.

'I'd better be going' was what he'd said, looking at his watch.

'Come on, Lem,' she'd said, laughing. 'I'll drive you to the Tube.'

Dawn was staying with her parents that night because Marvin had the weekend at home and so Lem went back to Walthamstow. He had got under the duvet fully clothed, his long body laid out completely straight and still and listened to the silence of the house waiting for the sounds of Fay and Alan returning home. He woke in the dark at 3.00 a.m. fragments of a dream slipping from him: a small black bear at the bottom of the stairwell, the feel of Alan's arms lifting him asleep from the bed, Todd trying to force the bear out of the house with the poker and Lem seeing that he was too afraid to manage it. He had got out of bed to get some water from the bathroom, then stood on the landing listening. The downstairs light was still on so he knew Fay and Alan must be away in their fisherman's hut in Mersea. He opened the door of their room and looked at their double bed smooth and pale like a stone in the middle of the room. He went in and lay face down in the middle of it, breathing in the cinnamony smell of Fay and the musty tang of Alan. As a boy, at first, he could remember finding Alan's smell unbearably strong and would turn away from his rough face. Once he'd bitten Alan's hand, hard. He could remember the feeling of satisfaction as his teeth sank into flesh and the way the carbony taste of oil had made him leave go and look in disgust at this man who shared his mother's bed. Some afternoons after Alan had moved in, Fay would give him a sandwich and tell him to go out and play. Alan would stand in the doorway, tossing a football from one hand to the other, jiggling one leg, looking questioningly at his cuckoo of a stepson and say, 'Take the ball with you.'

But Lem couldn't go to the park because he always had to give something to the gang of boys who ruled it – his jacket, his bike, his Discman, his money, his skateboard, the fluff from his pockets – basically all the paraphernalia that Fay and Alan kept giving him to try to ease his passage through the battlefield of boyhood, and if only they'd been bloody looking, they would have seen that he had floundered and almost perished quite early on. He'd tried explaining to Fay about the way the boy fiefdom worked in Walthamstow, but she didn't understand and she wouldn't look at him, she would just start on about negotiating boundaries with them and talking things through with their parents. So instead of the park, he'd explore the great churchyard at the end of Church Path where he could be sure of meeting no one. The boys who ruled the park avoided the graveyard.

St Mary's church itself squatted large and locked, and was surrounded by towering horse chestnuts so that the wild and rambling place was always in shade. At the entrance was a sign which explained that the site held two plague pits, although their exact whereabouts were unknown. Lem used to like to scare himself at night, lying in his bed and thinking of the pits hidden somewhere not far from where he lay, filled with the corpses of the hurriedly buried. With the fear drumming inside his ribs, he would picture the scenes, carts piled with the dead, trundling up the path in front of his house. Alan told him that Vinegar Lane, which ran along one side of the graveyard where the almshouses still stood, was so called because the villagers would pour vinegar into the ditch dug round the churchyard in an attempt to prevent the contagion from spreading.

Before Alan, the churchyard had been a place Fay would

visit with him, holding his hand and crouching by the mossed slabs. Together they would trace their fingers over the lichened epitaphs, sounding out the names and the dates of the dead. His earliest memories of reading and of arithmetic were among those gravestones.

'Myrtle Withers 1736–1774.'

He did the maths. Thirty-eight.

'Did they know they were going to die?'

'Not always.'

'Are those rats, Mum?' he said, turning suddenly at the scuttle and rustle by the buttressed walls, his voice too loud.

'That's a blackbird, hopping in the leaves, look,' and she would snuggle him under her arm.

Lem couldn't be sure, but he liked to imagine the time of those graveyard visits together as a brief interval when he had Fay all to himself. A short precious time after Todd and before Alan when he felt a solid connection to her. The two of them alive among all the many who had died and been forgotten.

'A lot of them are scared, Mum, aren't they?'

'Sacred not scared.'

And there was the small grave of a child they always visited, the smell of leaf mould filling his nose. Fay would read aloud the inscription on the stone while Lem held his breath, waiting for the hit of grief it released.

> Samuel Reeve 1780–1785
> He was the pilot of our bark
> Without him the wrack is total.

When he was older and used to visit the graveyard alone, he would place twists of stick and twine and grass on the grave and then run, scalp prickling, out of the shadows and stones and back towards Church Path.

The woman by the doors, who was still being kissed, had

grubby heels. Each time she flexed one foot the back of her sandal dropped down and Lem could see that her feet needed a scrub. Still, it was not an unattractive foot, not like Dawn's, he thought with gratifying spite. Dawn's feet had a needy, hopeless look to them. The male half of the couple was throwing glances at Lem, his eyes shifting his way as he kissed the woman's upturned face. 'What you looking at?' With a flush of shame, Lem stopped staring, bitterly aware that Steve or Todd or Alan would not have done so. He looked at his watch. 7.45.

4

Seven Sisters

DEAN HAD SEVEN sisters.

Seven Sisters was a godforsaken, traffic-choked, treeless place where hardly anyone got on the train at all. He thought of Devora's god-daughter, who must be back from her honeymooning by now and living the marriage in one of the streets way up above his head somewhere.

'She lives on the Seven Sisters Road,' Devora had said.

They had been doing break duty at the front gate one morning. The sun was appearing from behind the clouds every now and again. It was one of those months when it had rained for days on end, November maybe, or March.

'Dean has seven sisters. But they all live with his mum, back in Ireland.'

'The Seven Sisters Road, though. Nearly as bad as the North Circular. She's got a flat above the Bank of Greece. Not the most beautiful of locations to start your married life.'

'It must have been beautiful once,' said Lem. 'The Seven Sisters were seven trees.' He tried to remember the date but couldn't. That irked him. There must be a date.

'What kind of trees?'

'Elms. Although I'm not sure what they look like.'

'You don't see elms any more. Very tall and majestic. Think of a Constable painting. There's bound to be an elm in that. They're like a cross between an oak and an ash.' She stepped into the path of a six-foot-tall boy who had a girl's squealing head tucked under his arm. He was dragging her towards the fortress gates where Lem and Devora stood guard.

'Joe, whatever you are doing to Nicola, she doesn't like it, so stop.'

'I'm only cuddling her, Miss.' He yanked the girl around so that she faced the other way.

'That's not cuddling. Let go of her. And why are you hanging round the gate? The bell's about to go.'

'I got to go dentist, Miss.' Joe gave the girl's head another yank and let go. He put his hands in his pockets and tugged his trousers downwards, nodding his head to an inaudible soundtrack.

'Let me see your note, then.' Devora held out her hand.

'She's got my stuff.' He grabbed the girl again, who was hovering just within reach. 'Nicola. Where's my bag?'

'I ain't got your bag.' Nicola stepped forward and kicked him hard behind one knee so that he sank lopsidedly. He flailed at her and she shrieked and jumped away.

'What you mean you ain't got my bag, man? I give it you.' Joe spread his hands and moved from foot to foot. He wiped his forehead with one big palm and shook his head. 'Come on, Miss, let me out. I got to go dentist. My tooth is killing me.'

'Note, Joe.' Devora stood her ground, one hand holding the gate shut until Joe gave up and sloped off towards the main school building. 'What is it with boys and bags, for God's sake? I mean, when, how and why did it become an act of emasculation to be seen wanting to succeed in school? I don't get it.'

Lem watched Joe go, lolloping and limping like a friendly, confused bear. 'My bag was thrown in the kitchen bins at my school on the first day,' he said. 'It's not easy being a boy. In fact it is almost impossible.'

'You think it's easy being a girl and having to carry two bags all your life?' Devora turned on him. She was a little alarming when she overreacted like this. 'That is why my bottom is the size it is, Lem. Pack–pony rump, that's what that is', and she gave it a slap.

What was the point of her getting like this with him? Women didn't understand. They just didn't get it. Devora should just shut up every now and then and look around her. He opened the gate and looked up the road to the turning into the school car park, where some kids whose names he didn't know were squawking and darting their heads back and forth round the corner, hoping he would come over and chase them. He turned back and sneaked a look at Devora's bottom. She was right, there was something a little animal about it. He remembered now. There hadn't been a date. Seven Sisters was a legend, which meant that it was probably really old.

A flock of students flapped past them screeching like gulls; coats, bags, crisp packets and sweet wrappers flying in their wake.

'It's a bit like being in a musical in this place, Lem. Know what I mean? Random outbreaks of apparently meaningless song and dance.'

They were silent for several moments and Lem watched her face as she tipped her head back and closed her eyes to soak up a moment's sun. He looked up at the sycamore above their heads. A grey squirrel was poised head downwards on the trunk. He tried to retrieve the scattered facts about the Seven Sisters from the *Dictionary of London Place Names*.

'People think the elms were planted by seven sisters to mark the spot where they said goodbye to each other.' He placed his toe over one chewing-gum patch on the path and then on four more, one to the north, the east, the south and the west.

She looked across at him and then squinted upwards again. The sky darkened and the sycamore branches hissed. It was going to pour.

'Sounds a bit unlikely. Where would seven sisters be going

all at once?'

A football flew over the wall and thudded into the road. Lem looked the other way and could just see what looked like Joe's legs clambering over the ten-metre-high car park gate.

'Maybe they didn't leave.'

The boy was having trouble managing the row of spikes at the top of the gate, one leg over, the other waving for a foothold. Lem couldn't bear to watch.

'Maybe they died. Perhaps there was a witch hunt.'

'No.' Devora was standing close to him, face on, inches from his chest. 'Seven Sisters sounds special, not sinister.'

He counted the seconds and thought about the kiss.

'Maybe it's nothing to do with people. Maybe it's to do with trees. Something special about a group of particular trees that has been remembered.' She widened her eyes and then laughed. 'Ooh, it's making me feel all funny, Lem', and the first raindrops began to fall, large and heavy and wet. She pressed herself against his side, crossing her arms over her breasts, hugging herself. 'History is very sexy, don't you think?'

But then they were standing side by side, touching, both aware of the line of contact between them that ran from their shoulders down their arms ending at their hips, with the word sexy in the air around them like a force field. He waited, counting the seconds again, knowing she would deal with it.

He got as far as four and, sure enough, she thumped him on the chest with her forearm, stepped away triumphantly and said, 'Tree worship. That's what it is.'

They began walking, with rapid steps back towards the main school doors as the rain intensified. 'That's it, you know, Lem. The Angles and the Saxons and the Jutes, the northern hordes fleeing the cold and the dark. The ones who are responsible for all our impossible spellings. They worshipped trees, I am sure of it.' She laughed, suddenly energised, punctuating her reasoning with little leaps across puddles and mud slicks. 'So I bet that elms were special trees, and of course seven is a magic number and so Seven Sisters was a holy place.' They were running now, the rain so heavy that it hammered on the pathway. 'And now look at it.' She grabbed his arm as they leapt clumsily over a small flood, colour flushing her cheeks. He steadied her and laughed. He wanted to kiss her mouth. 'It'd be like coming back in a thousand years and finding that St Paul's Cathedral was a roundabout . . .'

A jam of whooping kids shoved and pushed themselves at the main doors.

'It is.'

'No it's not.'

Her hair was drenched, she blinked hard against the drops, face shining. He could feel a drop of water make its way over his collar bone and down under his arm. Someone got the other door open and the crush subsided, kids falling into the foyer shrieking and laughing.

'But it is. St Paul's is a roundabout.'

'Oh God, you're right,' she said. 'We're history.'

A deafening thunderclap set up another bout of student screaming and Devora said, 'Oh', and leapt like a girl up the steps and through the doors while he ran behind her shouting, 'Dean's got seven sisters, you know', thinking that maybe musicals weren't so far-fetched after all.

Battyman.

Seeing it like that, in the wrong kind of whiteboard pen, the kind that does not wipe off, had caught Lem off guard, because it was the morning after the night that Dawn had called him the same thing when he'd lost her keys.

'Lem,' she'd said, her jaw held rigid in derision. 'You total battyman.'

It wasn't just the loss of the keys, of course, it was the loss of his sex drive. He couldn't really account for it himself and while he was used to people calling him gay since his own school days because he didn't play football and Fay made him do his homework on time, he couldn't in all honesty summon much enthusiasm for the idea of gay sex either. He had thought about it of course. At times it had seemed to be the suddenly simple solution to his problems, and yet he had done nothing about it. Not really. Not unless you counted the time Dean had helped pull his sweater over his head at the reservoir and both his sweater and shirt had come off, and before he could untangle his arms, Dean had drawn one fingernail hard, so hard it hurt, down from Lem's sternum to his belly and said, 'Streaky rashers.' With his scalp prickling and his groin melting, Lem had scrambled to his feet, pointed at the water and shouted, 'Did you see that? There's something massive on the end of your line.'

'It's simple economics. The law of supply and demand,' Devora had told him one break time when he'd found her studying a newspaper article about the national decrease in desire. 'The Lost Libido, you see,' she said triumphantly tapping the page. 'It explains everything.'

Lem was too tactful to mention Mr Devora and Miss Work Experience or, indeed, Steve, who was at that very moment bearing down on the new art teacher who was turning in small circles near the noticeboard and dripping coffee from a polystyrene cup.

'Now that sex is everywhere, like chewing gum, it's flooded the market, see?' continued Devora. 'Consequently, its value has dropped – supply has outstripped demand.' She looked up and watched Steve, then added, 'Oh, don't be fooled by all that. He's just going through the motions, bless him.'

Lem considered telling Devora at that point that Steve lived in his car but he had promised not to and he was congenitally incapable of breaking a promise. Not that he had ever been given that many promises to keep, yet nevertheless he had somehow retained a child's sense of the sacredness of a secret. Perhaps he should become a priest, he thought. Presumably faith could be studied and learnt just like everything else. Steve's car secret had emerged the night he had given Lem a lift home after a department meal and had asked whether he could borrow Kinloss Court on Saturday evening while Dawn and Lem went out.

'What do you mean?'

'Don't ask. Just do me a favour.'

'What if we don't want to go out?'

'Please, just this once.'

'But why?'

'I've got a date.'

'What?'

'For Chrisakes, man, I need a place with a bed in it.'

Lem watched the traffic for a bit, imagining Steve in their bed.

'What's wrong with your own place?'

'This is my place', and Steve had indicated the back seat with a lift of his head. Lem twisted round and looked at the sleeping bag, electric razor and empty cans of Stella. He thought about what Dawn would say if she found out.

'It's complicated, mate. Temporary. Debts and stuff. Don't tell anyone, will you? I'm sorting it out.' He looked tired and smaller than usual. 'Please.' He looked over at Lem and then added, 'I'll make it up to you.'

Lem thought for a moment about what Steve might be able to give him in return. There was Steve's bravado, he could do with some of that. And there was his macho charisma with which he controlled the most unruly classes. Just one look at the six-foot, six-pack swagger of the man made teenagers sit meekly in their seats and pay attention. But he couldn't very well ask for any of that.

Battyman.

It was the calmness of Dawn's voice that had made him realise she was more than angry. And it was then that it had dawned on him, if he was not very much mistaken, that she and he were nearing the end of the line. Very much mistaken was what he had been all his life, and that included his conception, as Fay had made clear on a number of occasions.

'Wasn't brilliant timing,' she said, peering critically at something through the kitchen window, looking at anything but the space that he was filling.

Lem watched her slim back at the sink that was repeatedly crossed by Alan's short busy frame moving to and fro across the kitchen, opening cupboards, sliding cutlery into drawers. Alan always wore checked chef's trousers at weekends, something that Lem found infuriating. Why couldn't he just wear a pair of badly fitting stone-washed jeans like any normal stepfather? As Alan stowed a pack of paper towels in the cupboard under the sink, his head level with Fay's thighs, Lem considered the question of how and why, then, he had been conceived. No one spoke and the room filled up with the unspoken sexual act between Todd and Fay.

Alan finally straightened up and broke the silence. 'She hadn't planned to spend the next twenty years in Walthamstow sketching villains, is what she means', and he went over to the kitchen table where Lem sat and cuffed him quite hard across the back of the head.

'Uh,' said Lem, rubbing his head and offering Alan the wan smile that he knew the man needed. Why don't you just piss off and leave me alone with my mother? he said to himself.

Alan tossed a loaf of bread up in the air, snatched it on its way down and chucked it in the bread bin. 'Y-e-s!'

'I hadn't intended to still be doing the job I just did for a laugh when I first left college,' said Fay, watering the plants on the windowsill.

Lem wasn't sure whether Fay was any good at art. How did you tell? Her courtroom sketches all looked the same — bewildered faces with crayoned flesh-tone shading and wiry hair. One or two of the notorious cases were stuck to his bedroom wall with masking tape. Even so, their ordinariness was what caught the eye; there was nothing in their faces that betrayed the unspeakable acts they had perpetrated. Most of his bedroom though was filled with the giant canvases of thick-layered acrylic or oils, which seemed to Lem noisy and completely incomprehensible.

The train decelerated to a rumbling crawl, juddered, squeaked and then stopped. Passengers raised their eyes from their papers. Lem checked his watch. Given it was Tuesday, he'd probably have to cover that Year 10 English class again. The very idea that in less than an hour he would be standing in front of a class of overtired, malnourished, love-hungry, hormone-hyped adolescents created a shrinking sensation low down in his guts. How could he have forgotten something as basic as a pair of pants? If only he'd trained to be an ambulance driver or a tree surgeon. Or a poet. A poet would be good. Chances are it would all be over by the time you were twenty-six.

'Like a frog in a frost,' she had said, half turning her head towards him.

'That's not really telling me very much though is it, Kakeka?'

That lesson with them last week had been particularly bad. It was a cover lesson for the permanently absent English teacher. Seeing that he knew many of the class because he taught them maths, and seeing that he appeared to be teaching them English by default this year as well, he would try to involve himself as much as he could. He'd been feeling a little on edge that day even before he entered the classroom and when he'd tried helping Kakeka, he'd made the mistake of relaxing momentarily in the warm refuge of the Serious Student. He squeezed behind her chair and tried to lean over her work with her, but there wasn't enough room between the tables and the radiator and so he was stuck. She looked back down at her page and then up at him. He tried to shift the table next to her along a little bit, but it was unaccountably heavy, its legs immovable on the industrial ribbed carpet.

Across the room, in front of the teacher's desk, Emily was sorting photos out on the table in front of her.

'Put those away, Emily,' he said, getting down on one knee beside Kakeka, a position he regretted immediately, but once he was there he decided he might as well stay put.

'Put what away, Sir?'

'Your photos.'

'Why? Miss lets us if we've finished our work. Don't she, Kakeka? Isn't it that Miss lets us if we've finished?'

Kakeka blinked once at her, eyes like planets.

'Show me your work then, Emily.'

'It's only rough, Sir. I got to do it in neat at home.'

'You haven't finished then.'

With a slither, Emily's photos fell to the floor. Babies, friends, brothers, sisters and a pet rabbit lay scattered over the carpet. Delighted guffaws and an obscene comment erupted from the middle of the room.

'You what?' Emily got to her feet and glowered accusingly at Kemal and Osman. They sneered at her and leant back in their seats, muttering as she crossed the room towards them.

Lem looked up. 'Emily. Go and sit down, now.'

She ignored him, but deciding against giving the boys a thump, collected up her photographs, then roamed over to where Salma and Rina sat on the opposite side of the room, facing the windows. They were tucked into a corner as far away from the centre of the room as possible.

Lem sighed. 'Emily,' he warned, remembering that this was precisely what Devora said you should never do. Emily's circuitry, she claimed, had been wired to require her name to be repeated in just that tone at regular intervals from the moment she woke to the moment she fell asleep. If it didn't happen, how would she know she still existed? 'Emily.'

'I'm bor-row-ing a pen.' All of Emily – her body, her voice, even her hair – exuded absolute indignation and complete disbelief that a teacher could be so extraordinarily unreasonable, not to mention stupid.

She helped herself to Salma's pencil case, rummaging in its contents until she found something that pleased her. Salma raised her eyes from her work and watched without speaking.

'These are crap.' She dropped the pens onto Salma's book and squeezed herself with some difficulty round to the back of her chair. Opening the wall cupboard, she began opening boxes and riffling through papers, 'Where does Miss keep her pens?'

'Emily.' He raised his voice, sick of the sound of himself. He sounded like a bloody dog trainer, for God's sake. Salma and Rina were watching him. So was Kakeka. He got to his feet and started trying to squeeze himself round the backs of the chairs so that he could get to Emily and the cupboard. Just as he was crossing the room, Kemal and Osman started braying like donkeys, flapping their hands and trying to push their chairs away from where Jason sat grinning.

'Kemal, get on with your work.'

'Sir! It was Osman.'

'There's a bad smell round here, Sir. I can't concentrate.' Osman got to his feet and staggered to the door, clasping his face.

Kemal threw his upper body across the table and wailed like he was in a Greek tragedy, 'I need oxygen, Sir. I can't breathe.'

Jason leant back in his chair and said, 'Sir, can I go toilet please Sir?'

'SHUT UP YOU LOT!' bellowed Saskia, raising her head from her arms. 'I'M TRYING TO SLEEP!'

Calm descended immediately and Emily sauntered back to her seat with a fistful of pens, muttering and tutting to herself.

'Oof,' Lem said, returning to where Kakeka sat and struggling to open a window. He managed to get it to open the regulation Health and Safety three centimetres. He knelt down beside her again so that he was the same height as her.

'Where were we? Oh, yes. Like a frog in a frost.'

She stared at him, then turned away and looked back down at her page again. 'You said, Sir. You said, try and use a simile.'

'Yes, well, it is a simile, I think, but how effective is it? What's it actually telling me?'

He was stalling for time. He liked Kakeka. Her whole family of several sisters and brothers were polite and conscientious. They gave him hope and their mother should get an OBE. But now Kakeka had had enough. She dropped her pen onto her page, leant back and folded her arms.

'It's not mine anyway,' she said, staring up at the ceiling.

'Ah well, there you are then,' said Lem, shuffling forwards a bit on his knees.

'It's Keats's.'

Lem looked at her.

'KEMAL'S GOT HIS HEAD STUCK SIR.'

Lem concentrated on not looking up.

'SIR!'

'What makes you think it was Keats's, Kakeka?'

'SHIT MAN SIT DOWN YOU MENTAL OR WHAT?'

'I read it, Sir. He said it in a letter to his girlfriend. Said he'd rather die in the heat of the moment, like Romeo, than leave her coldly like a frog in a frost. But don't make me say her name, Sir. I ain't saying that word.'

Lem straightened his back. How did Kakeka know about Keats? What on earth was she doing reading Keats's letters, for God's sake?

'Still, Kakeka, frog in a frost, even if it is Keats's, is not a very *effective* simile, is it? For one thing, frogs can't live in frosts, can they?' All the energy was draining out of him down through his knees and into the stained carpet. 'They'd die,' he added.

He held onto the table to steady himself and withdrew his hand quickly. The under-surface was layered with pads of gum.

'They're reptiles, I mean, amphibians,' he continued.

'So what you saying, Sir?' Emily had leant across to join in. 'You saying that all frogs die in winter? How do frogs as a species keep going, Sir, if all frogs die in winter? You know, like, suddenly, bam, all frogs dead?' She shuffled her enormous body forward on her chair and said, 'Come the spring, right? Come the spring, no frogs. I don't think so.' She did the infinity head wave again and Kakeka started to giggle. 'Course frogs don't die in the winter. I seen them down the reservoir. My dog finds them. They don't die. They whatsisname, *habitat*, innit?'

'SIR! SIR!'

'Right!' shouted Lem, unable to ignore the mayhem going on around him and manoeuvring himself out from behind the chairs. 'Right! Look! Just listen everyone, please—'

'Goin' anger management,' said Alice, shouldering past him, avoiding physical contact by a hair's breadth and heading for the door. It slammed inches from his right ear. The second corner of the poster on the door about Targets and Attendance flopped downwards. Osman laughed. Kemal lit a match. Jason said, 'Shall I clean the board, Sir?'

Perhaps he should retrain as a plumber. At least that was a job where you got to carry a toolbox around and your skills would be in demand. At least that was a job with a clear target. Here is a leak. Mend the leak.

Saskia had woken up again and was waving her hand in the air, an urgent expression on her face.

Lem looked at her hopefully, eyebrows raised as he began gathering up his things.

'How come, yeah,' she pointed to the poster of Great British Writers on the opposite wall. 'How come they all had poppy eyes in them days? Was they all ill or related, or what?'

Lem looked out of the window at a crane swinging a portable classroom into position. Crane driver would be another option.

'Oi, Sir! I'm arksing you a question, Sir.'

Although a bit of a responsibility, all those heavy weights.

'Oi! I arksed you a question. Them poets and what have you. They all look the same. Poppy eyes and long noses. How come white people don't look like that no more?'

Salma sat motionless in the midst of the chaos, writing carefully in blue-black ink. She seemed immune to what was going on around her and Lem wondered what her parents were thinking of, bringing her to London for an education. Surely there was better than this in Tehran, he thought, before remembering that Salma's family had to leave Tehran in a hurry. He turned on the class; he knew he didn't have it in him to live the lives that half these kids' parents had to live and rage arrowed through him.

'Right, everyone. Just stop what you're doing and LISTEN.' He banged the table with his fist.

To his astonishment a silence fell on the room. All eyes were on him, apart from those of Salma, who continued writing. He took a deep breath in and opened his mouth. This was what it was all about. The joy of a captive audience. If only he had thought of something worth telling them.

'If you really think that—'

The rest of his sentence, what there was of it, was drowned out by the sound of an industrial hammer drill boring through nine inches of reinforced concrete. On the other side of the wall, they were demolishing Food Science and turning it into Languages. He found there was a perverse pleasure to be had in the pandemonium of demolition that had accompanied all his teaching this term. It made manifest the absurd impossibility of the job, without it being entirely his fault.

Lem surrendered to the mayhem and decided that Dawn was right. This was not much of a job. Not that she'd ever said that, but there was a look she applied to her face whenever they were with other people and everyone was asking, 'And what do you do?' Lem sometimes used to want to say, 'I ride the Tube', because that's what he was doing whenever he stopped to think and it seemed to take up hours of his life. It was almost a profession. That and trying to go to sleep. I ride the Tube and I toss and turn. Oh, and I have an encyclopaedic knowledge of London place names that I don't know what to do with. Walthamstow. Place where guests are welcome (1075). But he didn't of course. Instead he would say, 'I'm a teacher', and watch them calibrate his worth. That's when Dawn would let that look slide over her face. She'd put the tip of her tongue up to one pointed incisor, smile lopsidedly and raise her head. Then she'd wait to be asked what she did and say, 'I work for the Ministry of Defence', which would always elicit a chorus of Rights, Wows and OKs, and Lem would feel a breeze of pride on her behalf during the pause between them asking, 'And what does that involve exactly?' and Dawn gradually meta-morphosing it down through Crown Protection, Customs and Excise, Military Police and Canine Procurement Sector, finally telling them that she worked in the office which trains sniffer dogs for the military and the Home Office. Their bright open faces would fall a little at that point and they would be on the verge of moving on to another subject until Dawn added, with impeccable and well-practised timing, 'Explosives', take a gulp of VodkaandOrange and look sort of thoughtful about Semtex.

5

Finsbury Park

'I USED TO lay a place for your ghost.'

Todd's heavy cheeks had a yellowish tinge where they met the worn skin just below his eyes. He couldn't be sure, but Lem thought he saw Todd go a shade yellower when he told him that.

'You what?' They were sitting side by side on the big comfortable sofa, feet up on the table, watching television at Todd's house. Dawn was at her family's for the weekend. Marvin crisis. Lem not invited.

Expensive perfume filled the room and Helena appeared in the doorway. She smiled at them, blonde head on one side. A ghastly gold lamé bag was hitched on one shoulder and her shoes were leopard-skin points. Helena bought whatever jokes designers dreamt up to make women look like lunatics.

'You boys be good now.' She blew two kisses, eyes flicking to the wine bottle and Todd's glass. 'Molly would love you to say goodnight to her, Lem. She's still awake.'

Lem half got to his feet, then felt unaccountably tired at the sight of the curving, carpet-clad staircase through the doorway. He liked Molly, in a way, but after a couple of minutes with her his eyes would start to glaze over. Helena's daughter liked to introduce him to all of her Beanie Babies and each one had a name and a whole life story. Anyway, the au pair was up there with her, wasn't she? He gave Helena a weak smile and sank back into the sofa. How did Todd get his sofa so deep and so comfortable? It was the kind of sofa you could sink into all day. Unlike the sofabed at Kinloss Court, which had an unwelcoming habit of letting you slide bottom first onto the floor.

Todd turned his head towards Helena without taking his eyes from the screen. She left and closed the front door very quietly. They heard the click of the latch and then her heels on the steps outside.

'You look lovely, darling!' Todd shouted towards the window and then he sighed, emptying his whole body, it seemed, of air. Lem thought of Fay stretched out on the tartan rug under the apple tree, a book face down on her stomach, rubbing her eye with the palm of one hand and saying, 'Well, Lem, if your father hadn't squandered his vast salary on weddings, wives and houses, you very probably would be able to afford something more enticing than Kinloss Court. But as it is . . .' And then she had picked up her book again, pulled her glasses back down off her head and continued reading.

Lem wondered about talking to Todd about Helena. He didn't think it would be good for his father's health if he mislaid another wife. He smirked at the joke and then he thought, What if it's hereditary, this mislaying thing that Todd seemed to do? At the edges of the days, he could feel the doubt creep up on him. To be frank, the laying was not much good despite Dawn's best efforts, and you couldn't say she didn't try. Maybe Gulliver men just weren't cut out for this relationship business, in which case why did Todd feel compelled to keep replacing them? Lem scratched his head and realised he had no idea what Todd looked like naked.

'You used to lay a place for my *ghost*, for God's sake?'

'Not when you first left.' A giggle almost escaped him. 'But a while after. Once I started noticing you were gone. You know, not coming back.' He really wanted to laugh properly now. Empty his lungs and his body of the tension and bloody misery of it all. He wanted to be shaken up, fall apart, unravel. He turned his face to the television and laughed at that instead.

'Who the bloody hell put the idea that I was dead into your head?' Todd jerked himself upright and emptied the rest of the bottle into his glass. 'Get your feet off the table.' He flapped at Lem's legs. 'It's the sort of thing that drives Helena mad.'

Lem stopped laughing and put his feet on the floor. He felt cold and a bit sick and wondered whether Helena or the au pair had done anything about food.

'I knew you weren't dead, but—'

'What did your mother tell you had happened to me, then?'

Lem remembered that for the first year he hadn't really noticed that Todd wasn't there. He tried it out in his head. I didn't notice you were gone, Dad. It didn't matter much that you were gone. Dad, you were gone before you left anyway. He looked at Todd, who was breathing noisily through his nose and switching silent channels. He decided against trying any of these out loud.

'Not that she wasted any time.' Todd threw the remote control down and looked about five all of a sudden.

Lem stared at the painting on the wall above the fireplace where a molten sun burnt the vapour off a dawn on the Thames. Domes and towers dissolved in the evanescent light transforming London into Venice. Somehow, despite the brashness, Todd seemed to know about beauty.

'What did you think was going to happen? You left.' His mouth filled with saliva and for one horrible moment he thought he might cry. 'Once Alan came, I worried about you being forgotten,' his voice barely a whisper.

Lem pointed the remote and pressed the button, but instead of the television changing channels, the gas fire whumped into life, pale flames leaping.

Todd said nothing. Now he looked about a hundred and ten.

'Look, it was just that when Mum asked me to lay the table, I'd put an extra place for you. She never used to say anything.' He stood up and hesitated. He needed to go and see what was in the fridge.

Todd swallowed noisily then fumbled in his pocket, tugging out a large blue handkerchief. He blew his nose like the elephant in *The Jungle Book*.

'Jesus Christ,' he said.

The braking motion of the train at the approach to the station swung him about as if he were on a horse and he thought of one of those Sergio Leone heroes swaying into town at a devastating slow canter once upon a time in the west.

Once Upon a Time in the West was Fay and Alan's favourite film, the one he remembered them watching on anniversaries and birthdays, knotted together on the sagging sofa in the back room, the hiss of the gas fire and the lament of the harmonica filling the air. Fay and Alan would watch the screen, absorbing the long still shots of Charles Bronson and Henry Fonda and their slow, dry dance of death. 'An opera of violence,' Alan used to say, although Lem knew it was written on the video cover, but Fay would always move in closer under his arm when he said that. Lem remembered wanting the feeling, wanting the feeling he knew they had, sitting there together in front of the screen. Now, whenever he heard that harmonica melody it triggered the fluttery sensation in his belly, a sensation that had felt sometimes like hope and sometimes like dread. But the truth was, he told himself now, those evenings made him feel that he was a visitor to his mother's marriage who had overstayed his welcome.

The train crawled through the dark and then came to another halt inside the tunnel. A collective sigh went through the carriage, half anxious, half resigned. Finsbury Park would be packed with people at this time of day; everyone braced themselves for the invasion, drawing feet and elbows, bags and papers closer in to their bodies.

'Finn's Manor, 1235,' he had said to Dawn one rainy rush hour to relieve the tedium of the perpetual traffic jam outside Finsbury Park Tube. He was nonplussed by how dull they had become together and how quickly it had happened. Within a year it seemed, they had reached the stage where they rarely managed to create a conversation that took them to new places, allowed them to impress or to flirt or to reveal the hidden parts of themselves. Why the hell was that?

'I'm not interested in what some Irish geezer did here a thousand years ago, Lem.'

He pressed on. 'An Irish manor house? In England?'

She had taken a deep, warning breath in and the vertical vein that he used to love appeared down the centre of her brow.

'In 1235?' he added, trying to tempt her out of herself with a smile.

She tensed her arms on the steering wheel and did her boggled look. He considered telling her why an Irishman would be unlikely to have owned a manor house in Finsbury Park in 1235, but Dawn suddenly swung to the left and was nipping along the bus lane. This is illegal, said Lem to himself. You will get fined £400.

The windscreen wipers were whacking to and fro, visibility was poor and Dawn had switched the fan heater on to Hot at full blast. He put his finger on the window button on his left and tried to achieve a slice of cold air. While his window remained mysteriously shut, Dawn's opened and closed at speed, admitting rhythmic blasts of rain, wind and traffic.

'Lem-a-a!'

She stabbed her own button repeatedly so that both windows went up and down, and all at once they were trapped in an auto-farce that made him laugh until she said, 'It's not funny, Lem'. He thought then how dangerous electric windows were. You only had to put your head out to check something and lean your elbow on the button at the same time, or someone else had only to lean their elbow on the button and your head would be sliced off. He slid a look over at Dawn's neck.

'For God's sake, it's like having a child in the car.'

They crawled along for several minutes without speaking, their child sitting invisibly on the back seat behind them. Lem read the back of her windscreen Animal Liberation Front 'MEAT IS MURDER' sticker. It said, REDRUM SI TAEM and he had a fleeting memory of a horror film where REDRUM kept appearing in blood on windows. He watched the pavement crawl by – the mini-cab offices, estate agents and pubs – and tried to conjure up an image of Finn striding about the fields and dales of Finsbury Park deciding where to build his manor. He was just opening his mouth to ask whether she would like to have lived one thousand years ago when she narrowly missed maiming a cyclist. He waited for her swearing to subside while in the wing mirror he watched the cyclist wobble, struggle and finally tumble in a heap into the bus queue.

Dawn turned up the radio. A singer was wailing inconsolably about love and Lem stared at the volume knob, fighting the desire to tell her the next bit about Finn's Manor. The more he read about the history of the places around them, of the lives lived and of the survival of these names through time, the more he began to feel that he barely existed in his own life. Dawn's stubborn refusal to be curious about things she didn't know dismayed him, and it occurred to him with a weary slackening of his spine that he no longer liked her very much at all.

'Finn,' he said, looking at her, 'is a Scandinavian nick-name.'

By now they were trapped behind the Number 19 bus that

had pulled in to a bus stop. She looked in her mirror and calculated the distance between them and the cyclist, who Lem could see had now remounted and was pedalling furiously towards them. Dawn stroked her eyebrows straight with the middle finger of her right hand.

'Really,' she said with emphatic disinterest, staring fixedly ahead once more.

Lem swallowed and thought how it seemed that Dawn had too little knowledge and he didn't have enough. Perhaps Dawn was only interested in money and sex and he didn't have enough of those either. It was depressing. She put her indicator on and began trying to pull out from behind the stationary bus, prompting a barrage of horn blowing.

'Fuck off, fuck off, fuck *off*,' she sang, strangely cheered.

'So Finn,' he ploughed on, 'was a Viking.'

He looked out at the gridlocked grime of the Blackstock Road and tried to imagine the verdant pastures of Finsbury Park when Finn pitched up, having made the treacherous sea crossing from the icy wastes.

'And this area was convenient for Londinium, presumably,' he added.

Dawn turned up the volume on the radio. Someone was extolling the virtues of smacking your bitch up and Dawn drummed the steering wheel with her fingers, nodding her head in time to the beat.

'Just goes to show you never know how things will turn out,' he said, flinching just a little.

The lovers by the door had been edged along inside the carriage by the press of people getting on at Finsbury Park. Now they stood inches from Lem, their foreheads touching, making a close private space between their faces so that they weren't kissing any longer but looking, first into the other's eyes, then down at the other's mouth. Lem let his eyes travel down the length of the woman's long narrow back, past the spherical lift of her bottom, down to the hem of her skirt, which shook a little at the backs of her knees; he followed the line of her calves, a sheen of sweat across the taut curve of skin, and then he let his eyes rest on her feet, which were placed either side of her lover's foot. He studied the rhythm of her secret dance; the creased stained sole of her right foot as the heel lifted up, dropped back halfway, then rose up again in a twist and back down over onto its edge as she moved her pelvis against her partner's thigh. He felt the ache settle in his balls and behind his eyes, and he swallowed at the sensation of all the liquid in his body being drawn down towards his groin. He clasped his fingers closer, feeling the head of his cock nudging his palm, and hoped that the suited man standing in front of him would not take his eyes off *The Times*. Her buttocks tensed and relaxed in tiny movements that made her hem tremble and when the train started with a jerk that made everyone lurch, her partner caught Lem's eye again so that, with a dart of shame, he looked down at the floor in front of him and prayed that the heat and heaviness between his legs would retreat.

Through the throng of people, the darkened windows opposite offered up partial reflections of faces. It was safer to study these and he thought of Dawn seated scowling at her make-up mirror and of the time he had said, 'A reflection is not the truth, Dawn, you know that, don't you? It's a distortion.' She had looked at him like he was stupid and at that moment, at that very moment, he had the feeling that he was suffocating and he got to his feet with the words 'I'm leaving you' filling his mouth like marbles. He had taken a breath and got the first word out, 'I'm—', but her phone had rung and he had waited, watching her as she sat half naked in front of the mirror, holding the phone between her chin and her shoulder while she mascaraed one eye; and when she laughed her left breast shuddered and shook gently, so that he felt nostalgic for the girl she had seemed to be once, and the man he might have become with her all that time ago on the boat in Mersea, and he had sat down again and said nothing.

'Why don't you get a motorbike, like Alan?' Dawn had started to say to him. Well, the truth was he just didn't think motorbikes were safe. Scooters were even worse. Shocking in the rain, and in point of fact it annoyed him a bit that Dawn showed not the slightest concern for his physical safety in continually nagging him to get a bloody motorbike. All right for Dawn, the journey to work, she never got the Tube. She tuned in to Heart FM and drove the Peugeot to Hendon. Dawn loved to drive. In fact, she rarely used public transport because she said it was dirty and dangerous. He knew for a fact that she had never been on a bus. Buses were for losers, she said. Alan wasn't afraid of the motorbike of course. And nor was Fay, although strictly speaking she didn't actively ride it; she rode pillion, which was, Lem knew since covering the Year 10 English lesson every Friday afternoon, an unusual example of a noun and a verb. You hardly ever got that in the English language apparently, although when he'd challenged the class to come up with examples of nouns that were also verbs, he had precisely three seconds of glorious thoughtful silence during which he basked precariously in a rare sense of superiority, certain they'd never guess *pillion*, before Saskia put her hand up and said, 'You Fuck.' There'd been a silence and then she'd continued, 'That's a noun and a verb, innit though?' And then there'd been the explosion of shrieks, screams, yells and the as yet unnamed sound of fifteen-year-old boys expressing shock, delight, contempt and triumph. When he was a pupil it would have been called punching the air and whooping, but it was so much more complicated than that now and involved much trouser hitching, crotch cupping, finger epilepsy and head jerking.

Marissa, the new maths teacher, had been very sweet to him the day of the noun-that-is-a-verb riot in his classroom. She'd been in the next room and had come in thinking the class had been left without a teacher, and afterwards at break she'd made a point of sitting next to him and told him about the time that class had lit a firework during her lesson. Steve had sat the other side of Lem pressing his arm and thigh hard against his leg, mumbling obscenities *sotto voce* the whole time. 'You're in there, mate, bloody hell, what I wouldn't give for a bit of that', and making sizzling sounds with his tongue when he wasn't stuffing a greasy sausage roll into his mouth. Lem watched Marissa's hands as she talked. They hovered around her head a lot, strumming the twisted silver of her necklace, stroking strands of hair and scratching just inside her ears. Her eyes shone and so did her hair, and Lem had started to develop a dread that she expected something of him.

'Baby I'm Bored,' she said with a short shriek.

She talked fast and entirely in the present tense, the words punctuated with whoops and smiles like solar flares.

'I have one of those signs in my rear window,' she was telling him. 'Like, it's a laugh, yeah? Because it looks like those Baby on Board signs that parents have, but mine says Baby I'm Bored? The man at the garage give it me. He's always giving me things,' she let out another shriek. 'No-o! Lem. I do not mean in that way!' And then her whole body shivered with laughter.

He looked at her shaking her hair and combing it with her fingers and said, 'My girlfriend used to have a car', by which he meant that he no longer had a girlfriend or a car, but he realised that wasn't quite how Marissa understood it.

'I think it's sort of different,' Marissa told him, another smile snapping across her face like a sheet. 'Baby I'm Bored? You know, reassuringly non-reproductive.'

She leant back in her chair, raising one arm in the air and exposing a smooth caramel stomach pierced at the navel by a gold stud. She ran her hand up her stomach and down again, rubbing her palm back and forth under her waistband. 'That's the big turn-off for guys, isn't it?' she said.

Lem turned his large hands over and looked at his bitten nails.

'Is it?'

'You know,' she said, 'the way most women just see men as sperm donors? That is *so* wrong.' She put her hand, the one that had been down the front of her trousers, lightly on the back of Lem's forearm. It was still warm from the heat of her skin. 'Men should stand up for themselves. Whoo!' She stood up, punching the air. 'They deserve a bit of respect as well.' And then she said, 'Don't, whatever you do, mention sperm donors when Ameena's around.' She paused a moment for Lem to ask why, but he was trying to decode her necklace, which had letters in it and seemed to be saying 'ass' something. Marissa continued, 'Apparently she's been trying for a baby and it's not happening.' She nodded meaningfully.

The bell went and, like parts of a machine, people began standing up, gathering their overstuffed bags and seventeen pieces of paper and Biros and memos and bunches of keys and folders. Lem stood up with nothing and wondered where on earth he'd left everything. Marissa put her hand on his arm.

'Remember, you are more than just a sperm bank.' She raised her fist again. Lem hoped she wouldn't, but she did, 'Whoo!' And then she joined the heaving jostle in the too-small corridor, shoving and shouting its way towards the next two lessons before lunch.

'Jeeze, man,' hissed Steve in his ear. 'She got the hots for you or what? You going to ask her out then?'

Lem wished he'd move further away and not press his arm up against him like that when they were walking in front of the kids. He fell back, allowing Steve to walk ahead. Steve had the stiff-arsed walk of a cowboy with bruised genitals, a gait which Lem used to think was an affectation, but since discovering that Steve lived in his car, now suspected might be the early onset of rheumatism or gout. He wondered if Marissa knew where Steve lived. Lem thought of the night Steve had cried in All Bar One and said he wished he had what Lem had with Dawn and then he'd leant forward, Lem assumed to be sick, but it had in fact been to kiss Lem roughly on the mouth. The inside of Steve's mouth had tasted of old pennies. Neither of them had mentioned it since. Best not to.

A large television mounted on a six-foot trolley zigzagged down the corridor towards them. Lawrence's face appeared from round the side of it, a ring binder and a cascading sheaf of paper under one arm.

'Just borrowing this,' he said, and then came to grief against the wall-mounted fire hose. Complete gridlock ensued and Lem found himself immobilised between the adolescent bargement that commenced and the Year 8 algebra wall display in a corridor that must have been designed in inches, then constructed in centimetres by mistake.

'Well? Did you ask her or what?' Steve said over his shoulder.

Lem shook his head and pulled his mouth up at the corners. He ought to check what that expression looked like actually, because it was intended as a sort of economy smile, smile-lite, but it was just possible it could be interpreted as a snarl. After all, isn't that how some monkeys show aggression?

'Come on, Lem, what have you got to lose?'

'She's just not my type,' he said. 'Too clean and shiny.' But his words were engulfed by the calls and shouts of the students that surrounded them. They left a little space around Steve, he noticed; in fact not a single one of them made physical contact with Steve's rigid frame and he was also doing that thing where he used his eyes to silence a child in mid-yell. They hadn't taught Lem that on the PGCE course.

The double doors at the end of the corridor wouldn't open because there were kids jamming both sides. Lem turned his body, craned his neck and started to take tiny steps in the other direction. If he took the long route round, down the stairs, along past Technology and up again through Science, it might be quicker. As he turned the corner the faces of boys that he recognised surrounded him like a shoal of fish, SIR SIR WHERE ARE WE SIR? SIR, I AINT GOT MY BOOK SIR and a tide of jostling bumping surging hormones swept him onwards into the crush at the top of the stairs. ARE WE WATCHING A VIDEO? TELL HIM SIR HE JACKED MY PHONE SIR.

Increasingly Lem wondered why it was that society clung to the notion that compulsory education after the age of thirteen was such a good idea. Who exactly was learning what? 'Send them all away to an island for four years and let them get it all out of their system,' was Alan's advice. 'They'll be begging to be allowed back into polite society by the time they're eighteen.' 'From what you've told me, Lem, it sounds like they've all had their hearts broken,' Fay added. 'I doubt they're old enough for that,' said Alan. 'I meant by their parents, actually,' she added, finishing the purple shading on the inside corner of a defendant's eyes. 'But no doubt one leads to the other.'

When he thought of other professions, he marvelled at the sheer courage and skill required. He thought of Fay sketching in the courtroom, looking up and looking down, studying the eyes and mouth of the accused, trying to get the way they did their hair – the hair was the hardest, she always said. He imagined her checking the clock and worrying whether the likeness was too sympathetic or too demonic, unsure whether it would be used in the papers or not. Or he thought of how Alan earnt a living, thundering along the tarmac day after day, appearing out of the haze of fumes to rescue the stranded, bending beneath bonnets in the wet filthy roar of the M11 and saving them with a few turns of his torque wrench. And then there was Todd, whose day, frankly, he didn't understand at all. Lem had visited his TV production company several times. Todd himself seemed to do nothing, but all around him were women, and a few men, looking up at computer screens, talking in clipped assertive tones down the phone, striding purposively from one end of the office to the other. Todd's office was sectioned off from the rest of the company with glass and blinds and was full of witty and pointless objects, many framed declarations of success and recognition and two large leather sofas. How did someone like his father actually conduct his working life? How had he learnt to command such an immense salary and attain the status that allowed him to shack up with women repeatedly? Fay always said that there was no secret. 'Your father had one good idea in 1980,' she told him. 'In those days,' she said, 'television was a small pond and he was a big fish. A good idea was rewarded out of all proportion to its worth. Since then he's been able to pay other people to have the good ideas. Usually women.' And then she would add, unable to stop herself, 'Anyway, he didn't actually marry me, which is why we live in Walthamstow and he lives in . . . wherever it is that he lives now.'

'That's Francesca,' Todd told Lem, during one of their father-and-son lunches, watching the disappearing back of a lithe woman with hair like an advert, clip-clopping her way to the Ladies. She had passed their table with a smile and a 'Hi, Todd.' He turned back and cast his eye down the wine list. 'Very bright. Very ideas-*fertile*.'

Yet even if Todd didn't come up with the ideas himself, whole days still had to be filled, budgets conjured up, expertise and knowledge displayed, meetings chaired, new territories conquered, confidence exuded, reputations maintained, deals done. Todd's world of work involved a lot of questing and striving and thrusting. If he was honest, when Lem thought of all that, he got close to what he imagined was a panic attack. It felt like that time one February, the year he had met Dawn, when Todd took him up in his Tiger Moth and performed loop-the-loops over the dank fenland landscape. He had known then what terror was, sitting behind his father in the cramped cockpit, encased in the flimsy skin of metal. The engine laboured during the vertical climb into the grey, and Lem wondered if Todd was planning to kill them both. He thought of Fay and of how she would receive the news. She would be brave, but furious at Todd and his childish pranks.

At the top of the climb they had paused in a sudden silence, father and son lost in space, then there had been a spinning, gut-annihilating dive which forced his forehead into Todd's back. With his face crushed into the oiled sheepskin of his father's flying jacket, he had yelled, 'Dad!' at the top of his lungs so that Todd brought the plane out of its dive and they swooped in a graceful curve low over fields and ditches. Then it was like nothing he had ever done before, better than the fair or flying to Spain. It felt as though he was in an airship and he understood how little can be seen from the ground and how even less can be understood down there, but that up here everything was mapped out, the lie of the land was clear. Todd shouted, 'All right?' and Lem shouted back, 'Yes', grinning and nodding his head like an idiot because suddenly it was the best feeling, defying gravity and death with this man, this father of his, and he wanted it to last for ever. The plane roared up for the beginning of another looping dive. 'I love you, Dad,' Lem bellowed, but above the scream of the engine he couldn't be sure that Todd heard.

The train stuttered its way out of the tunnel and into the lights of Highbury & Islington station, strobing the faces of waiting passengers so that they looked like frames in a film.

Islington was Gislandune and was very old, he remembered that. They were under what had been Gisla's hill a thousand years ago, but was now a giant roundabout with a McDonald's and The Famous Cock Tavern, where you could drink twenty-four hours a day and where Dawn once had her handbag stolen. Highbury was just boring. It meant high manor, which in Lem's opinion was as unimaginative as Green Park – a seventeenth-century name for a park that was green.

When the doors opened, the lovers disconnected themselves and looked about them. The whole of north London seemed to be getting on and the crush and push of people entering the carriage meant that now everyone was pressed up against everyone else, whether they were lovers or not. Lem felt glad of his seat – there were some perks to living out in the back of beyond. The doors remained open and the train engine ticked monotonously. Every now and then another passenger sardined themselves into the carriage. The doors slid shut and then opened again. And again. Someone was obstructing the doors with a limb or a briefcase.

Please stand clear of the closing doors.

A tiny change in mood or pressure in the carriage made Lem look to his right. By the middle doors, the sea of people parted miraculously as, automatic weapon clasped across his flak jacket like a crucifix, an armed officer stepped into their midst.

6

Highbury & Islington

IT WAS MARISSA who had first told him the rumour about the suicide bomber in Year 10. They had been invigilating an exam. Lem liked invigilation because it gave him a whole hour of silence and space in which to do nothing but think. He enjoyed pacing the aisles to the rhythm of his own musings, passing rows of silenced students hunched over their Ordnance Survey maps and photographs of the Kalahari Desert. Occasionally one would interrupt his reverie with a whispered request for a tissue or more paper, and Lem would be happy to perform these small acts of kindness in return for a rare glimpse of their suffering and vulnerability. He couldn't understand what the fuss was about exams. Ameena was always up in arms against them. Too many tests, she said, but Lem suspected that the students liked them as much as he did. Ameena said they were just sick, the whole institution was sick, and what they were really enjoying was the chance to do penance, to be punished in the eyes of the Lord for ever daring to question their place in the British caste system. The Sports Hall became a kind of church at exam times and it always amazed him that the kids actually did sit there shivering in silence for three hours.

'The last thing exams are, are measurements of academic ability,' Steve told Lem once, on a rare occasion when he wasn't talking about sex. But then the object of his attentions was Marissa, on her first day, and she was sitting between them in the staffroom. Marissa had brought up the subject of league tables.

'Exactly,' she had said vehemently, eyes bright and turning abruptly towards Steve.

Steve had given his head a little shake in a good impression of sincerity and ploughed on, running his hand through his hair.

'I mean, basically it's a social measure, isn't it? You know, if they—'

'Exactly! Just reminding everyone where they stand in life.'

She had turned back to Lem then and given him a blinding smile that scattered every thought in his head because he knew what she wanted. She wanted him. He opened his mouth and then merely inhaled.

During invigilation, Marissa and Steve seemed to encounter some sort of problem with stillness and silence. For a start, Steve was incapable of adjusting the volume of his own voice and pursued Lem mercilessly in order to try to deliver the tale of the previous night's sexual adventures, most of which these days were probably celluloid, not that that made any difference to Steve. Increasingly, Lem realised, Steve spoke only in Pornish and it had occurred to him that the man might need help from something like Porn Anonymous, if such an organisation existed. As Steve trailed after him saying, 'And I'm telling you, she was hot and ready', Lem thought that for Steve, the biggest torture of all would be to have no one to tell. Like a modern-day Ancient Mariner, the albatross round his neck was sex.

Lem walked up the far aisle where Richard, who was six foot four and whose knees came up above the level of his desk, was supporting one arm with the other, waving it about like a giant crustacean. Lem leant down close to catch the mumbled question.

'Sir? What's Nigeria's primary export, Sir?' Richard pointed at the question in front of him with his pen.

'Well, that's what they're asking you. You have to look at the diagram and work it out.'

Richard looked up at him forlornly from under his hood and Lem tapped one finger on the drawing of three barrels of oil next to the coast of Nigeria.

'Cylinders, Sir?'

'No, think geography, not maths.'

'Rum?'

Lem shook his head and wished he had let Steve deal with this one. Richard squirmed in his child's chair. 'Did you do Nigeria, Richard?'

'I was away, Sir. My mum died while we were doing that.'

Lem let his forearm rest against the boy's shoulder. It seemed to happen rather a lot in this school, parental death. He tried and failed to imagine what that must be like. Richard cleared his throat. Lem could smell the boy's feet and he noticed he had spelt Nigeria wrong.

'What do you cook chips in, Richard?'

He pushed back his hood a little, looked up at Lem and smiled. 'Oh,' he whispered. 'Oh. Oil. Oh, yeah. Thank you, Sir.' And he bent eagerly over his paper again.

Lem went back to the front of the hall where Steve came and stood with him, rocking on the balls of his feet, legs wide apart as if straddling some imaginary conquest. Marissa appeared at the far end of the hall, trying to close the squeaking doors quietly. She smiled and walked with quick strides towards them, looking to the left and the right. Lem noticed that the kids sought out her gaze as she passed and offered sad smiles in return for hers. The boy at the front watched Steve watching her. Marissa came and stood in the space Steve made between them.

'Did you hear about the suicide bomber in Year 10?' she whispered, jewellery tinkling around her wrists and neck.

'What?'

'Apparently. Some girl whose brother was killed in . . .' She hesitated and jingled some more. 'One of those places . . .'

A hand went up at the back of the hall. Lem took a ream of paper and left them to it, studying the bowed heads of the girls in hijabs as he did so.

'The kids in her class say she's almost qualified,' Marissa continued when he returned to the front of the hall.

'What's her name?' Steve asked.

It could just be the lighting in the hall, but close up, Steve's waxen face looked unhealthy. The skin around his mouth was sore and there were brownish hollows beneath his eyes. Marissa inched away from him, towards Lem.

'Can't remember her name,' she whispered. 'I've a feeling she's in one of your classes though, Lem. Wears all the gear and that.'

He thought of the students in his Year 10 class that wore the hijab. Hawa from Eritrea, Nazimah and Salma from Iran, Shaheedah from Pakistan and the new girl from Russia whose name he didn't know. Surely none of them. They were devout, but they didn't seem angry. But then, how would he know? He had barely spoken with them.

'Salma something, I think.'

'Someone's having you on, Marissa,' Steve said. 'Who told you? If it was the kids, then you can forget it.'

The man standing in the carriage directly in front of Lem jerked his head back in a helpless contortion and suddenly let loose a sneeze so violent it was visible. The sneeze triggered a spate of coughing in the woman next to him and Lem held his breath and began to count.

He thought of the common on a wintry morning, running behind Alan and Fay, knowing he had to circle them some-how but not enter the bubble around them, watching the shape of their breath as it hung in the freezing air like misty lungs. He remembered thinking how big their exhalations were compared to his short shredded puff and then thinking that perhaps that was what the soul looked like. He thought now how everyone in this carriage had no choice but to inhale one another. That in his immune system the battle had no doubt already begun, white blood cells engaged in fatal combat with that man's cold virus, a battle which, whether it was lost or won, would leave him weakened and weary for the week ahead.

As the train swung everyone suddenly towards him, he was reminded of *The Sound of Music* and Julie Andrews in the convent, then the scene where the family hid in the cemetery while the Nazis searched them out. You never saw nuns any more. It was a very long time since the West had seen wimples.

Sister Maria, that was what Julie Andrews had been called. He wondered whether France, having banned the hijab, would also have banned Maria's wimple. But then wimples were for women, not schoolgirls. It was the idea of adolescent girls concealing themselves that upset the French, according to Ameena.

'The French are afraid of the idea of intelligent women,' she said. 'Capitalism would fail in the face of an upsurge of intelligent women.'

Lem had been surprised to hear her say this, because he had rather assumed that Ameena would approve of the ban and even suggest their own school should follow suit. She was always going on about women's rights and it seemed to him a bit unequal if the men didn't wear it too. He kept quiet, fearful of being drawn but listening carefully, trying to remember the details of Helena's conversion to Islam. Fortunately, Marissa was one of those people who panicked on seeing any gap in a conversation and would charge at it like a nervous horse. She blundered into all the traps Ameena laid for Steve.

'Oh, but it's a symbol of male oppression, isn't it?' she said. 'I mean, why should they have to cover their heads? It's medieval.' Marissa ran her hand up through the back of her hair, making her belly-stud glint. 'And anyway, I don't think religion has any place in schools. I agree with banning – what is it they call it – conspicuous signs of religion? Well, you don't get much more conspicuous than a headscarf.'

'Rubbish,' said Ameena who was slitting open her mail with a ruler and now punctuated everything she said with ripping noises and well-aimed lobs of junk mail into the bin by Marissa's legs. 'Capitalism is the religion of the West and most of the kids we teach are plastered in conspicuous signs of that – Dolce & Gabbana, Adidas, Burberry – do I need to go on? Girls who wear the veil are asserting their right not to trade in the only thing the West values in a woman – her appearance.'

'Don't be so ridiculous, Ameena. That is bullshit,' said Devora, looking up wearily from her marking. She had taken to doing her marking in the maths office recently. Her broad back looked hunched and tired. Grey roots were showing beneath the auburn. 'Are you telling me that I'd be happier in a headscarf?'

The paper slitting ceased. Ameena studied Devora and said, 'Actually, yes.'

'Whoah!' Steve raised his hands and stared at Lem. 'Ameena didn't mean that, Devora.'

'What, and I'd be more intelligent too?' A blush was rising up Devora's throat.

'Well, do you teach any stupid girls in headscarves?'

Ameena simply appeared not to feel embarrassment, thought Lem.

'Of course I do.'

'Not many though, do you? They are nearly all high achievers. The point is that Western women waste ninety per cent of their brainpower on worrying about how they look.'

'Well, why don't you wear one then?' asked Devora, slapping down an exercise book.

'I did until I was twenty. Then I decided not to. It was my decision. But that's what I'm saying. There shouldn't be a law against it. Headscarves are not harming anyone.'

'No, but Islamic fundamentalism is,' said Marissa. 'There's that girl, Salma Musad in Year 10, who's a suicide bomber.'

Lem froze. Devora stared. Steve put his hands up in the air again. Ameena turned to Marissa.

'You really should not repeat rumours like that. Seriously. Just think if the local paper got hold of such a story. They'd have a field day. They've had it in for this school for years.'

The muscles around Marissa's mouth loosened and her flesh paled in response to Ameena's words, so that Lem wondered at the physiological effort normally expended by our bodies just to keep us looking like we aren't falling apart. He tried to make his own face look like he had Islam, sexuality, freedom, class, poverty and multiculturalism completely sorted in addition to an awesome grasp of mathematics.

Ameena meanwhile seemed to have no desire to dismantle Marissa and she turned back towards Devora and resumed her letter slitting.

'But now you come to mention it, the other thing that the French are afraid of is that some people might die for an idea.'

'I never knew you were a religious zealot,' said Devora, picking up another book, licking her index finger and turning the pages.

Steve was suddenly involved in some complex texting and Marissa was trying to pull her T-shirt down over her belly.

'I didn't say the ideas they were ready to die for were worth dying for, I said that what terrified the French was that an individual might contemplate doing such a thing. It goes against everything we've been taught in the West, against everything we teach.'

'The reason we don't need to die for an idea, Ameena, is that people have already done the dying for us. Why do you think we have a democracy? How many Islamic democracies can you name by the way?'

Lem was fairly sure Helena would not be prepared to die for anything, but he decided to try to begin to explain about her curious conversion two years ago.

'My dad's ex-wife . . .'

Blank stares all round.

'Your mum, you mean?'

'No, my ex-stepmother, Helena,' said Lem, wishing he hadn't bothered, 'converted to Islam at the age of forty-five.'

'Did she marry a Muslim then?'

'I think it was a way of putting an end to the marrying. It's something to do with her job too.'

'Which is?'

He blushed. 'Top secret.'

Steve laughed and so did Devora and Marissa. Ameena smiled and Lem wished he had said something more outrageous, like 'She's a double agent.'

'You must tell Melanie,' said Devora, making him feel better. 'She's looking for speakers for International Women's Day.'

Then they stopped talking and looked at the door.

How long Salma had been standing in the doorway, Lem had no idea. Her tired, austere face was focused on him and in her hand she held her maths book. He got up from his chair when he saw her and went towards her, wiping his damp palms on his trousers.

'Sir,' she began, dark eyes meeting his and ignoring the silent tableau behind him. 'You told me to come and see Ms Patel about starting AS maths a year early. I've been having extra lessons . . .' She smiled apologetically. 'Sorry if I'm interrupting your lunch hour, Sir.'

Lem got up and took her book, remembering vaguely that he'd told her to come at the beginning of lunch break and now it was nearly the end of it. An eddy of annoyance with Salma swept through him. This girl, or woman. It was hard to get your bearings as far as that was concerned. What did she want from him, with her diligence and her manners? She would never complain that he hadn't marked her book for a term, but on the other hand, if he passed it over to Ameena, which he was now going to have to do, Ameena most certainly would.

'Have you had any lunch, Salma?' was all he could think of

to say. She shook her head. Lem turned towards Ameena. 'Salma was wondering about doing the GCSE a year early.' He flapped her book in Ameena's direction. The bell went. Normality returned to the office as everyone got to their feet and began to leave.

'It's OK, Lem,' said Ameena. 'I'll deal with this.'

Lem knew he'd missed his chance. If only they'd all slow down a bit or shut up for a moment so he could gather his thoughts. If only his heart didn't quicken and his scalp didn't prickle and his belly twist at the prospect of joining in. He had wanted to finish the tale of Helena's conversion to Islam two years ago. He wanted to tell them that Todd claimed it was further proof, should anyone need it, that the woman was certifiable. He wanted to imitate the way Fay insisted Helena had always worked for her American father and was rumoured to be part of a CIA plot to maintain Europe's support of the war on terror. He wanted to parody the way Fay would close her eyes against Dawn's disbelief and say, 'You wouldn't believe what the CIA have done. Nothing is too fantastic for that outfit. They recruit and train people to carry out attacks in Europe . . .' How Dawn would shake her head, and how Fay would stop talking as if there was no point in wasting her breath on someone whose political life was focused entirely on the rights of small mammals. He would like to make them laugh, show them how Fay would say all of this in a flurry of washing up bubbles and much thwacking of rubber gloves on the draining board, while Alan whistled, but without the actual whistle sound, and bustled about tidying things in an energetic and noisy manner. But here he was, speechless and a bundle of nerves. He had run out of time and the bell was going for afternoon school. He was even incapable of describing Helena's relationship to him, seeing that none of these people had met her and anyway, he wasn't sure whether the whole world of Helena wasn't really just a figment of Fay's overactive and vengeful imagination.

'You'll really like Helena,' Todd had said, the day he had taken Lem for lunch and told him he was getting married again. 'Very smart. Bright, you know.' He leant back in his chair and surveyed the wine list critically. 'Her father's a big shot in American intelligence. All very hush-hush. But Helena's what I call *feminine*. Looks after herself, if you know what I mean.' Then he'd leant forward and winked so that Lem had lowered his eyes and flailed around for something to say back, but all he could come up with was, 'Nice jacket, Dad.'

'We'll have a bottle of the—' and then Todd said something that sounded badly mispronounced so that the waiter had to bend towards the wine list, looking politely at where Todd's finger was hovering. 'Red OK for you, Lem?' Todd's face appeared from one side of the wine list. 'Oh, you don't drink, do you?'

Lem shook his head, wondered whether it had been wise to have had that joint when he had woken up that afternoon, and then the wine list was snapped shut and handed to the waiter with an exchange of manly nods. Mispronounced or not, Lem marvelled at his father's ability to keep finding wives and choose from a wine list. How the hell do you know what to have? he wanted to ask.

'Do you like it then?'

Lem glugged at his Coke. 'Mmm?' He was having difficulty keeping track of the conversation.

'The jacket.' Todd jiggled his head from side to side and splayed out the cuffs.

'Oh.' Coke bubbles rose up his nose. 'Yeah. Nice.'

'Here. Have it.' Todd wrestled it off his shoulders, shrugging it down his arms and causing the woman at the next table to slide a look his way. 'Go on. It's getting too tight for me anyway. Here. I'd like you to.'

Blushing, Lem took the jacket and crumpled it onto his lap. 'Thanks, Dad.'

One of the good things about meals out with Todd was

that Lem was likely to be on the receiving end of one of his random acts of generosity.

'Anyway, she's dying to meet you.'

Todd finished off his aperitif and a silence opened up between them. He brushed the dandruff off each of his shoulders. Lem made the I've-reached-the-end-of-my-drink noise through his straw. Todd moved his chair noisily away from the table and began buttering another roll.

'Do you work out at all, Lem? I've got to get back in shape. Your mother all right, is she? Now what do you fancy to eat? University OK?'

'They all watch *What's Your Poison?*' said Lem, staring at the menu. Could the lamb really cost thirty-two pounds? he wondered.

'Unbeatable format, those hospital reality shows. Just developing another one. *So Up Yourself.* All done with fibre-optic cameras. Amazing where they can get them these days. Fancy the squid?'

Now, several years later, Lem was wearing the denim jacket because he felt it might bring him luck although he knew this was irrational since, being a mathematician, he didn't believe in luck. Probability, yes. Luck, no. Nevertheless, for a long time he'd worn a pair of grey silk boxer shorts that had belonged to Todd. He'd found them in Fay's bedroom wastepaper basket one day when he was about seven, along with a pair of glass cufflinks, two odd socks and a tie. The silk boxer shorts had been one of the things Todd had forgotten to take with him when he left. Lem was one of the other things of course, as Fay used to joke. Lem had taken the silk boxers and they had become the thing he kept under his pillow, bringing them out to nuzzle in the half dark of his bedroom at bedtime. He liked the slippery feel of them and their faint scent of shower gel.

Putting on Alan's shirt, though, was a new departure for Lem and not something he had made a habit of. It was a little on the small side, but it had appealed to him hanging so crisply on its hanger on the bathroom door. He didn't know what was happening to his own shirts lately. He had dropped them in the laundry basket in the bathroom as he'd always used to do, but they didn't seem to have resurfaced.

But God, he was ravenous. When he hopped out at Euston he'd have to sprint to Upper Crust as well and get one of those breakfast baguettes down him. There was so much of him to fill, that was the trouble. 'All arms and legs,' Dawn used to say. No matter how much he ate, he never filled out or really stopped feeling hungry. Not as badly as he did when he was a teenager, but food was still never far from his mind. 'It's like feeding a bottomless pit,' Alan would laugh. 'You're eating us out of house and home,' Fay would add, looking into the fridge over Alan's shoulder and resting her chin there.

7

King's Cross St Pancras

SANCTUM PANCRATIUM, 1086.

He tried not to think of the things that had happened here.

Ecclesia Sancti Pancratii, 1183.

The fire in 1987 that had killed twenty-seven. Fay watching the news, hand over her mouth. It should be called Battlebridge, not King's Cross at all. The cross, a brief monument, the king, George IV (1820–1830), womaniser, drug addict, national embarrassment. The 7/7 suicide bombers that killed fifty-two, twenty-seven at King's Cross. Battlebridge, circa 800, where King Alfred fought the Danes. The Saxon altar buried here circa 600. St Pancras, child martyr beheaded in Rome.

The day of the bombs he had walked all the way home. Four hours it took. Alan had rung him. Then Todd. He hadn't realised till then how far out of it Walthamstow was.

Pankeridge, alias St Pancras, 1588.

A four-hour walk from Brixton to Walthamstow, it was practically Essex.

Wilcuma and stōw, Wilcumestowe, 1075. Safe place where strangers are welcome.

'Is there anything more boring than men talking about sport?' yawned Devora, interrupting Steve's account of the previous night's match.

'Yes. Women talking about love,' Ameena replied, getting up from her seat and leaving the cheese-plant area.

Steve saw Lawrence and leapt to his feet to go and talk to him. Lem hoped Ameena and Steve weren't going to make a habit of coming to the staffroom at break. Devora had got to a crucial moment in one of her stories and he was about to find out what was so special about Philip. He luxuriated for a moment in the happiness that only teachers who have a free period before lunch know.

'Where were we?' Devora shuffled closer to him so that his right knee could touch her left knee if he wanted.

'The Little Chef on the M25,' he said, placing red ticks across a page of scrawled sums and watching the way the taut denim on her thigh tapered to the cap of her knee 'The first time you met Philip.'

'Oh, yes. I suppose you're wondering whether I've gone completely mad, aren't you? I know it's a bit risky, so near a motorway and all that. But he travels a lot for his job, and since he separated from his wife, he's on the road more often than not. And anyway, why would I want to drive all the way down to Sevenoaks? Little Chefs nowadays are quite nice, you know. Very friendly. Have you been to one recently?'

Lem shook his head, nodded and leant forward to take a sip of tepid coffee.

'Well, his emails were different somehow, right from the first one.' He let his knee move towards hers. 'I felt I could hear his voice in them, if you know what I mean. He sounded gentle, a little hurt and quite wary really, for a man.'

She put down her cup and her leg moved alongside Lem's, warm and human. Then Steve was there, throwing himself onto a seat opposite them, legs splayed to their full extent, exhaling a gust of stale beer and cigarettes.

'I don't know why I do it, I really don't,' he said, rubbing his face in both hands.

Lem moved his leg away, lifted his arm, elbow upwards,

and scratched the back of his neck, smiling crookedly towards Steve.

'Aren't you supposed to be teaching?'

Steve yawned and adjusted his crotch. 'They're doing Investigations in the playground.' He leant back, bent his knees and put his feet up on the opposite chair.

'Well, shouldn't you be with them?' Devora crossed her legs and sat up straight.

Steve looked at them both, checked his watch, felt in his pockets and then winked at Lem. 'Lend us a quid, Devora, darling.'

'You still owe me from last week.' She reached into her bag and pulled out her purse.

'Do I? Tell you what, Devs. Buy you a drink after the staff meeting tonight. Just you and me.' He winked at her and caught the coin she threw him, clambered over the back of the chairs and fought his way through the cheese plant.

Devora watched him go. Steve's powerful form seemed to press its shape into the air so that you couldn't help but be aware of the way his body was put together.

'Where was I?' she said.

Lem leant towards her a little to catch the scent of her. She smelt sweet, like hay. He opened another book and commenced ticking, happy to be alone with her again, lulled by her confessions.

'I always have to have a little talk with myself before I actually meet them, sort of pluck up courage and that. But with Philip, there was something about him straight away that made me think he might be The One.'

Still ticking, he watched Devora's throat as she swallowed another mouthful of tea, the swell and spasm of skin and muscle. He didn't like to think of Devora in the Little Chef car park with some internet-surfing saddo. She stared out of the window behind him and Lem could see the pores of her face through her foundation. He'd like to clean all the make-up off her. He ducked his head in the continuing silence and ticked steadily. She rubbed the nails of one hand with her thumb, swung one leg to and fro and continued.

'He had sad eyes, you see. I could tell that he'd been through a bad time. His wife had taken the children to live in Manchester.'

Lem scribbled, Where is your homework, Stefan? on the bottom of a page.

'Anyway, after a while I said, "Shall we go in and have a coffee?" because I didn't see the point of just sitting in the car park. We went in and got a nice table for two by the window next to the kids' play area.'

Devora's phone beeped twice from the depths of her bag between her feet.

'That'll be him. He's always texting me.' Her face came alive, years lifting, to reveal a glimpse of girl as she retrieved her phone and read the message.

Lem contemplated stealing the phone from her and texting Philip something bad like, Get a pair of concrete trunks and take a dive, Granddad.

Outside, the sky had darkened and the wind was making the sycamores dance, sending sheets of newspaper and white plastic bags flying upwards. He loved the weather when it was wild because it gave him hope that nothing was certain after all. It had been a day like this that Dean had taken him fishing up in the Lee Valley just north of the M25. It was September and they had walked through dry bleached fields towards the reservoir, skirting the woods of beech and oak. Warm gusts raced through the trees, sending showers of acorns pattering down onto the dead leaves on the woodland floor. He had stopped to pick one up, feeling it small and smooth in his hand as he followed Dean along the edge of the wood. At a break in the high hedgerow they rounded a corner and there before them was the rippled sweep of water, the sudden reach of scumbled sky and a buffeting wind that took his breath away.

The train came to a standstill in the tunnel so that people started to shift and move like livestock in transit. Lem felt anxious, suspended as they were in a subterranean limbo, and he wished Dean hadn't told him that he wouldn't go on the Tube even if it was free. What, he wondered, was the delay about? The police officer by the doors adjusted his earpiece as his radio buzzed and crackled. No one wanted to turn their back on that gun, apart from the lovers who were still oblivious and had found a bright blue pole to lean up against. The man had his knee bent in between the woman's thighs so that her skirt was riding up. He had grabbed a handful of her hair at the back of her head and was pulling her face up and back towards him. Her hair was coarse, tangled and dry as if she had no moisture to spare, and he thought of the feel of Dawn's thin hair, which was mouse-coloured like his own. 'Everyone's is from these godforsaken islands,' Fay had said. 'It's the curse of the Britons.'

Right now, this minute, thought Lem, it was quite impossible to understand that there had been a time when he and Dawn had been like that couple by the pole. Where did all that energy and momentum go to? he wondered. If matter could be neither created nor destroyed, then they must have put it somewhere, mislaid it, had it stolen or something. He tried to remember the first few months when they couldn't stop having sex, when he'd just been grateful that she had made him feel normal, that he appeared to have managed some sort of connection with someone, although he realised now with a numb sadness that pleasure, like pain, was hard to recall once a short time had elapsed. 'What could be the point of that?' he had asked out loud not long ago when he and Steve and Devora were hurrying back from the café one lunchtime. Devora had thought about it for a moment and then said, 'Maybe that's why it's called making love, Lem, because it has to be about more than sex.' And Steve had jumped in front of them, turned and shaken his head, pointing his finger at her sternly, no humour in his face.

'Romance, Devs,' he said, 'is the worm in the bud. You have to kick the habit.' And he barred her way so that she had to stop walking. ' "It's the invisible worm that flies in the night in the howling storm." ' And then they had all been separated trying to cross Brixton Road and the hurricaney October wind had whipped at their hair and hurled the day's litter high up into the air, and when they reached the opposite pavement Steve was back to normal and walking with his head turned backwards, watching the audacious slow roll of a passing woman's buttocks.

'What was that Steve thing all about today?' he had asked Devora later and she had said, 'Slippage, Lem. Character slippage. It happens sometimes. People slip out of role.'

ANIMAL RIGHTS BOMB SENT TO CHARITY SHOP, read the headline on the newspaper opened out opposite him and Lem wondered whether Dawn was one of the silhouetted protesters in the photograph. Her recruitment to the Animal Liberation Front had been a turning point in their relationship, a signpost that pointed firmly towards the end. They came to it the day Dawn had met Laura standing behind her stall of tortured animal photos on the Finchley High Road. Mesmerised by the images of monkeys with electrodes in their brains and bandaged beagles being rescued by a gang in balaclavas, she had listened wide-eyed to Laura's despatches from the laboratory front lines. Perhaps Laura had caught Dawn at a weak moment or perhaps Dawn, like Lem, sensed that there was a hole where passion and principles should be in her life. Defending guinea pigs and her friendship with Laura had filled that gap, and Dawn had set out on an increasingly extreme road of animal activism. At the end of that road stood Ian, waiting with two silenced children and a kennel full of springer spaniels.

The conversion had happened just after the pig-sticking scene in a film they had watched at the cinema by mistake one chilly night last September. It was a bleak and depressing story and not their kind of film at all really, but the 6.15 and the 8.45 of the latest Julia Roberts film at the Finchley Hollywood Bowl were full. There was a Kate Winslet season on at the Phoenix in East Finchley. It was Dawn's idea to go because she loved *Titanic*, and the film that was screening was billed as a love story, though neither of them had heard of it. It was a period piece and the first ten minutes were in black-and-white, which put the damper on an already unpromising evening, although Dawn didn't stay very much longer to find out.

Lem had been conscious of her sighs and shuffles from the opening shots until the Rachel Griffiths character, Arabella, had to kill a pig, and for a short while Dawn went completely still. Arabella had gone out into the mud and snow and chased the pig round the yard, brandishing a large knife. It had started squealing and it was difficult to convince yourself at that point that it was acting. Dawn stopped chewing popcorn, tightened her grip on Lem's hand and buried her head in his shoulder, which was, he knew, his cue to put his arm around her and whisper, 'Shall we go?' But by now he was oddly involved in the doomed intensity of the scene, in the determination and courage of the woman, of the man's desperate love for her and of the life-and-death struggle of the pig. There was something about the squealing that left you in no doubt about the pig's state of mind, for it was uncannily close to the sound he imagined a human might make in similar circumstances: conscious, visceral terror. The couple were hopeless at the business of killing, but in the end it was the woman who managed to get the knife in the pig's throat and hack away at it until it stopped screaming. There was an awful lot of blood and the pig, which was quite definitely dying, was suddenly hanging upside down from a cross-bar with blood streaming from its neck in a steaming rush, one imploring eye roving the limits of its vision for some means of escape from the end of its story. All at once, Dawn's seat harrumphed back on itself and she shoved her way past legs, feet, bags, coats, popcorn, cups and cans, sobbing, 'I'm not watching this, I'm not watching t-h-i-s', and stumbled her way up the dark aisle to the exit.

As stormings-off go, it wasn't the most elegant of exits and, as with all stormings-off, it attracted a small audience who, once Dawn had disappeared from view, Lem was aware were focused with quiet interest on him, curious to know how he would react. Should he sit out the rest of the film with the gaping vacancy of Dawn there for all to see, or should he 'Sorry, sorry, sorry' his way along the row after her and be shouted at out on the pavement? On screen, Jude was skulking in the kitchen watching the blood-letting through milky glass and Arabella was hacking away at the twitching pig's throat, trying to catch the clumping gush in a metal bucket. Lem wanted to sit there in the audience for ever, for the lights never to go up, for the screen never to grow dark. The fact of Dawn's absence faded fast and he realised that he was going to stay to the end.

He knew Dawn was capable of breaking off diplomatic relations between them for a period of up to a week and he couldn't help admiring the sheer force of her fury as it manifested itself in silence, sighs and assorted slammings and bangings. What though, he often wondered, was she so very angry about and could it really be all his fault?

Soon after that film, while the Cold War between them was still officially on, they had gone to have lunch with her parents. Sunday lunch in Arnos Grove was a kind of tradition and, like all traditions, its meaning had long ago been lost, if indeed it ever had one. The event consisted of Dawn and her mother talking in the kitchen while Lem sat with Dawn's dad in front of a muted television set. Dawn's dad didn't speak much, except to the television and to Bandit, the obese yellow Labrador with artificial knees.

Looking at them from the opposite wall was a framed photograph of Dawn's brother, Marvin, smiling in his Sea Cadet's uniform. Next to it was a portrait of Jesus standing on a blue lake, one hand raised in benediction. Lem sat in the armchair next to the older man, looking out at the damp square of garden with its neat lawn and abandoned swing. He couldn't help noticing that the actual lunch was absent although he knew something was cooking because the microwave peeped at one point and the smell of vegetable lasagne battled briefly with the smell of Labrador, but no food ever found its way out of the kitchen. When Bandit began to moan, Dawn's dad went over and hauled the animal round to lie on its other side, then changed channels and asked the newsreader whether he would like a beer. Lem said, 'All right', and began reading Dawn's animal welfare magazine.

Not long after, Dawn had gone on her first Animal Liberation Front demonstration with Laura. Lem had been with them the evening before when they were making their placards. They were going to join a protest outside the home of a man who bred guinea pigs for a research laboratory near Cambridge. The protest had ended with the police being called and Dawn had come home smelling of smoke and petrol. He was never sure whether she had actually been involved in the arson attack on the breeder's home or just caught up in the fracas. Dawn told him she'd signed an agreement vowing secrecy, but once she'd had a couple of VodkaandRedBulls she tended to talk non-stop about whatever came into her head.

'So the guinea pigs are being used for research into the human brain?' Fay had asked Dawn once when she'd come home with Lem on a rare visit to Walthamstow.

'It's disgusting, isn't it? They're fascists. They all deserve to die.'

Fay emptied a bag of crisps into a bowl and brought them to the table, offering the bowl to Dawn and then Lem. 'It can be disgusting, dementia, yes, but thank goodness someone's still prepared to research it,' she said, sitting down opposite Dawn.

Lem clenched his teeth. This could only end badly.

Feebly he rallied to Dawn's defence. 'I think Dawn just means that—'

'It's all right, Lem-a.' That was always a bad sign. When she added that extra syllable onto the end of his name. She drained the rest of her drink. 'I can speak for myself, you know.'

'I knew someone who died of dementia once,' Fay poured herself a glass of wine. 'It took them years. Love your hair by the way, Dawn.'

'Do you? Thanks. Lem hates it.'

Lem crammed a handful of crisps into his mouth. 'I only said that I liked it the colour it was.'

'The point is—' Dawn reached for the vodka bottle.

'Sorry, do you need topping up again?' Fay took the bottle and poured some into her glass. 'It started with confusion, you know, getting lost on the way back from the post office, that kind of thing—'

'But it's not just that he's breeding them so that they can die a horrible death in that laboratory in Cambridge, right? The point is, right? The conditions he keeps them in are appalling. I mean, inhuman, yeah? Like a concentration camp.'

Lem got up from the table and started opening and shutting cupboards.

'Then a year later, she was doubly incontinent . . . well, you work with animals, Dawn, so I have no need to tell you what that was like.'

'Mum, when's Alan back?'

'The thing is, right? The thing is, they can cure dementia and all those other things without torturing animals.'

Lem got up and filled the kettle. 'Anyone want a cup of tea?'

'She had no idea who anyone was in the last two years. Not even her own daughter.'

'But cutting up animals just because you're a sadist is not right, is it?'

'Then she lost her speech—'

'There's this one guinea pig, right? I saw it with my own eyes. It had its head shaved and a hole the size of this crisp cut out the top of its skull.'

'By the end she could only crawl on her hands and knees. Crawl and cry like a baby.'

'Tea anyone? Dawn? Mum?'

'And the human brain's nothing like a guinea pig's anyway.'

Fay drank her wine and allowed a silence to answer that one.

'They're quite organised,' said Lem. 'They've got a website . . .'

'Oh, I should think they need to be,' continued Fay. 'Arson, hate mail, destruction of property. It must take an awful lot of planning and time.'

'No, but,' said Dawn, 'it's a democratic organisation, OK? It operates democratically with suggestions from all kinds of people. We got four hundred phone calls a day during the guinea pig campaign.'

'Really? Could I have the phone number then?'

Dawn shook her head. 'I'm not at liberty to divulge that information.'

'Why so secret if it's a democratic organisation?'

'Because, Fay-a, we live in a really sick society, yeah? Just because I'm in the Animal Liberation Front, I probably have my phone tapped, did you know that?'

Fay got up from the table and went out into the hall. She came back in with the framed photograph from the hall table, which she handed to Dawn. 'That's her when she was about your age. My mother. On her wedding day.'

Dawn took the photo and looked at it. She looked at Lem and then at Fay. Fay smiled at her, 'So who did your hair then?' And Lem wanted to shout at Fay, to shake her and shout, 'Shut up!' in her face because by despising Dawn, by making no secret of her feelings about Dawn, didn't she see she was forcing him to stay with her, to bloody well end up probably marrying her? And anyway, it was hard to disagree with Dawn on the subject of torturing animals. He could even find himself liking that about her; it came from a passionate, uncomplicated place inside her; the place he had held onto that night in the boat in Mersea.

'Not long after that, she started coming home late smelling very strongly of dog.'

It was November, a few weeks before Dawn left. Devora was coaxing the story of Ian and Dawn from him, although Lem much preferred it when she talked about herself.

'Things bad at home, Lem?' she would prompt, when he collapsed beside her at break time. Somehow, with every line he offered, he felt he was writing the tabloid story of him and Dawn. It was so much easier to tell it in headlines than in the small, everyday acts of intimacy that had also been them.

'Where does she say she's been when she comes home late?'

'Round her parents.'

Devora raised one eyebrow. He shrugged.

'And why is she spending so much time round her parents, allegedly?'

And then he'd had to tell her about the exorcism.

'What?'

'Dawn's mum got the priest round to exorcise him. Marvin, Dawn's brother . . .'

'You mean they thought he was possessed?' Devora's face was incredulous, the face she used when students said they hadn't done their homework or that they had overslept.

'Dawn's mum thought he might be. It was before he was sectioned. He came home from school one day when he was seventeen, except he hadn't been in school, he never really went because he was too stoned. But he came home, sat down in front of the television and didn't speak for a fortnight.'

She put her hand on his arm and said, 'Oh, Lem.' Then,

sure enough, the bell went and the two of them started to get up from their seats. He tried to remember what day it was and who he was teaching next.

As they left the staffroom, Lem stumbled to keep up with her, through the two sets of swing doors and down the crush-filled corridor. He was aware of not wanting to enter into the futile struggle of another lesson, but more than that, he wanted to stay close to this woman.

'Where are you going, Lem?' She was laughing at him, stopping and half turning to face him at the top of the stairs. 'Your room's that way.'

The stairwell was a jumble of people clambering up and shuffling down, screaming greetings, threats, questions and just screaming. Lem found himself pressed against the wall with Devora by his side. She looked at him and said something inaudible. His solar plexus ached. Here was another of those moments when a decision must be taken, the correct lines spoken and he was struck dumb with the agony of hesitation, feeling the moment slip like mercury from the if to the never.

8

Euston

LEM CHECKED HIS watch and calculated how many minutes he had. If he could do it in seven he might make it. It was a risk, but if he ran, seven minutes should just about give him time, and he knew that once he had on a pair of underpants, he would feel less vulnerable and more able to face the day. He got to his feet and shuffled towards the doors, turning his body this way and that in an effort to avoid either causing offence or giving the impression that he was just giving up his seat rather than trying to get off the train. He stood with his back to the simmering vat of want that was the couple, checked his watch again and slow-stepped it with the sea of others off the train and through the platform exit.

At the bottom of the escalators, to his left, he could hear a man's voice, loud and imperious, saying, 'Excuse me, excuse me.' Lem turned to look as a broadside shove and then a tap against his leg with a stick followed the voice. The man was blind and he walked without hesitation towards the beginning of the escalator. A space opened around the blind man as irritation gave way to concern, then fascination. His beard was well trimmed and he wore a purple tie. Lem thought he would at least get a guide dog if he were blind. A short woman in her fifties almost put her hand under the man's elbow, looked as if she was going to ask him if he would like some help, and then didn't. Another woman did attempt to guide the man as the queue for the escalator doubled up for those travellers who had extra specially urgent destinations that they absolutely must get to without further delay, so that those who were watching the blind man feared he might miss his footing.

'No, no,' the man's voice boomed, half turning his face to her. 'Steps and stairs are my favourite thing. No uncertainty or nasty surprises there. Escalators are even better, don't you think? Beautiful things.' And up he glided, head raised slightly as if listening to something the rest of them would never hear.

Lem followed him up and through the ticket barriers, where the blind man never faltered. Lem hesitated for a moment while he read the exit signs, took the one that said British Rail and Way Out and found himself in the mainline concourse. Liverpool, Dundee, Edinburgh, Perth. The destinations board flickered and changed and Lem thought what it might be to board a train to somewhere else, somewhere north of London, far north, where no one knew him, where perhaps he could live a different sort of life. People did it, he knew that because Todd had made a documentary about it. The good husband and father kissed his wife and children goodbye at breakfast, put on his coat, picked up his briefcase, called goodbye at the door and disappeared. Got a train to Aberdeen and then a flight to Vladivostok or somewhere and began a new life, because in the still dark of the night he found he could no longer ignore the way his wife looked at him when he came in the room or the way his children became bigger and ruder with every passing day, and escape suddenly became a matter of life or death of the soul. Only last month he had read about a mother of two who had left her flat in Balham to go and buy a bikini for the family holiday and never returned. Of course it was possible that these people were dead, but Lem knew from the documentary that when people went missing it was almost always just that, because something was missing, not because they were dead.

The blind man was tap-tapping his way towards one of the kiosks that sold socks, a kind of sock shop, which was indeed what it was called. Lem followed him over the marble floor, where impressions of prehistoric shell and claw were clearly visible if you knew what you were looking for, and he reminded himself that this was supposed to be a flying visit and that if he didn't concentrate, he would be late for work.

Inside the kiosk he stared stupidly at the displays for a moment, forgetting what it was that he wanted. Ties? No. Socks? Not really, although he did seem to be a bit short of the thick, comfy clean ones. He turned, his face inches from an armless torso clad in white Calvin Kleins. That was it. Pants.

'But do you have them in red?' the blind man was asking, handling a pack of three-for-two black socks.

'If it's not out, then we don't have it.' The young assistant behind the till was busy with some sock stocktaking and did not want to assist, much less look up. Besides, it had only just gone eight o'clock and she hadn't had her Starbucks yet.

Lem wandered further into the kiosk and took down a packet of black boxers and then a packet of white ones and dithered. White looked better, but only as long as they didn't turn grey. When Dawn washed them they always turned grey, but Fay had some system going whereby white stayed white. Black was too much of a statement, too much the kind of thing that Steve would wear, verging on the seedy, but which had the advantage of keeping its colour. If only Devora were here to advise him. She would have a view on which pants to buy.

A patter of falling sock packs to his right made him look round. The blind man had swept one row of cotton-rich to the floor and was sauntering out of the kiosk. And a few feet away, suddenly and very close, hovering in the entrance, was the very last person he wanted to see right now, Dawn's best friend, Laura. Firstly, he did not want her to see him choosing underwear. It was all too humiliatingly bound up with

Dawn's dumping of him for Ian which, although not a complete surprise, he suspected had been hastened by Laura. Secondly, he dreaded her. He couldn't really say why, but he sensed something out of control about her animal liberation zeal. And thirdly, he probably had bits of breakfast in his teeth, which, coupled with the black boxers that he was now holding, would completely condone the fact that she had persuaded Dawn to jettison him.

She wore a grey tracksuit with Too Busy to Fcuk branded across her rump and she looked agitated, cutting the air with her palm stiff and straight like a cleaver. She kept her head down as she talked into her right hand and marched towards the doorway of the kiosk. Lem cowered near the Calvin Kleins.

'What do you mean, you've overslept? The train leaves in twenty minutes.'

He watched her, mesmerised as she shouted and backed into someone looking at the window display. She appeared not to notice the collision and for a few moments she looked directly at him, but if she saw him she showed no sign. Instead, she took a step sideways so she was in front of the glass, tipped her head on one side and turned her face without moving her eyes. She was silent while she examined her profile critically. Giving her hair a quick finger-comb, she turned her back again and resumed ranting.

'The whole point is that we have to get there before nine-thirty.'

She threw her head back in exasperation as she listened to the reply.

'The bag is packed and ready. We left it in the cupboard under your sink. You are in serious trouble if you don't get here.'

There was another pause during which Laura wheeled round and slammed the palm of her hand up against the glass, inches from Lem's face. He jumped and his heart began to skedaddle about like a pinball.

'Listen, if we don't get in and out before Security changes his shift we're shafted, so get up here now.'

He prayed that she wouldn't come into the kiosk. Shifting her bag from one shoulder to the other, she kicked at the floor with her toe and said, 'No, Dawn', and then she swung round and looked up and directly into Lem's eyes.

'Just get here, Dawn, or you're done for,' she said and cut the call.

Lem moved sharply to his right so that he was screened behind a rack of thongs and novelty socks and tried to calm his breathing. There was nothing he could do about his bolting heart. He looked down at the packet of boxers he held in his hand and very much wanted his loose and lost libido to be encased in their firm weft and weave, if only Laura would get out of the way. He peered out from the side of the display rack and found that Laura had gone.

Quickly he took the boxers over to the cashier and put a ten-pound note down on the counter, his eyes sweeping the concourse for Laura's grey tracksuit. There was no sign of her and, without waiting for the change, he hurried out of the kiosk and across the main concourse. He checked the time: 8.11.

People wandered alone in the vast space looking in vain for seats and litter bins and staring up to check the train times. Manchester, Wolverhampton, Liverpool Piccadilly. This had all taken much longer than planned. A police officer with a sniffer dog watched him as he jogged as casually as possible towards the men's toilets clutching his slippery bag in one hand, backpack in the other. The toilets were situated beneath a Scottish Tourist Board screen on which a man in waders was fly-fishing, standing strong against the current, suicidal salmon hurling themselves up the waterfall behind him.

The very first time he went fishing with Dean, they had taken a train out to Ramsey Island in Essex to fish for flounder. It was the August bank holiday and they had sat opposite one another on the train silently watching the Essex landscape strafe by the window. When they got off they hitched a lift and were dropped near the marshes, where the air smelt of salt and mud and a sea fret obscured the horizon.

Lem liked the fact that Dean didn't really do small talk, in fact he barely spoke at all that day apart from the occasional invocation of subject-specific nouns. 'Sea lavender . . . scabious . . . cuckoo pint . . .' They had walked along a grassy track towards the water, their breathing heavy with the weight of the fishing gear; Dean's voice trailed backwards, juddery as his soles pounded the turf. 'Campion . . . marsh samphire . . .' At each name he'd tip his head in the direction of the plant. When the track eventually turned to black glutinous mud, their steps became slow, heavy and squelching. 'Seablite . . . pink thrift . . .' He concentrated on placing his feet precisely in the prints of Dean's Docklands', counting their steps and treading the same sure path.

They had stopped by the water, among the reed beds, and Dean had started pulling the equipment out of his canvas bag. Lem squatted near the edge, his back to the wind, which snatched at his coat and hair, listening to the hiss and shiver of the reeds. Every now and then, the sun would break through the restless clouds above and light would ricochet off the water as if it were sheet steel so that everything, the grasses, his own shadow, Dean's hair, had a momentary intensity and detail like a vision, before dropping back again into ordinariness.

Lem studied the water seeping up towards his feet, which were half submerged but held safe by the spreading roots and stems. Curious as to whether it was fresh or salt, tidal or still, he dabbled his hand in it and tasted it. It tasted brackish, like someone else's spit. Then a movement around the base of his trainers made him start and look down thinking he might be sinking, but instead, with a volt of fear, he saw he was standing among snakes. He rose suddenly upright and let out a yell.

Dean stepped over to the place where he stood and looked. 'Eels,' he said, 'There', and he scooped up a palmful of the glibbery, writhing creatures. Half fish, half snake, they slithered and fell from his hand. Dean held Lem's arm tight so that he wouldn't move as a rope of eels, almost invisible apart from their eyes, writhed through their boots.

The eels vanished, headed in the direction of the eastern stretch of metallic sea where the power station crouched on the horizon, indistinct in the haze. 'No one knows where they go,' Dean said. 'But it's a long way. And you see this?' he added, laughing and smearing the slime from his hands down Lem's parka. 'That's osmotic protection. Nothing can get in or out. Means they can go just about anywhere.'

Later, Dean had set up his line for him, cast it into the water and then done his own. Then they'd just sat there, Lem on an upturned bucket and Dean on the bait box. Staring at the surface of the water listening to the whisper of the reeds and the screech of birds, they sat, barely moving, like a couple of monks at prayer.

'What do you think?' Dean said, after a while.

'It's great,' Lem replied, without lifting his eyes from the water. 'This is just great.'

Watching the floats on the water that day in Essex, Lem felt his lower jaw relax, his shoulders go soft and his lungs empty for the first time since, well, since when? Since he was eleven probably.

'Do you grind your teeth?' the dentist had asked him last time he'd visited. 'Are you aware of headaches, soreness around the jaw?'

'Nugh.'

His mouth had been wide open at the time and filled not only with the dentist's fingers, but with at least three dental instruments as well.

'What is it you do again?'

'Uh uh ea uh.'

'Aspirate, please.'

'Teacher,' said the dental nurse, moving the aspirator towards Lem's gullet so that he felt he was going to drown. Was that thing supposed to suck water in or spray it out?

'Oh, a teacher. An awful lot of teachers are grinders,' said the dentist, swivelling away on his chair to select another tool. 'An awful lot of grinders,' he murmured, bending back towards Lem and lowering his masked face inches from Lem's nose.

That night Lem had got into bed, fallen asleep and woken the next morning with his jaw clamped together like a vice. His whole face ached all day and it felt as though he'd been trying to wear away the inside of his own head.

'Do I grind my teeth in the night, Dawn?' he'd asked her the next morning. But she was still in a strop about the fact that Lem had borrowed her keys that day and then lost them at school. Maybe she actually was asleep, but Lem was pretty sure she was pretending. For one thing she was silent, which was not usual for Dawn, and for another, her face looked like the idea of slumber rather than the absent, forgotten look that it assumed when she really was asleep.

What was it that he was so worried about exactly, that was making him gnaw away at the inside of his head during the night? he wondered. He had a lot more going for him than plenty of people he knew, like Marvin for instance. He had a flat, a secure job and a steady girlfriend, although the words 'steady' and 'friend' didn't always seem right. But really, what else could he ask for? Things were all right. Things were fine.

On the down escalator, he took the stairs two at a time, luxuriating in the security and comfort of his brand new underwear. The southbound platform was still crowded and he made his way down to the far end in the hope of getting a seat when the train arrived. Staring at the rails, he watched a mouse wandering below the tracks and felt the draught of the approaching train before he heard it. When the train hurtled out of the far tunnel towards them, the mouse carried on its foraging, apparently unconcerned. Lem looked behind him and took a step back from the edge.

9

Warren Street

THE TRAIN WAS packed so Lem stood with his back to the open doors among a crowd of people, arms raised to the handrail above their heads. He twisted round and looked out at the platform behind him and then he saw her, Salma, throwing herself between the doors of the next carriage just as they closed. He looked at his watch, a vague disquiet shifting at the base of his belly. That Salma was on the train was neither here nor there, he told himself. It wasn't as if it was the first time and there was probably a perfectly rational reason for her being this far north. She was just a child, for God's sake.

If he leant forward just a little he could glimpse Salma standing in the crowd, head leaning against one raised arm. Her eyes were lowered to her lap and her pale, beautiful face looked tired. He had asked her one time; had just come out with it as she came into the classroom at the end of the day for his lesson. 'I saw you this morning, didn't I, Salma?' he'd said, very relaxed, nothing threatening or even definite. Plenty of space there for her to either deny or confirm it. But she stopped alongside him without looking at him, eyes down and just sort of waited, not saying anything, just waited for him to unsay it. And so he had. 'Or someone very like you,' was what he'd said. 'I suppose it could have been one of your sisters.' She had still avoided his eyes, maths books clasped to her chest in both arms, and then she'd moved on into the classroom.

He remembered the odd freeze-frame he had seen some months back on Warren Street platform. He couldn't be sure, but at the time he'd thought it was Salma, facing the train but hanging back just inside the passageway that led to the platform. As the dense crowd shuffled past her she stood alongside a woman in a soft leather jacket and cream head-scarf who had her back to the train. In the confusion of people around them, the image of these two became difficult to see with any continuity, yet in a series of interrupted stills Lem saw what looked like a scene between two clandestine lovers or a couple of spooks.

Despite the crowd flowing past them, the woman with the cream headscarf remained immovable, staying close to Salma while Salma kept her eyes to the ground, her head tilted towards the other woman, one hand hanging down at her side. There was something familiar about the tall woman; Lem had the sense that he knew her and wished she would turn round so he could see her face. She looked Western and wealthy and wore her headscarf draped loosely in a style more reminiscent of Marilyn Monroe than any piety. She dipped her head and a tress of blonde hair fell from the side of the scarf before one gloved hand tucked it back inside. Then he saw them touch hands without eye contact, the way lovers might secretly squeeze each other's fingers in company. Warnings and reminders from the Tannoy bounced incoherently off the tiled walls of the station, and the woman looked quickly down the platform while hitching the thick brown leather strap of her handbag securely up onto her shoulder.

It was then that Lem saw a brief instant of a pale, equine profile and knew it was Helena. With a quick movement, her hand withdrew into her clothing and then extended again with a white envelope which Salma took, withdrawing her hand back inside the cloth of her jacket. The doors had begun their warning shudder and hum and Salma moved towards the train. Lem had looked back at the entrance tunnel for the Helena figure, but she was gone. Salma too was out of sight as the doors slid shut.

Helena didn't look like the other people he knew. Something about the quality of her skin and hair marked her out as different. At first he thought it was the fact that she wasn't English, or that she didn't live full time in England and was not smudged with the grimy sadness of most England dwellers. But Fay, at the kitchen sink in Walthamstow one day, put him straight on that one.

'What you are seeing, Lemuel, is breeding. And breeding is all about money.'

What she was saying sounded bad. Helena had been all right and he hadn't liked the way Todd had treated her.

'She's not a racehorse,' he said. 'And don't call me Lemuel.'

'Same principle though, which is probably why the aristocracy have always had a thing about horses.'

'Move over, Lem, please,' said Alan, 'bread making to be done.'

'Helena looks like that because for generations the men in her family have all been virtual millionaires, allowing them to breed with the most beautiful women available.'

'Don't touch that, Lem, it's yeast.'

'The offspring are raised on only the best food, the cleanest air and the kind of education that imbues them with complete and utter confidence in themselves and their place in the world.'

'Yes, but—'

'That's why she looks like that. And, with the help of science and surgery, will continue to do so for many years to come.'

Lem watched Fay rinse out a glass vase and turn it carefully upside down to drain. Rainbow bubbles slid down its side. She flicked the foam from her gloved hands. It was beyond him how Fay and Todd had ever had anything to do with each other. He really wanted to ask her what that was all about, but instead he said, 'Why did Helena marry Dad?'

'If you stay sitting there, you're going to get covered in flour,' said Alan.

'Oh, they just came across one another when they were stumbling about in the debris of their burnt-out marriages . . .'

'Helena is quite a vulnerable woman,' said Alan, adding a pinch of salt and throwing the rest over his shoulder. 'Fragile.'

Fay stayed quiet. Lem watched her back.

'In some ways they were quite well matched, I've often thought,' he said. 'Todd probably couldn't believe his luck when Helena's father gave him access to the CIA—'

'Ah, yes, that singularly uninformative in-depth analysis of the CIA.'

'Say what you like about her,' said Alan. 'She certainly knows people in high places.'

Lem wondered why Fay never sat down at the table. Having finished at the sink, she crossed over to the sofa and began taking books out of the bookcase, wiping each book with a cloth.

'Yes, well, documentaries apart, Helena needed to give her daughter a family home, when she wasn't at boarding school at least, and probably thought Todd was more successful than he actually was.'

Lem wished she would stop hating his father. It cut him in half.

'What Helena couldn't tolerate was Todd's philandering. She seemed to think it would stop with her, but men like him just can't help it. He probably lives in terror of the day when one of those young women will say, "Go away old man", and in the meantime he is compelled to keep playing the goat.'

It was 8.19 and he was going to be late and Lawrence, the deputy head, wouldn't know, so no cover teacher would be put in front of his first class, which meant that they would get restless and then become noisy and unruly and incidents would occur, probably involving Saskia or Emily or Jason, which would require large amounts of paperwork and tedious reprimands. Lem struggled to take a breath at the thought of it while the woman pressed up against the front of him attempted to turn the page of her newspaper, which she had positioned parallel to the ceiling.

The last time he had seen Helena with Todd was at a restaurant somewhere near Hoxton. It was in the early days of his relationship with Dawn and they had locked hands under the table, eating one-handed and sending squeeze messages back and forth between them. The only thing on the menu seemed to be roast hog and mushy peas. Dawn was looking red-faced and frowsy from too much wine. Lem had loved that look, just as he had loved the way the fabric on her blouse strained across her breasts and the way her lips and teeth became stained with red wine. She seemed childlike and unconscious in those days. He wondered which had come first, him not loving that look any more or her not liking how she looked. By comparison, Helena was like a piece of modern sculpture: sleek, rigid and brittle. Her voice slid between east-coast American and west London. She drank several bottles of sparkling water, which she urged Dawn to do as well if she wanted to save her eyes from bagging.

Todd tucked into his beef, marvelled at the bloody flesh and declared it was done to perfection. Every now and then he'd order another bottle of red. He and Dawn were getting completely pissed and her eyes were doing the swollen slide down the sides of her face that happened with wine.

'That's why I prefer vodka,' she said to Todd as she returned from the Ladies. 'There's something in wine. Look at my eyes, they've gone all wonky.'

'Well, I think you look very *au naturel*, sweetheart,' Todd said, waving his fork in the air.

Several times during the meal Helena had picked up her bag and headed off for the toilets where she stayed for some time, reappearing eventually with a reddened upper lip and a runny nose. On one of her returns to the table she found Dawn and Lem trying to recapture one of Dawn's breasts that had escaped from her blouse.

'Enjoy it while you can,' she'd said to Dawn as she sat down. Lem had tried to push Dawn upright and offered Helena some more water.

'Dad's just popped out to take a call,' he said.

'Yeah, yeah,' said Helena who, while not drunk, was most definitely not behaving normally.

'Want to see these?' she said and had pulled apart the wraparound top she was wearing. 'Birthday present from your father. Cost a fortune.'

Wine spluttered out of Dawn's nose and Lem froze. Most vivid in his memory of that moment was the sight of Helena's swollen breasts sitting high up on her chest, pointing upwards and looking like they might explode.

'Three hundred and twenty cc of silicone in each one. Going under the knife again tomorrow.' She took another gulp of Badoit. 'Not smiling enough, apparently.'

'Wow,' Dawn said, extending a fascinated fingertip. 'Does it hurt?'

'Not at all.' She gave them a slap. 'All the nerve endings are cut. Can't feel a thing—'

And then Helena had started to cry, really cry so that her face became a fudge of fingers and lips, and at first Dawn had started to laugh because that was what she thought Helena was doing, and Lem had remembered thinking how strange that no one had taken much notice when she'd exposed her breasts, but many heads swivelled when the crying began.

Todd had reappeared carrying Helena's coat. He'd waved his Visa card at the waiter and within a few minutes all four of them were out on the pavement in the cool autumnal night with Helena clattering about on her heels and blowing her nose noisily into a paper napkin. Todd folded her into a taxi, they waved goodbye and the next Lem heard of Helena, she and Todd had got divorced, Helena had returned to America and then converted to Islam. It all seemed a little far-fetched as far as Lem was concerned and, while he had wanted to ask Todd about Helena since then, there were aspects of their story that he just did not want to hear about. And anyway, he preferred Todd without her.

Back in Kinloss Court that night, Lem had kissed every inch of Dawn's soft and spreading flesh. At that moment, drunk on champagne and red wine, he loved the imperfection of her, her lardy body, erratic moods and lack of general knowledge; all the things that made her fallibly, hopelessly human. They attempted to make love, but lost interest halfway through, given that Dawn was drifting in and out of consciousness. He lay awake in the dark, one hand on her hip and the other under her neck. Right now, here with this rude rough girl, high above the roar and tremor of the North Circular, he felt safe and tethered. He hugged her tight and thanked God they were not Todd and Helena.

But that was then, and then didn't stay now for very long.

'You don't tell me things.'

The sound of Dawn's voice sent suddenly out there into the grainy dark above their heads halted his reverie. He lay still in the silence, watching the bubbles rise in the tangerine glow of the tropical fish tank, and wondered how long she had been awake.

'What?'

His voice sounded weak and disembodied and he wondered about all the other voices that had drifted up to the ceiling in this room. He gave her a squeeze, but she shrugged him off and inched away, opening up a space between them.

'You don't tell me things.' She was making swallowing sounds with her mouth and throat. 'You know. Stuff.'

Lem rolled over onto his back, conscious of the gap between the two of them, and he felt misery settle on his chest like a stone. The Spider Love, was what Devora called it. The moment when you realise too late that love is fragile, needs to be made, remade and mended each day. After that point, she said, the garden becomes a dark place to be. He needed Devora and her words. He badly needed some words now.

'I mean, where's this leading, Lem?'

In the rhythmic headlight sweep of the room he could see that the side of Dawn's face was wet. She was doing the motionless, silent crying that Lem knew was much more serious than the other, howling kind. His hangover was beginning to take hold.

'Are you getting your period?'

He tried to remember whether this was one of the things Devora said he should never ask a woman or not.

'It's late,' she said, sniffing into the pillow.

Lem loosed his jaw and blinked into the semi-darkness. Everything had been fine, really more than fine these last few months. But now, with a handful of words thrown up into the air, it was all falling apart.

He put one hand out towards her body and let it rest there. What was this part of her? A shoulder? A hip? He looked over. It was her knee, raised up almost to her chin. If only she hadn't brought up the idea of pregnancy. As soon as the idea that this might be for ever squatted between them, the spell was ruined. But he couldn't tell her that. If she was pregnant, then he supposed he would do what was expected of him. He would batten down his soul, padlock it away and sit it out.

There had been early summer mornings, he remembered, when he visited the churchyard at the end of Church Path, when cobwebs would stick and tear across his forehead and cheek as he crept his way among the tombstones, visiting the regular places. Each time he would feel the guilt of the small catastrophe he had caused, coupled with an irritation at the stoicism of the spider that made no complaint but scuttled away to weave another fragile web in some equally vulnerable location. Devora used to say, 'We're all trapped by the idiot human heart spinning its gossamer hopes over and over.'

'Maybe this time . . .' Devora had sung along to the Liza Minnelli number on her car cassette player as she drove them erratically back from the pub that Friday night. 'Maybe this time it'll happen . . .' She had a surprisingly powerful voice and Lem had smiled to himself as they careered down the quiet midnight road towards her house. 'Maybe this time, he'll stay . . .' He'd never heard the song before and felt a wing of elation lift him as Devora jumped the lights and accelerated up Brixton Hill.

The whole contraception thing was a bit of a confusion to Lem. Now they were living together, condoms didn't seem right somehow and anyway, he hated them. Dawn said she quite liked them because they made her feel like a teenager, but for Lem condoms were associated with sex with people you didn't know. Anyway, Lem had assumed that Dawn had been in charge of the contraception department.

The bad stuff that had filled the silence between them was beginning to set and he roamed his mind for some clue as to what Dawn had said she was doing about contraception and, more importantly, what he should say in response to the news about her period.

He lifted his head and pushed back the duvet, which she had tugged up around her neck. Heat rose up off her boiler of a body.

'Dawn.'

'What?'

'Are you . . . ?'

'What?'

'You know.'

'What if I am?'

She moved the duvet down a bit so their bodies were almost touching again in the gloom. The musty air around them waited. Words. He needed words. Devora would know what to say.

He watched the fish and thought about Devora's egg harvests, assisted hatching and urine from nuns in Italy. She had not spoken much about the five years of IVF that she and John had embarked on, but just enough for Lem to see how the repeated hammering of hopes and hormones could destroy a marriage. 'It was bonfire night that I realised we were finished,' she said. 'We were in the local park, explosions blossoming the black sky. All around were parents shouldering small children, heads back, looking up, all laughing and saying, "Ooh, aah." Our fifth attempt had just failed, I could smell the blood on my fingers and I felt wasted, all used up. I knew we were never going to be parents.' Her voice had wobbled at the memory. 'Right then I knew it in the smell of gunpowder and mulled wine. It was the death of us, of the most fragile and intimate part of us, and now sex lay like a corpse in the bed between us.' He had watched her shyly as she bent her head in a small shuddering sigh. He took little sips of her face and body and thought about what she might look like naked. Most of Devora was not small and neat like Fay, but curved and solid with heavy breasts and a large rounded bottom. But from the knees down, she had legs like a young girl, skinny with bony knees and little feet that she always displayed with pride in strappy high heels.

He closed his eyes and smelt the burnt-honey scent of Devora as he put one hand on Dawn's waist. She shifted towards him a little and he moved his hand down to her thigh so that she lowered her knees. He could see Devora's naked knee and the soft shadowed skin of the inner thigh of her right leg as she put her foot down on the clutch. Dawn twisted towards him, put her arm around his neck and raised her head to kiss him. He heard the clink of Devora's bracelets as she brought her left hand up to the wheel again and watched the movement of her lips over her teeth as she sang the words. He buried his face in Dawn's neck.

'Love you,' he said.

10

Oxford Circus

'Is there anyone on the other side?'

Lem knew how stupid he must look shouting at the door, but it rattled and shook a little every now and again as though someone on the other side were trying to open it. He had tried the lock with a different key, yet still he couldn't get the door open. There was someone on the other side, he was sure of that, because he thought he could hear a key and muffled shouts, but it was difficult to be sure because the fire alarm was being tested again, the kids were screaming and whooping and the chairs were being scraped and chucked about.

Noise was the dominant sensation in his life, he realised. He looked down at the gigantic bunch of keys in his hands and thought how Dean or Alan would tackle the problem logically. Take a key and work methodically through the bunch, eliminating those that failed to open the lock. Cursing at his ineptitude, Lem wondered why it was that he could not perform such a task himself.

He got as far as two keys and was interrupted by Jason saying, 'Sir, Sir, I ain't done my homework, Sir.' Lem ignored him and continued the struggle, but Jason, swimmy eyes a few inches from Lem's shoulder, would not be ignored.

'Sir, my mum says you have to give me detention, Sir. You said you would.'

Lem's skull ached from the jaw joints up to the cranium. He realised he'd forgotten to breathe for quite a while and so took a deep breath and looked at Jason. A thin stream of phlegm ran down the channel that joined the boy's nose to his lip. At one corner of his mouth was the beginning of a cold sore and in each eye a sty was brewing.

'All right, Jason, have a detention,' he said, dropping the bunch of keys and longing to let loose a torrent of swear words.

'Aw, shit, Sir,' he whined. 'When?'

'Tomorrow. And don't swear.' Picking up the keys, he tried to remember which ones he had already tried.

'I dint swear, Sir.'

'Yes you did.'

'When, Sir? What?'

'Shit, Jason, is a swear word.' Lem felt himself sag at the entrance to the Alice in Wonderland-like tunnel of Student Behaviour and School Rules. He stuck a key in the lock and turned it.

'No it int, Sir. Shit? Shit int swearing.'

'Yes it is.'

'Is it? Fuck. Oops, sorry, Sir.'

Lem concentrated on the key and on not responding to Jason.

'I can't do tomorrow, Sir. I've got football.'

Lem was sweating despite the fact that it was nearly winter. Was it nearly winter? He always found it hard to remember the season. What with the way this building was heated and the lack of natural landscape in his life, perhaps that wasn't surprising. Come to think of it, wasn't it actually early summer? It didn't seem to rain any more, that was one thing. Through a classroom window he could see the grey concrete and razor-wire-topped walls and he tried to recall the last time it had rained.

'I can't do tomorrow, Sir. I've got football.'

Lem felt his patience shredding and he cursed the crazy key

culture that he had to work in. It was becoming quite impossible since he taught in what used to be a corridor, but was now a series of interconnecting rooms. The stream of people passing in and out of these doors had made teaching even more unlikely than it was in rooms where the doors stayed shut and the population of the room remained roughly the same from one minute to the next. And so a decree had been issued, and after much drilling and hammering, locks had been fitted to the doors so that they could not be used by students trying to shortcut through to other lessons that they were late for. There were many problems with this solution, not least of which was what to do with the latecomers for your own lesson and what to do with the legitimate temporary absentees, of which there were many – Steel Pan lessons, Voice lessons, Mentoring sessions, Violin lessons, Counselling sessions, Drama reheasals, Citizenship trips and emergency menstrual events, not strictly legitimate, Lem felt, but equally he didn't feel able to argue about the necessity or otherwise when Emily said, 'Got to go change my tampon, Sir.'

'Sir? I can't do detention tomorrow, Sir.' Jason was jiggling about from one leg to the other, tugging at his crotch.

'Well, Wednesday then, Jason.' The sharp odour of urine wafted up Lem's nose.

Keys were always going missing at school. In fact, the enormous bunch of keys necessitated by Lem's professional life was out of all proportion to the importance of his job. Everything had to be locked: drawers, doors, cupboards, gates, filing cabinets, fridges – everything. The latest City Enterprise Initiative had meant that the school did actually have thousands of pounds' worth of state-of-the-art technology, but no one knew how to use it and, even if they had known, the inflexible seating, blinding direct sunlight and inaccessible socket situation in the classrooms would have rendered it useless, in addition to which it was all locked away in a steel room and only one person had the key to that, and he had been off sick since the previous term and the school keepers said a new key could not be cut without a memo giving notification of the key code. In the end it was easier to leave the room locked for eternity. Perhaps in thousands of years' time archaeologists would discover it and get completely the wrong idea about schools in the early twenty-first century.

'Aw. You're mean, you are, Sir. Can you write it down for me, Sir?'

'Give me your diary then, Jason.'

'I lost my bag, Sir.'

'Well, what shall I write in then?'

'You can write it on my hand, Sir.'

And then Lem had almost left his keys in the staff toilets. He'd gone in there to fill the kettle and to escape from Jason, who trailed him like a gosling repeating, 'Have you got a pen, Sir?' until Lem wondered whether it wouldn't be doing everyone a favour if he just locked the child inside the service lift. He had put his keys down on the sink, executed the tricky kettle-filling procedure, which necessitated holding the kettle spout at ninety degrees to the tiny tap that dribbled lukewarm water very very slowly, then walked back into the department office to boil the kettle.

'Sir? Have you got a pen? I lost my bag.' Jason had his palm outstretched ready for the detention reminder to be tattooed into his skin.

Once Lem had plugged in the kettle, he realised with a dart of anxiety that he'd left his keys in the toilets, sprinted back, felt absurdly cheered to see them lying there, picked them up off the porcelain, jogged to the office and realised there were no clean cups. He kicked the door shut behind him and stood still, marvelling at the blessed silence. It was brilliant having a room with no kids in it.

'Jason Cluney's been looking for you, Lem,' Ameena told him without looking up from her desk. 'Says you want to see him. Where's that coffee?'

He looked at the clock, noted that Steve was helping himself to Devora's HRT cake again and sprinted back to the toilets. There was unlikely to be any time to make a cup of coffee now, but he decided to persevere only because he had gone to the effort of asking Ameena and Steve whether they would like a cup too and of course they had said yes. Lem found three dirty mugs and gave them a cursory rub and rinse under one spluttering tap, musing to himself as he did so that if the public sector was serious about improving the sickness record of their workers, one thing they could do, apart from getting rid of the public, would be to provide dishwashers and a large supply of new crockery.

'Did you say Wednesday, Sir?'

Lem hurried back down the corridor and into the maths office, only to find the door shut and locked. Putting the mugs down on the floor, he fumbled around with his key ring to find the office key. Once he'd got it in the lock, he turned it so that the door opened, bent down to pick up the mugs, stood up and went into the office to make the coffee, kicking the door shut behind him before Jason could open his mouth. It was only when he realised that the milk had turned to festering, blue-splotched yogurt and that he'd have to unlock the stationery cupboard where the UHT milk was kept, that he realised he'd left his keys in the office door. Dashing to the door just as the bell for the next lesson sounded, he saw with a belly-wash of nausea that the keys were gone.

The really very terrible thing about this fairly ordinary calamity was that attached to his work keys were Dawn's keys. Dawn's keys to Kinloss Court, to the Peugeot and to her new work placement at the Military Defence Animal Centre at Melton Mowbray. He had picked them up by mistake that morning instead of picking up his own keys, and now someone had the keys to several kilos of Semtex, heroin, cocaine and Winalot.

Lem felt suddenly bad about Salma and wondered where she

was. He leant forward and tried to catch a glimpse of her in the adjoining carriage. It was ridiculous to have had such thoughts about the girl. She was just a girl. He began to wonder whether he hadn't imagined the Helena scenario at Warren Street. The platform was packed after all, and his vision never clear. Salma was devout and had chosen piety instead of whatever altar Marissa thought she should be bowing to.

'There wouldn't be all this fuss about headscarves and fundamentalism if it were nuns we were talking about,' Ameena had said, coming into the office a few days after the previous hijab conversation. It was not unusual for conversations in that place to be fragmented, sometimes stretching over several days. Lem had prepared himself to join in this time, he had rehearsed the Helena story in his head enough times. He badly wanted to impress Devora. He put down his pen and opened his mouth to speak, but Devora got in there before him.

'A return to medievalism isn't going to do anyone any favours, especially peasants and women,' she'd said. 'Just watch.'

'Me and Lem would be sorted then,' Steve had said, rousing himself from the Sports pages. 'It doesn't sound so bad, does it, Lem?'

'Maybe most men actually like a bit of mystery,' said Marissa. 'Covering yourself up from head to toe and only revealing your entire self to your man is really rather sexy when you think about it.'

'Steve, what makes you think you would not be a peasant?' asked Ameena. 'You and Lem would be little better than slaves in your medieval utopia.'

'Fundamentalism has all the superstitions and iconography of medievalism. That's why I'm against it. We've been there before,' added Devora, the flush appearing at her neck.

'Praying five times a day does not make a girl a potential suicide bomber. It's still a woman's choice. If she wants to wear the veil, why on earth should that upset you?'

'Choice? We're talking about children here. What choice do you really think they have? You won't get me covering myself up. I'm invisible enough as it is.'

'Well, I can see the attraction of the hijab,' continued Ameena, stacking her pile of stuff on her desk and scratching her bottom with her Biro. 'Western women are suffering from exposure.'

'Tell me about it,' said Steve, wheeling his chair back a bit from the desk and putting his head on one side for a better view of Ameena and her Biro.

'As in *dying* of exposure, Steve, as in *over*-exposed, and yes, I am scratching my arse here, not – though you may find it hard to believe – performing miniature pole dancing. Yes, Michael, what do you want?'

'You told me to come and see you, Miss,' smirked a boy at the door, an expression on his face that mirrored Steve's and was that of a small but very precisely circuited brain failing to compute the contradictory information before it that was Ameena: Asian, babe, bitch, pussy, mother, whore, hag, teacher.

'I told you to come and see me yesterday after school, not now in my lunch break. Go away.' Michael swayed slightly on the balls of his feet, almost put his heels down by mistake, sucked his teeth and sauntered, groin first, hands last, out of the door. 'And take that hood off!' she called after him.

'Hijabs for boys,' muttered Devora. 'You won't catch the French trying to ban those.'

'You mean,' mused Marissa, still several sentences behind, 'the way most women in the West literally expose their bodies?' She sucked the tip of her pencil. 'But surely that's liberating, isn't it?'

'Course it is.' Steve swivelled the other way and levelled his gaze at Marissa's cantilevered breasts, pierced navel and naked knees. He opened his mouth as if to speak, but was intercepted by a look from Ameena and nothing emerged except for a yawn followed by a boyish grin.

'And talking of visibility,' added Devora, looking in dismay at the toppling tower of books still to be marked on the desktop in front of her, 'maybe suicide bombing is one way of achieving it. What do you think, Lem? Shocking prospect, no?'

'Yeah, get a word in edgeways, Lem. Any views?' Ameena looked at him, challenging him to live up to his job as, just occasionally, and very scarily, she sometimes did.

Lem scrunched up his toes inside his trainers and summoned the response he'd been rehearsing in his head.

'Devotion can hardly be a crime—' he began, but the second bell cut through his words and he was grateful, for in truth he did not know what to think, let alone say. All he knew was that half his classes never stopped filling the space with their voices, a stream of unstoppable stuff of everything that entered their minds. The stage whereby human children learn to internalise their thoughts at around the age of three just didn't seem to have happened with those students. And then there was the other half, who simply never spoke. It was impossible.

The carriages swung one way, then the other, like the twister at the fair which he had loved because Todd used to crush him under his arm till it hurt and they would yell together for the duration of the ride. Now it meant that Salma jerked violently into view at irregular intervals so that he saw her as if in a slow-motion film, first with her eyes down to the floor, one arm raised to the bar above, then with her head half raised and holding her bottom lip between her teeth so that she looked troubled, and finally with her face turned towards him for just an instant, but enough for their eyes to meet and for her to blink twice in recognition before the metal-framed window of the connecting door lurched hard the other way at another bend and Salma vanished from sight, obscured once more by the suspended bodies of the standing passengers.

He looked up to check the Tube map on the wall opposite him and found his look intercepted by the gaze of a handsome woman clutching the metal pole to his right. She was so tall she almost had to stoop to avoid the ceiling. Her head hung down and she was looking directly at him out of frank, curious eyes. Something about her unlipsticked mouth and long neck reminded him of the underwater sea-urchin woman in Rhodes. He'd been squatting underwater with his mask and snorkel, retreating from the thong throng on the beach. There wasn't much to see under the sea, it had to be said. It was grey and silty and dotted with the occasional sea cucumber. Every now and then a shoal of small colourless fish would dart by in a jerky synchronised swim. It was all a very long way from Dawn's illuminated tropical fish tank. He'd been trying to crouch on the seabed, but was only managing a slow-motion bouncy squat as he listened to the muffled buzz of speedboats.

A tiny tide of seawater slid about in the rim of his face-mask. What he really wanted to do, he thought, was to feel what it was like to swim naked. And why not? There was no one around. That lot on the beach never ever swam, as far as he could work out. They dived in a lot and then came lumbering straight out again gasping, tossing their hair and flicking foam from their arms and bodies. Lem surfaced partially to take a breath and check that the coast was clear, then sank out of sight again. He slipped his thumbs down the waistband of his swimming shorts and lowered them halfway down his bottom. Instant transformation. He felt that if he could just swim untrammelled he might attain a sense of release. He kicked his way out of his shorts and lowered one arm to grab the nasty nylon. Bliss. He jerked and kicked about a bit, imagining himself to be a dolphin, and then, feeling even more daring, he lay on his back on the surface of the water with his arms outstretched and felt the sun warm his skin. Suspended in this way, completely naked, he felt a delicious aquatic abandon. Flipping over, he kicked his way down again and took a couple of strong underwater strokes, exhaling powerfully in a tumult of noisy bubbles.

And then she just loomed up at him from below, sea-urchin woman, dark hair floating out from her face-mask, mouth smiling around her snorkel mouthpiece, eyes wide open and friendly. She had a sea urchin and a knife in one hand and a plastic bag in the other. Tactfully she rose to the surface with one slow beat of her flippers. Lem struggled back into his shorts and rose to the surface too. Treading water, he spluttered and smiled at her. She said something in Greek, pushed her mask back onto her dark wet head and scraped the flesh out of a spiny shell. Holding it out on her knife, she offered it to him. 'I've just eaten, thanks all the same,' Lem said, and she shrugged and dripped the black meat into her mouth, tossing the urchin over her shoulder. He knew that if this had been a film, the next scene would have them swimming underwater to the promontory, where they would clamber out, gobble up more urchins and make slithering love in the ruined windmill. But instead he said, 'Nice, isn't it?' and gestured around at the scenery. And then added, 'Just lost my watch', and pointed down into the depths. 'You want?' she said, pointing over to the rocks, and she jackknifed down to the seabed. A perpendicular tail of flippers was the last he saw of her.

He turned back towards the beach and saw Dawn waving a bottle of retsina at him. He took a deep breath and dropped below the surface, looking for the woman in the bubbling swirl and wondering how far he could get without coming up for air. When he rose to the surface he squinted across at the beach again, just in time to glimpse what looked like Dawn being sick onto his towel and shorts. He turned onto his back and flailed wearily towards her.

Lem studied the pattern on the armrest, which was different from the rest of the seat – turquoise and green rhomboids fitting tight together – and thought of him and Dawn in bed in Kinloss Court and how they would lie in the same position night after night, a repeated pattern themselves, their geometry making dents in the mattress. 'Dawn, I'm lost,' he would whisper sometimes and then he would lie there, not daring to breathe, unless she wasn't sleeping either, but just lying there like him. Often in the night, he would feel himself detach from her and imagine instead all the other people lying asleep in Kinloss Court, many many of them, placed horizontally at different levels, pointing north, south, east and west like souls in flight or the frozen bodies in *Coma*, and he would feel that it was with them that he belonged, not with Dawn at all.

Green Park

THE TRAIN STOOD still with its doors open onto the platform, sides rattling and electrics humming. Lem could hear a telephone ringing down the other end of the station. The public address system inside the carriage beeped, breathed, rasped and then trailed off in a hiss. Passengers' glances crisscrossed the carriage. The hiss died into silence.

Lem wondered about jumping off the train and making a run for it. He could change onto the Piccadilly Line and in three stops he would be at Todd's office in South Kensington. Surely Todd could find him a job at Sunspot Productions, in Development or Expansion or Realisation or Research. There was bound to be something he could do. After all, it seemed to take an awful lot of people to make one television programme.

'Come on come on come on come *on*.' Todd clicked his fingers at the Sunspot Development team gathered round the conference table, each with the day's newspapers in a pile in front of them. He squeaked back and forth in his executive chair that Lem knew for a fact had cost £3,000, because Polly, Todd's PA, had told him. 'Ideas. We need ideas. We know which formats work, but I sense we're getting stale here. We're playing safe and going over old ground.' He swung melodramatically round to the right and upended his palm at Lucinda, a small intense woman sitting next to Polly. She was leafing through the *Mirror*.

'Well, I think there might be something in this piece about spanking . . .'

Yeps and mmms of agreement rippled round the table. Todd raised his palm into a stop sign.

'Hold on hold on hold on. *Spanking*? Spanking as in . . .' He offered both opened hands to the room and allowed a pause for one of the others to fill, but they all looked at him hesitantly. A job in Development might be more boring than actually watching the television programmes, but all of them were grateful for the tentative foothold it offered on the lower rungs of the television ladder.

'Not spanking as such,' said Lucinda with care, 'we're talking . . . we're talking *smacking* really, aren't we?'

'Smacking, yes.'

'Oh, yes, smacking is the—'

'. . . is the term generally—'

'. . . generally used, yes.'

'Smacking, spanking, all much of a—'

'We're talking hitting children, yes?'

'At the end of the day, a smack's a spank though, yes?'

So far, Lem had written 'spank' on his pad, then crossed it out and written 'smack'. Polly looked over his shoulder and beamed at him, offering a throat pastille that he shook his head at, a can of Sprite that he nodded at and a chocolate-chip cookie that he didn't respond to, in case it had nuts in it. Work experience at Todd's office during one of Lem's university vacations had been all right really. Not as exciting as he had hoped, but it had been a chance to spend time with Todd. Lem shifted his chair a little closer to his father and turned his pad away from Polly.

'Got you. Right. Yes. Go on.' Todd swung sharply to the left and held his coffee cup outstretched. Natasha, sitting halfway down the table, reached for the pot and refilled it. Lem wondered where all the men were.

'So,' began Lucinda slowly. 'How about we take a child from a smacking family and send it to live for a week with a non-smacking family . . . er . . .'

There was something just inside Todd's right nostril that was distracting him. He was trying to reach it with his thumbnail, but this wasn't easy because the whole room kept looking up at him to check that the ideas were developing to his satisfaction. Lem thought about giving him a nudge or the screwed-up tissue in his pocket and felt all at once sorry for his father's puffy eyes, thinning hair and straining paunch. The whole process of living seemed to be exhausting him.

'That's not going to work, is it?' he said, hand hanging down by his side and flicking away at his thumb with his middle finger.

'Perhaps not,' conceded Lucinda, shaking her head. 'The swap format is wrong possibly, but I was thinking—'

'How about,' began Emma over the other side of the table, 'we get some adult smackees, put them in an isolated environment, subject them to various tests and humiliations, then—'

'. . . and another group,' interrupted Yasmin, 'of smackers on a parallel island, camp, house, whatever—'

'But how *sexy* is spanking?' said Todd and everyone looked down at their pads and papers. 'I mean, as an idea . . .' He picked up another croissant. 'What else have we got in the papers?'

'How about Celebrity Sperm Race?' Hank from Production had wandered into the room.

Todd stopped chewing. 'Go on.'

'Celebrities give a sperm sample, we dye it so you can tell whose is whose, create a chemical lure like the hare the dogs chase at Walthamstow, and viewers put bets on the winner.'

'Most virile celebrity wins.' He finished his coffee and crushed the cup, tossing it in the bin on his way to the door.

The room fell silent.

Todd spanked the table top once. 'Absolutely bloody brilliant.'

Lem looked at his fellow passengers and wondered which of them, if any, would have the potential to be a hero should the need arise. Definitely sea-urchin woman and perhaps the man opposite with the suit and grey hair who was reading *New Scientist* because you could tell that, apart from knowing about science, the man was fit. That looked like muscle bulging inside his sleeves rather than flab. Lem's own biceps were becoming fairly impressive, thanks to all the book lifting and carrying he had to do at school, and he thought of the story of Devora's husband whose attempts to stave off age had been assisted by a pair of dumb-bells. Devora said the beginning of the end was heralded by the clinking of metal weights and rhythmic panting from the landing outside the bedroom. As signs go, I suppose it was at least clear, she had told Lem one day as they strode fast to the café one lunchtime.

Just occasionally, when the weather was fine and they both had an easy afternoon ahead of them, they treated themselves to lunch at Zorba's, which was a ten-minute walk away near Brixton market and sold good coffee and greasy food. It was there, one intensely sunlit day not long after Easter, that he'd almost but not quite managed to coax the rest of Devora's tale of the magical massage in Thailand out of her.

Steve had wandered past just as they sat down and Devora had tapped on the window, calling his name through the glass. Don't look this way, Lem had thought. But Steve was looking in the estate agent's window next door and appeared not to see them, although Lem figured he must have followed them down the road. Once they were seated, Devora had seemed set on talking about Marvin, Dawn's skunk-scammered brother. Lem looked up at the clock. They had twenty-five minutes and he really did not want to discuss this with Devora. There was no point. Devora's generation just didn't understand about cannabis. They thought they were doing today's youth a favour by being very liberal and saying dope was OK. But dope today wasn't what it used to be in their day, and how do you explain that to forty- and fifty-year-olds without making them all smoke the kinds of spliffs that Marvin had smoked several times a day since he was thirteen? The stuff you got to smoke these days was a different drug altogether from the hash that Devora and Alan fondly remembered.

'It must be to do with puberty, don't you think, Lem?' Devora was saying.

Lem looked up at the menu on the wall. 'Probably.'

He really wished Devora had not said that word. If she had to talk about it, couldn't she call it something else? The Aborigines probably had a word for it. The Aborigines probably had a whole desert devoted not only to entering it but coming out the other side, but not of course the English, or more specifically Walthamstow, where one was left to blunder alone through the tulgey wood of—

'Lem?' Devora tapped his arm.

'What? Sorry. Baklava?'

'Dope, Lem. I mean, if this stuff is really as strong as you say, then I wouldn't be surprised if some neurological catastrophe is triggered concerning puberty and identity.' Devora sat down and started sweeping away the sugar grains. 'If it's interrupted or derailed, then maybe they're left in a kind of limbo. You know, the more I teach, the more I think we have seriously underestimated the fragile nature of masculine identity. It may be too late. We've spent so long worrying about the girls that . . . ooh . . .' Devora's mobile beeped twice and she stopped to thumb its keys.

Lem studied the menu again. He felt hollow. He badly needed filling up. Moussaka and chips with baklava for desert should do it.

'Oh. Message from ex-husband: what is vet's number?' She waved the phone in front of him then tossed it into her bag. 'What a prat. Come on, let's order.'

Catching sight of himself in the mirror behind Devora, he tried to flatten his hair a bit. He looked like he'd just had a shock and he thought of whey-faced Marvin, who was sometimes in and sometimes out of the unit. Marvin had always seemed to perk up a little on the Sunday visits to Arnos Grove when Lem was there for lunch. The two of them would stand in the garden, each listening on one earpiece to Marvin's Discman while Marvin chain-smoked and spoke too loudly. Since Lem and Dawn had finished, that whole side of his life had fallen away from him like a split log that someone had taken an axe to. He supposed he would never see Marvin again.

'So, what happened with the massage then?' he asked, emptying a sachet of sugar onto his tongue and noting a warm glow begin in his groin.

'Well, something very strange happened to the time, for one thing. I went into the hut at two o'clock and the next thing I knew it was three hours later. Nirvana was what happened. Some sort of tantric state—'

And then Steve was sitting next to her and helping himself to the froth off her cappuccino and saying, 'Tantric state, Devs? That'll be Lem's conversation, won't it?' and he guffawed happily, looking from one to the other, grinning like a greedy ape.

It wasn't until the next night, in the flickering light of the fruit machine, that Devora recounted the remainder of the massage story. They were in the pub, tucked around the corner table away from the others who were crowded around the screen watching the match. The place smelt of beer and bleach and carpet.

'So, go on,' he said.

'Lying in the dim light of the curtained cubicle, which smelt of sun on hessian, I just felt the weight of my marriage fall from every cell of my body. I knew I didn't have to fear his judgement, you see, Lem. Outside I could hear the small pony I'd seen earlier clip-clopping about the rocky path, blowing its nose and huffing and puffing nearby, and in the distance the waves breaking on the shore like a heavy sleeper. I just waited there for him to begin while he moved gently about the room preparing his oils and towels.'

Lem checked the bar. Steve was safely occupied by Marissa. He hoped Devora's preamble wasn't going to take too long. He assumed the massage was more than just a massage. He let his eyes drop to her breasts, then her belly and the top of her jeans. She looked better in a skirt, he decided, because of her hips.

'It reminded me of when I was a girl. I must have been about eight or nine and I'd gone to the doctor's with my mother. He'd sat me on the edge of the bed and tapped my back and chest with his knuckles, like this.' She cupped her hand over his heart and knocked on it with the other and Lem saw that the wine had made Devora dull. Dull and rambling. 'I always used to like that, but they don't do it any more. I have no idea what he thought he was listening to, but there was something pleasant about the knocking of his hands against bone. Deep breath in, he always used to say, and I'd stare at the sharp caps of my knees on the edge of the bed, see the tips of my toes dangling. Remembering the girl I was then, years before I'd even thought of boys or marriage . . . well, the tears just fell. They trickled into my ears and hair as I thought to myself, There must have been a day, a day I didn't notice, when that gamine girl that was me just got up and left.'

Sadness pulled at the corners of her mouth and Lem looked away into his drink. Perhaps there was a time when he would have put his arm round her, been able to offer some comfort, maybe more, who knows? But just recently, that time seemed to have gone.

'Do you know?' she continued. 'I've come to understand that marriage is bad for women. It really is. Show me a married woman who doesn't look old before her time. Can you think of one?' Lem thought of Fay, but decided against mentioning her. 'It's a bit like a boat tour you decide to take on holiday. They always seem like a good idea, but every boat tour I've ever taken has become a mind-numbing voyage of pointlessness and you pace the deck oblivious to the view, just desperate to get off.' She swallowed the rest of her wine and grimaced. 'God, this stuff's poison. Anyway, the point is, in Thailand,' Lem sat up and nodded, 'I lay there and remembered what it felt like to be inside a body that didn't hold you to ransom and how, when you become a woman, it is with a certain fear and dismay because from that point you're no longer free. I can remember the day I looked in my pants at the swimming-pool changing rooms, down past the scribble of pubic hair and saw with a shock the ferrous stain in my knickers—'

Lem reached in alarm for his beer glass and knocked it over onto the table. 'Whoops! Sorry.'

'Well, then I understood the ache in my belly and my breasts . . . the sinking feeling in my heart . . .' She stopped talking and began to cry, saying, 'Oh, don't take any notice of me, Lem. I don't know what's the matter with me lately.'

He knew he should say something, but nothing came to mind. The drink seemed to have stolen the familiar Devora and put a smudged, rudderless one in her place. He wanted the old Devora back with her humour and her courage.

She twisted the stem of her empty glass. 'The funny thing was that, having remembered that moment, I then realised that for the next thirty years I forgot it. Forgot myself.' She spread her hands out on the table and studied the backs of them. 'It's not the same for boys, I don't think, is it?'

Lem wondered whether he should ask if she'd like another drink.

'I mean, the way you are looked at – judged – once you reach puberty if you're a girl . . .'

Lem looked at her over the rim of his almost empty glass, glugged the last mouthful and then looked away again for fear that he might be looking at her the way men look at girls once they reach puberty.

'Nobody looked at me at all,' he said.

It must be half time. Marissa had disappeared and the crowd had thinned. Steve was still standing at the bar, his eyes on the mirror behind it, moving his head slowly from one side to the other to check his profile.

Now Devora was looking at him, eyebrows raised, glass in hand. 'I said, would you like another drink, Lem?'

'I'll get them.' Lem struggled to his feet and put his hand in his pocket. 'Oh, er . . .'

Devora put her hand on his arm.

'No. My turn. You stay there.'

He counted the paces it took her to walk to the bar (eleven) and watched her stand alongside Steve, saw him turn his body outwards towards her as she stood on her toes and leant across to give her order. Her bottom looked pretty good in fact. He waited for the crude gesture from Steve that he knew would follow. He waited but it didn't come. Instead, Steve leant towards her and said something into her hair which looked gold under the low bar light. She looked up into his face and opened her mouth to laugh. Lem looked away and thought of Alan kissing the back of Fay's neck the way he did when she stood at the sink and he thought of the boredom, the hours and hours of boredom that seemed to span his childhood. A boredom that resulted in an escape into ever more banal numerological observations. Insects used to feature quite frequently, he seemed to remember, as he watched a fly supping at the puddle of beer on the table.

'Do ants ever go to sleep?'

The glare of the pool and the press of the sun during a fortnight in Spain with Fay and Alan. He was lying face down on the sun lounger in a stupor of boredom, studying a group of ants dismantling a dead fly. Alan roused himself from his prone position next to Fay, stood up, ran his hands down his hairless chest, adjusted the waist elastic of his trunks and slow-jogged towards the pool, calling over his shoulder, 'Come on, Lem. Race you!'

Lem turned his head and watched Fay watching Alan.

'Go on,' she said to him and he rolled over, sat up, and wrapped his arms about his sun-blocked chest.

'The water hurts my eyes.' His voice growled and soared.

'Go on.' Fay was already back in her book.

He followed Alan to the poolside and stubbed his toe on the low ledge surrounding it. He hopped on one foot, gasping at the pain of torn skin and nail.

'Mind the ledge,' said Alan, arms raised, balancing at the water's edge. Lem stood beside him. 'One, two, go!' and Alan had pierced the blue, leaving Lem windmilling on the hot tiles, flailing and finally falling into the froth and fizz of Alan's wake.

'It's one, two, three!' Lem shouted when Alan's sleek head surfaced. 'One, two, three, you fat cheat!' and he took a breath and swam underwater towards the other end. Alan turned back, plunged towards him and grabbed him under both arms, pinching the flesh.

'What did you call me?' he said wet and grinning, then threw Lem back down into the water, holding him under for just a little longer than was funny.

Devora came back from the bar, her glass filled to the brim with what looked like Ribena.

'Blackcurrant and soda. Can't take my drink any more. At the age of forty-five and a half, about the same time as the eyes go, my tolerance for wine went out the window. I have no idea what's going on in the liver department, but I can't do alcohol any longer. It's all most peculiar. You'd think by now my body would just give in and stop protesting.'

'Devora . . .'

She'd looked at him over her pint glass of ruby lozenge. The beer made him feel pleasantly distanced from his words.

'Carry on what you were saying about adolescence. You know, how it made you lose yourself.'

'Well, that makes adolescence sound like there was nothing to recommend it, which wouldn't strictly speaking be true. I quite enjoyed the power I suddenly found that I had. It's just that as soon as the looking begins, it cripples you with self-consciousness. Honestly, it's a disability. We should all have a special parking bay.'

'When you were my age . . .'

He tipped his head back and looked up at the ceiling. Ugly Edwardian plaster painted magnolia gloss. He carried on looking at the ceiling for fear of the expression on her face.

'I mean, how do you manage everything? A mortgage, a career, car, marriage . . .' He stopped because of course she hadn't quite managed that. God. Now he was pissed there was no telling what would come out.

Marissa had returned from the Ladies and Steve was safely occupied again over at the bar, bending forwards and backwards from the waist as he laughed at Marissa's tales of Most Men and Most Women. There was so little time. It felt like the last remaining grains were about to trickle through. The fruit machine on the wall near them pulsed and chirruped and he could feel the alcohol swimming through his brain, making him feel loose and reckless.

'People probably think I should go out with Marissa . . .'

There. The words were out now. Lying on the table between them like Scrabble pieces. It was her turn. He took another long gulp of yeasty beer.

'Lem.' She put her hand on his arm and rubbed it as though he was a child with a graze. He inched his arm away. Pity. He didn't want that. He could feel Steve's eyes on them.

'Marvin's back in the unit again,' he said. He didn't know why he was speaking of Marvin. Especially now of all moments. Marvin was the last person he wanted to talk to Devora about.

'Have you visited him?' She leant back in her chair, eyes glancing down at her mobile phone.

'No. Dawn phoned last night. It wasn't a long call, they never are, but, thing is . . .' He rubbed his damp palms up and down his thighs. Devora's nostrils flared as she stifled a yawn. 'Marvin could so easily be me.' And then before she could finish saying, Don't be so silly, he had pushed his chair back, said, 'I got to go', and stumbled from the pub out into the steady drizzle of the night.

12

Victoria

LEM SAID, 'We should have gone to Victoria Park. It's nearer the hospice and the river.'

Dean pulled the ring off another can and poured beer down his throat. He wiped his mouth with his sleeve, squinting into the distance from under his baseball cap. 'I like it here,' he said.

It was one Sunday a couple of months ago in April, a sunny day when the unexpected heat and light after weeks of cloud brought the humans stumbling out to lie down on grass like shipwreck survivors. All around them bodies lay crumpled alone, tangled in pairs or heaped in groups, parched faces upturned to drink the sun. Birdsong like liquid happiness, grass that glittered and an avenue of cherry trees caked with blossom seemed too much, Lem thought, remembering the morphined form they had just left and how he seemed to be slipping like sand through an hour glass, dematerialising in front of their eyes. He didn't realise Dean was going to take him to visit Mr O'Farrell before they went fishing. They had stayed by the bedside for half an hour and no one had spoken. Lem had leant yawning against the windowsill with the sun on his back while Dean sat by the bed watching the man's shallow breath lift the thin hospital blanket.

Lem had drunk one can of tepid beer and now he had a metallic headache above his right eye. He began tearing up the grass by his feet, resentment like clay forming in the pit of his stomach. Leaving the hospice on Mare Street, they had crossed the busy road and Dean had led him down Bush Road, then Sheep Lane and into the south gate of London Fields. The plan had been to go fishing in the River Lea to the north, through Victoria Park and up onto Hackney Marsh, but they had been sitting on the grass near the entrance to the Fields since they left Mr O'Farrell two hours ago and Dean showed no sign of making a move. Lem's bottom was getting damp; the earth beneath him was still cold and hard from the frost-locked winter and there was the unmistakable whiff of dog shit somewhere nearby. He cleared his throat and looked over at Dean whose face was turning red. Lem looked around him and tried to think of something to say.

'I think this was the last place you could graze your animals before the markets in London.'

Dean took another slug of beer.

With a sigh, Lem lay down on his back, balling his parka up under his head. It was too hot for a parka. He must remember to get Todd's denim jacket back off Steve.

'Hey, Lem. What you doing here?'

Opening his eyes, he squinted up at the sky to see Dawn's face looking down at him. Her hair was blonde and straightened so that it framed her face in slippery points like that news reader on Channel 5. She had on a thin blue dress that flutterered round her knees and clung to her thighs. She had lost a lot of weight.

He sat up, batted down his hair and said, 'Dawn.'

She smiled at him and looked around over her shoulder, shielding her eyes from the sun with one hand.

'I'm here with Marvin. He'd love to see you again.'

Lem looked over towards the sports ground where a familiar figure was standing with rounded shoulders, one hand in his pocket, the other holding a cigarette at chin level. He was looking up into a tree. Dawn shouted over towards him and waved.

'He's got a thing about ley lines and the earth's energies,' she said quickly. She chewed her cheek and waved at the motionless figure again. Her face was softer than he remembered it. 'He's got some sort of grid reference and we're visiting the axes of force fields or something.' Tucking her hair behind one ear she smiled at Dean. 'Hi, I'm Dawn.'

Dean stood up and shook her hand. 'Dean,' he said. 'James Dean,' and he raised his can of beer in salutation.

Dawn bent her knees and dropped halfway towards the earth, laughter spluttering from her. Lem had forgotten that laugh. It was a fantastic laugh, like the flinging open of curtains. He stood up too and hoped she hadn't brought Ian with her.

'And that's my brother, Marvin,' she said to Dean, gesturing at the figure approaching them with carefully placed steps. 'He's not been well.'

'Can you feel it too?' Marvin said, reaching them and standing square in front of them. Bloated and pale from the antipsychotics, he was clearly pleased to see Lem again. 'It's a sort of fuzzy whiteness, like you're weaving.'

Lem said, 'Well, this beer's given me a bit of a headache. Cheers, Marvin.'

'That's because they use aluminium in the can.' He paced to his left, then back again. 'It's not so strong here. I've got a feeling we need to go north.'

'So how do you two know each other?' Dawn and Dean spoke simultaneously and Dawn added, 'I mean, what are you doing here?'

Dean said, 'Well, you used to live with Lem . . .'

'The ley lines are connected to the earth's magnetic field.' Marvin lit up another Benson & Hedges from the glowing end of the one he was finishing.

'Yes, and you . . . ?' said Dawn.

'Pigeons, whales, honeybees, bacteria – they all navigate using the earth's magnetic field.' Marvin stared at the ground.

'So why can't I feel anything?' asked Lem.

'It's in there, but you've suppressed it. Being able to tune in is one of the advantages of my . . . condition.' He stopped abruptly as though listening for something.

Dean said, 'I was the other man' and there was a moment's silence, which Dawn broke with a laugh, holding out her hand for a can of Stella.

Lem checked the remaining passengers in his carriage as the train drew away from the station. A few local-government types and a couple of sleepy night workers sat opposite him. He pulled his mobile out of his pocket and read down the list of old missed calls. Dawn, Dean, Dawn.

The phone calls from Dawn had started as soon as she had moved in with Ian. Lem's phone would ring, he'd see her number come up on the screen, but when he answered there was no one there, just a lot of rustling, footsteps, sometimes a child's voice, the odd bark and snuffle. They'd happen several times a day. At the first one, his heart did leap a bit, he had to admit. He'd been lying on the bed at Kinloss Court next to a pile of unmarked books. The marking, he was thinking, was a form of torture. It was never-ending, and worse than that, everyone knew there was no point to it. The kids never looked at the corrections and the teachers barely looked at what they were marking. He was working out that if he actually set all the homework he was supposed to set (twice a week) for all the different classes that he taught (seven classes, which equals one hundred and seventy-five students) then he would never have time to go to bed. Well, that can't be right, can it? It was all a Kafkaesque performance that teachers and students were locked into by parents, who thought that marking and homework were what teaching and learning were all about. Not that most of the kids he taught did home-work, thank God. If they did, he really would never get to go to sleep. So he was lying there, listening to the ceaseless river of traffic outside the window and not thinking of Dawn at all, when she rang.

He had picked up his phone and looked carefully at the name before he answered, because he was trying to avoid Steve who kept ringing to ask him out. He had been a couple of times, but he didn't have it in him tonight for the pick-up routine in one of the heaving bars. And anyway, Lem had never in his life walked up to a woman and said . . . Well, that was the problem, what exactly were you supposed to say? He could not bring himself to speak the clichés that fell from Steve's mouth or engage with any of the bellowed responses. So, seeing it was Dawn's name being displayed on the phone, he pressed the answer button and said, 'Hello?' He listened for a long time, fascinated yet dreading what he might hear. Though he heard nothing distinct, he could just discern the faint burr of Ian's voice, the even fainter Welsh tune of Dawn's and some engine noise. He imagined them as he listened. Ian's forty-something body packed into the passenger seat of Dawn's Peugeot, the back seat covered in dog hairs and children's sweet wrappers. The children didn't live with Ian, but the dogs did. Eventually Lem put the phone down and then carried on staring at the ceiling light and wondered why it was spherical rather than cuboid and why it was that they had never got round to getting a shade for it.

After that first time, the phone calls had become a regular occurrence, so much so that he didn't bother listening after a while. He just said 'Hello?', got the muffled impression of a parallel world and hung up. He'd told Devora about it one day and she'd said, 'Oh yes. The phantom phone calls. I got those. I think it's just a form of her dreaming you. The unconscious self takes a while to come to terms with the seismic shifts that the conscious self has implemented. They'll stop after a few years.'

There had been one or two in the last six months when Dawn actually was on the other end of the line. Unfortunately the first call had come when he was in The Bird in the Bush with Steve, trying to talk to Lola and Dee, two women that Steve was working on. The drinks in that place were a fiver each and so it had cost a fortune to stand there being shouted at for two hours. His phone had made him jump, vibrating suddenly in his pocket. He couldn't see what the number was, but once he'd fought his way outside he heard Dawn's voice on the line crying his name. 'Le-e-m.' He said, 'Dawn? Dawn?', but all he could hear was the laughing and shouting behind him and the roar and scream of the road in front. He thought she'd hung up, but when he put his face against the greasy brickwork and hunched his body over, one finger stuffed into an ear, he heard her voice again, 'Are you out somewhere? Doesn't matter, I'll call you later.'

And that was it. He tried calling her back, but her phone was off. Then there was another time when he was going down the escalator to the Tube and Dawn rang. He only had time to hear her say, 'Lem, I'm scared, Lem' before he reached the bottom and the signal went. He ran up the other escalator and rang her back. This time she answered. She sounded normal and said she may have dialled his number by mistake and that she had to go.

Lem stretched his legs out in front of him and gazed round the carriage. He was hot and his palms were damp. He shrugged off Todd's jacket and put it on the seat next to him, pulling the top of Alan's shirt forwards so that he could blow onto his chest. Discovering that Steve shaved his chest had been as much of a shock to Lem as discovering that Dawn had been for a Brazilian down at Sheila's Health and Beauty. When Dawn had shown him, he was assailed by the image of Mercy Evans from primary school. Mercy's dad had a gun, so she said, and that was why she could demand money or chocolate with menaces from any child wanting to enter the toilet block at playtime. Most children, of course, didn't go to the toilet. Lem remembered that learning not to pee or shit during the school day is one of the first lessons you learn at school. Ask any child. School toilets have no locks, no paper, no ventilation, no cleaning and, more than that, it is where each child learns the strange and guilty truth about other people, which is that some other people like to smear their shit over cubicle walls and doors. Lem always suspected that Mercy Evans was one of these people. After all, she owned the toilets and her life was crap. Anyway, one day early in Lem's school career, before he'd learnt the never-go-to-the-toilet-in-school lesson, he'd encountered Mercy at the door to the mouth of hell and, as he hadn't any dinner money on him, she'd lifted up her skirt, pulled down her knickers and told him to get on his knees and beg for mercy.

Most mer-ci-ful beau-ti-ful God only wise – they had sung that at primary school. Or something like it. The pattern of the seat fabric was repeated in twenty-centimetre blocks. The apexes he supposed were intended to suggest direction and, where they interlocked, connection. The pattern was crude and predictable like a mundane song that got stuck in your head. No, it was Immor-tal in-vis-ible God only wise, In light, in-access-ible . . . He preferred the random distribution of white and blue spatters on the grey floor, or rather he preferred working out where the apparent randomness was betrayed by pattern. Most mer-ci-ful God only – he sat up straight. That was it. Most merciful Allah was what Helena had talked about in assembly on International Women's Day. The other speaker was Salma's mother who worked as a drugs counsellor in Finsbury Park. When Lem told Todd, he had not been very encouraging.

'Helena's coming to give a talk at my school.'

'Are you sure that's a good idea?'

Lem shrugged. 'It's for International Women's Day.'

'Well, she's international all right. London, New York, Qatar . . . What's she talking about?'

'Her conversion to Islam. Melanie wants to challenge the stereotypes.'

'Hold the wheel, will you.'

Todd took both hands off the steering wheel and lifted his pelvis up from the driving seat in order to swat the seat clean of crumbs. Lem grabbed for the wheel with his right hand so that the car swerved to the left.

'Bloody chocolate. Gets everywhere. ROUNDABOUT, LEM, ROUNDABOUT.'

Lem let out a yelp and the car veered right, then left, before Todd resumed control. Letting Lem steer was a game they used to play when he was a boy. Todd would give up the wheel, usually without any warning except to shout, 'Take the wheel, Lem!' Once, when he was seven, they had been driving back from his grandmother's on Easter Sunday. It was a bright sunny day, unseasonably hot, the kind that wakes up the lumbering bumble bees too early. The car windows were open and Lem was eating an ice cream. On his second bite, the car leapt over a humpback bridge and the ice cream hopped out of his hand. He stared at where it had landed, face down on the floor between his trainers, held his breath and tried to count to ten like Fay had taught him to do. He only got as far as three before a sob exploded from his mouth and nose and the slow wail of hot tears began. Todd, reluctant as always to slow down, looked at him once, twice and then three times before swinging the BMW onto the verge and bringing the car to a bumpy halt. Lem went silent, unsure of what was going to happen next. It wasn't that he was scared of Todd, it was just that he didn't know him that well. They both got out of the car, Todd cleaned up the ice cream with a chamois leather before tossing the whole lot over the hawthorn hedge. Lem stood on the verge, an occasional sob escaping him. Without a word, Todd picked him up and ran with him down the verge, leaping over the little drainage ditches and pulling up Lem's jumper. He stopped, turned round and blew a raspberry on the skin of Lem's belly so that the sob became a laugh, then sprinted them both back to the car.

International Women's Day assembly had not been a complete success. Two women in hijabs on the hall stage had proved too much for many people: the Turkish, Kurdish,

Afro-Caribbean, Pakistani and Bangladeshi boys were not inclined to listen to one Muslim woman lecturing them, let alone two; the white boys, and after a bit of chanting, the white girls also, wanted to know when it was International Men's Day; the Muslim girls were curious, excited even, but too reserved to sway the critical mass of the hall, and many of the staff had muttered about the inappropriateness of inviting a white Western woman to talk about Islam. The assembly staggered on, Helena explaining how two marriages and the pressures of living life as a Western woman had almost brought her to breaking point and that Allah had taught her to live in peace with herself. In Islam, she said, she had finally found acceptance and freedom as a woman. She finished by saying that if any of the girls needed support or guidance, she ran a fund that might be able to offer help. Salma's mother, an ex-nurse, gave a moving account (for those who could hear above the clatter of the lunch tables being set out) of the daily struggle against crime and oblivion facing the drug addicts of Finsbury Park. Melanie did a pretty good job of controlling the whole proceedings with laser-beam sweeps of her eyes and mercifully it was all over by quarter to nine. At the end of the talks, Helena and Salma's mother had been surrounded by Muslim girls laughing and talking loudly.

Melanie was Devora's closest friend, they had both been at the school since the start of their careers when, Devora said, teaching was much less complicated than today. If it wasn't for the fact that Melanie was head of English and therefore too busy to have lunch or break or go to the pub after school, Lem would probably see much less of Devora than he did. She was a tall angular woman in her forties, whose cross-genre dressing veered wildly between trouser suits from Next, teenager hooker wear and snowboard dudedom. Her sartorial eclecticism was mirrored by her mercurial temper. Some days, it seemed to Lem, she was tossing rapier-sharp witticisms left, right and centre, laughing and joking like an old soak on a bar stool, yet on other days she marched down the corridor grim-jawed and hollow-eyed, barking at the students.

Melanie had wandered across the hall to join them at the tail end of Parents' Evening. She sat down heavily on one of a row of low chairs with ripped corners so that, on impact, a few bits of foam rubber puffed out.

'Do you have anything like the apostrophe in maths or history?' she asked, sitting back in her chair with her arms and legs akimbo. Today her hair was dyed matt black with red wings at the front.

'Oh, you've done your hair,' said Devora.

'I mean, a thing, an idea, a concept that, if they don't grasp it by the time they have left primary school, they are never ever going to get?' Melanie put one hand halfway up to her hair and lowered it back down to dangle by her seat again. 'Yes, I know, the hair's a mistake . . .'

'No, it's not. Very *Sid and Nancy*. Apostrophes? Do you do anything like that, Lem?'

Lem thought how Devora's lipsticked mouth always drew the eye. Melanie never wore lipstick as far as Lem could tell. A girl was weeping across the aisle from them, her mother haranguing first Marissa and then the child. Marissa was turning the pages of the child's maths book and shaking her head. The mother was saying, 'Do you mean to tell me . . . ?' and the child was blubbing, 'But I was away for that one . . . and that one.' Apart from them, the hall was nearly empty. No one else would come now, it was *Big Brother* in five minutes.

Melanie said, 'I have just marked two hundred and eighty mock Key Stage 3 scripts and only seven students understand the apostrophe. We had an assembly about it, for God's sake. We've had a theatre-in-education company in to teach punctuation. We circle the mistake every time they write it and teach it in groups, in pairs, to the whole class. They do it in Year 4 of primary school. What the hell is the problem?

We've conquered most of the other things in the last five years – paragraphing seems to be understood by the time they are eleven now, capital letters for the beginning of sentences, even basic spelling has been dealt with, not to mention reading – they can all read now when they come to secondary school. But the apostrophe. They just don't get it.'

Melanie had the battered, storm-damaged look of a woman who may have been dazzling once, but had had her beauty consumed too fast by drink or love or a career in teaching. Lem thought how much more attractive Devora's lazy, slow-burning demeanour was even though, naked, he was quite sure that Melanie was rather magnificent. She sprawled upwards whereas Devora spread outwards.

He said, 'Catastrophe theory. That's the only *strophe* I can think of.' He wondered if they were all going to go to The Mitre for a drink. Steve was at the door chatting to the caretaker. The caretaker had his coat on, a fistful of keys in one hand. These Parents' Evenings were playing havoc with his men's rota. The lighting in the hall was chapel-of-rest dim and ranks of stacked grey polypropylene chairs lined the walls. Faded sugar-paper posters advertising last year's cake sales drooped from the walls. It was an unpromising place to come and discuss your child's future. The ones you really wanted to see rarely came anyway, thought Lem. If only he could get Saskia or Jason crying in front of their parents as Marissa had done with her students, things might change for the better in the classroom. Melanie swung her body round to the right and looked at him. 'Really? Who do you teach catastrophe theory to?'

'No one, actually.' Lem laughed soundlessly down at the table he was seated at. 'But I did learn about it once. At university.'

'I can't believe we are having a discussion about the apostrophe,' said Devora.

'We're not. I'm excising it from the curriculum. I don't care any more. Let's just whack one on to every "s" we can see. Catastrophe sounds more like what we should be teaching anyway. Go on, what is it, Lem?'

Lem pulled at his hair and attempted to peer into the marijuana mists of his final year at Lancaster. He saw his single bed, the lava lamp that Fay had given him, the sink and the mirror, but he was looking for the brown-eyed lecturer with the Yorkshire accent. The short one with the fraying navy jumper. He had a Soviet-looking haircut and large ears, but what the hell was his name? He had liked the man and had occasionally felt a faint tremor in those lectures, which he imagined now was probably the thrill of learning.

'Well, it's—'

Lem saw the screen at the front of the lecture theatre. Dynamical Systems Theory. That's what the little guy liked to talk about. There was a diagram on the screen of a ship at sea capsizing and another of prison riots. Melanie folded all her limbs in towards her as if packing away her possessions and said, 'But anyway.'

With a supreme effort, Lem said, 'Sudden shifts in behaviour characterised by small changes in circumstances.'

Melanie spread herself out once more. 'Say that again.'

He repeated the definition and added, 'At least, I think that's what it is.'

'Now that would be worth teaching, don't you think? I mean, they'd be interested in that. It must happen all the time.'

'The cusp catastrophe,' said Lem, concentrating hard and suppressing a sliding sensation of regret that he had not buried himself in his studies while he had the chance, instead of lying prostrate on his duvet for three years. 'Bifurcations. Equilibrium. Stable. Unstable.' He smiled, pleased with himself.

Devora got her mirror out and checked her teeth, rubbing her tongue across the front of them. 'Coming to The Mitre, Melanie?'

'See this piece of paper?' Lem held his appointments sheet in an S-shape.

Melanie nodded.

'Well, put your finger in that first fold and press down a little.'

She did so and Lem let the top of the S spring upwards so that the page flipped back straight.

'You've made what was stable, unstable. Just a small pressure, but enough to destabilise the equilibrium and create a catastrophe.'

Melanie looked impressed, but he was annoyed to see that Devora had missed it. She was twisted round in her seat, signalling to Steve to wait.

'Otherwise known as the straw that broke the camel's back, I suppose,' said Melanie.

'Coming for a drink?' Devora was putting her coat on.

Melanie stood up. Dark circles ringed her eyes. 'I think I need to go home to stabilise my equilibrium actually, Devora.'

Devora nodded and Melanie turned to go. When she was out of earshot Lem asked whether Melanie was married.

'Not married, no. But a long-term partner and two children. Rather a lot to manage with her job.'

'What's he like?'

'He's a she. An MP for somewhere out Bristol way.'

Lem watched Melanie leave and wished she had said yes to a drink. He felt suddenly stuck with Devora like he was stuck with his job. Devora didn't have the answer. But he had a feeling that Melanie might.

The train started and entered the tunnel for the final stretch.

This is the Victoria Line train for Brixton.

This train terminates at Brixton.

The night Lem realised Steve shaved his chest, Steve had come back to Lem's from school to get ready to go out together that evening. It was Steve's birthday and so some serious ribaldry, imbibing of alcohol and general bad behaviour were called for. Lem couldn't get a straight answer out of him about what age he was, but Steve had stood in front of the bathroom mirror at Kinloss Court, a greyish towel tight around his waist, and lathered up his chest before razoring the mat of dark hair. 'I am definitely going to pull tonight, Lem. Got to look my best.'

Steve had begun staying over more often than Lem felt comfortable with, although he could hardly say no to a man who lived in an Audi. It wouldn't be so bad except that he was exhausting. He blurted out sudden jabberings in the night, shouted imprecations and pleas and, when he wasn't doing that, he thrashed around like a landed roach. It had made sense in the end to leave Kinloss Court to Steve and move into Church Path while he sorted out the sale of the place.

As expected, Steve's birthday night out had been ener-vating and pointlessly protracted. They roamed from one bar to the other hunting women to pick up, but with no success. Steve was a little devastated. Even Lem could tell that and the evening ended rather badly with the chairs in the bar being stacked on the table, the lights switched on, the music switched off and Steve staring down at his distended Popeye body and saying, as he leant forwards on the edge of his leather armchair so that Lem could see a thinning patch at the centre of his head, 'Arrrgg.' Lem had brought his legs back sharply under him, not wanting to be spattered with vomit, and then Steve had lifted his head towards Lem, mouth open like the gargoyles on the buttresses at Walthamstow church and said, 'I love you, Lem, you're a—' and then he was sick.

Lem was relieved that Steve hadn't got any sick onto Todd's denim jacket, which Steve had helped himself to once he had moved in, and he made a mental note to ask for it back because Steve could be careless with clothes. They had got a mini-cab back to Kinloss Court, where he had had to heave Steve up the stairs and into the flat and onto the bed. This wasn't so different from the way his evenings with Dawn used to end, he told himself, toppling Steve's comatose form onto the bed and going down the feet end to tug at his trainers. He thought about trying to get the jacket off, but decided that would be an impossible task.

One small corner of the bed was free of the six foot of sprawled torso that was Steve, but very little duvet was available because most of it was underneath him. Lem looked at Steve's senseless face, pale lids sunk back into the sockets, the old-man gape of his mouth. He switched off the light, kicked off his own trainers, unzipped his jeans and went into the bathroom, locking the door behind him. It used to annoy Dawn, the door locking. She said it was weird, but the fact was, Lem could not pee unless he was alone in a locked room. He blamed Mercy Evans.

Coming back into the bedroom, he stood at the end of the bed in his pants, socks and T-shirt and looked around in the gloom for somewhere to lie down. On the back of the door hung his oilskin parka, the one he wore for fishing trips with Dean. He stumbled over trainers and then felt his way back over to the narrow strip of floor between the bed and the window, where he flung the parka out and lay down on it. In the light from the road he could see an old nightie of Dawn's and a porn magazine of Steve's under the bed. He stretched out his hand for the nightie and stuffed it under his head as a pillow. He thought about pulling out the porn magazine too, but those pantomime pouts and panties, teasing tongues and tits depressed him if the truth be told. He never could work out whether it was supposed to matter that the emotion in the pictures was fake. All he knew was that it mattered to him. He turned his face into the fur of his parka hood and his cheek against the cottony fabric of Dawn's nightie. He could smell the anxious scent of one of Dawn's body sprays and the mud of the creeks in Essex. Rolling onto his back, he slipped his arms down the sleeves and lay with his eyes closed, imagining the traffic to be the rush and bluster of the wind. In the rain, Dean's dark hair lay slicked against his skull, black lashes working fast against the drops, gaze steady on the red float in the dancing water.

'Tickle your arse with a feather,' Dean had said, still staring straight ahead.

'You what?' Lem had said.

And Dean had raised his voice, 'I said, typically nasty weather', and then turned his lowered head to look along his shoulder at Lem.

Lem saw the smile in his eyes before it reached his mouth. And when it did, a split second later, they both laughed, drowning out the sound of the rain and the wind. It felt good, laughing like that; made him feel like a man united, not a man apart and too far out to be heard.

13

Pimlico

'I WISH I'D known you when I was eight.'

Breathless from laughter, he had Dawn's arms pinned under his knees and was sitting on her stomach. Her hair was wet from the water-pistol fight and Lem felt the child's spiralling twist of glee when she struggled to knee him in the back. Her head was jammed up against the bathroom door and she was helpless, panting.

'What does Golden Virginia have in common with Pimlico?' He tightened his grip on her wrists. 'Go on, tell me.'

She laughed again and tried to wriggle free from under him.

'Your gun's empty,' she said and brought her knee up hard against his back.

He pointed his pistol at her forehead and pulled the trigger. A dribble of water ran down into her hair. Dropping his own gun, he picked up hers.

'Come on. Guess. Golden Virginia and Pimlico.' He gave her a little squirt on her neck. She shrieked and writhed away from him, turning her head and laughing up against the door.

'Is it something to do with the Freemasons?'

'Wrong.' This time he gave her a prolonged drenching down the front of her jumper. She stopped laughing.

He heard the wheeze start in her chest, which he knew

always made her think of Marvin and how they used to roll down the slope in front of their brand new house in Penarth after her father had cut the grass. She had told him how they would both be wheezing and giggling by the time they stopped rolling, till they saw their mother hurrying towards them, face twisted in anxiety, shouting, 'No, not on the grass, Marvin', and she'd be waving his inhaler at him. Dawn's asthma wasn't as bad as Marvin's, but he would let her have a puff. She said she loved the wet chemical jet at the back of her throat, the instant release of the spreading grip of the chest, but most of all she loved the fact that Marvin helped her before he helped himself.

'Lem, get off. I'm soaked. I don't want to do a quiz.'

Lem climbed off her and went into the bathroom to fetch a towel. He chucked it to her as she sat up and pulled off her jumper. She had no bra on. Every time he saw her breasts like that he felt a rush of tenderness for her.

She rubbed her hair with the towel. 'All you want to talk about is facts, Lem.'

He felt hurt. They'd been having fun, hadn't they?

'I wish I knew you when I was eight,' he said again, watching her breasts judder. She stopped rubbing her hair and he saw her smile.

'Really?'

'I missed you.'

Dawn moved towards him on her knees, flicking her damp hair back off her face. 'That is the nicest thing you've said to me in a long time, Lem.' She put her arms around him, lifted his shirt and kissed the zero of his belly. Tell her you love her, he told himself. Just tell her. He pulled away from her and cleared his throat.

'Dawn.'

'Mm?'

'It's not really Pimlico. It should be Pamlico. That's the name of the Indians who lived in North Virginia when Raleigh landed in the New World.'

'Lem.'

'Mm?'

'You're not telling me anything that I want to know.'

She got to her feet and went into the bathroom. Sitting on the toilet, she kicked her jeans off into a heap on the floor. Lem held the bathroom door open with one foot, one finger digging at his belly button.

'Don't you think it's weird, though? Not that there's a part of London named after a tribe of Indians that the English probably tried to wipe out in the 1580s so they could plant tobacco on their land, but—'

Dawn put her head in her hands. 'You're doing my head in.'

She stood up, pulled on a jumper and began brushing her teeth.

'– but that we don't know what the words mean any longer.'

Dawn spat into the sink and ran the tap. She turned to look at him, wiping her mouth with the towel.

'That doesn't explain why Pimlico is called Pimlico. Why not Raleigh or Virginia?' She stepped over him and went into the lounge where she flopped onto the settee and picked up a magazine. 'Are You Getting Enough?' she read aloud.

Lem leant back against the wall, put the gun in his mouth and pulled the trigger.

'I told Marvin and he was fascinated.'

'Are You Bored with Your Sex Life?' she read.

'He said it explained the feeling of panic he got when he studied a map of the Underground. A Stephen King kind of thing. That just beneath the surface there's a whole history screaming to be let out.'

'Does Your Man Do Intimacy?' She turned another page, licking her finger in the way that he hated. 'That's a laugh.'

'Devora says that if women read those magazines they get depressed.'

'You what?'

'Or was it the other way around?'

'Devora is hardly an expert on women's magazines. Her marriage failed, didn't it?' More page turning and a sigh. 'Let herself go, most likely. She probably could have done with a few magazines for bedroom tips, body toning and what have you.'

Dawn twitched her nose to the left, a facial tic that was becoming more pronounced lately. She was suspicious of Devora, he could tell that. And like all suspicions, it sprang from a seed of truth.

'How old is she?'

'Forty-nine, fifty.' He turned away from her. A fingertip of dislike was making its way up his back.

Satisfied, Dawn shook the magazine and said, 'Ten Top Tips for Toes.' She lifted her feet up off the floor, legs straight. 'I hate my feet. They look dead.'

And she was right. Dawn's feet were not a pretty sight.

'Lem—a!'

'They're lovely little feet,' he said, and knee-walked towards her to gingerly kiss the tuber stumps of her toes.

Devora liked to put her feet up on the opposite chair when they were in the cheese-plant corner so that they both gazed at them while she talked. They were long-toed, straight-boned feet like the ones on classical statues, but with pink painted nails.

'You'd think, wouldn't you, Lem, in a place like Thailand, that the bird life would live up to expectations.' Devora ran her tongue along the front of her teeth and then picked at an out-of-the-way molar with the third fingernail of her right hand. 'Funny really. I suppose I'd expected macaws or birds of paradise or something. But no. Just the incessant cawing of crows.'

She was just at the end of the bit about her trip to Thailand at Christmas with Don, the software consultant from Surrey.

Lem thought of his last holiday with Dawn in Rhodes

nearly a year ago. They had sat among the other couples in the hotel restaurant avoiding the bemused stare of marooned marriages. Isolation was the word that came into Lem's head during those meal times, but that wasn't right really, since the whole point was that they were together and a couple. Yet on that holiday he had felt more alone than he'd ever felt by himself, as though he were disappearing down the wrong end of someone else's viewfinder. He wasn't sure there was a word to describe the loneliness of couples.

'Don't get me wrong,' continued Devora, spreading her toes wide so he could see each metatarsal. 'He was very solicitous and everything. It's just that all he could talk about was his ex-wife. I didn't mind so much at first. Told myself, Give the man some slack, Devora, but after a while . . .' She gave her teeth another wipe with her tongue, 'Well, it just got to me.'

Lem never really knew whether Dawn had been having a thing with Ian at the time of their last holiday a year ago or not. It must have started at around that time because she had been very excited after she first started the new job. Getting dressed in the mornings took even longer than usual and in the evenings he would count the number of times she said the word 'Ian'. 'Ian (1) keeps Semtex in the top drawer of the metal filing cabinet along with the drug samples, although the drugs are in little lockable metal boxes like the one Lisa, that's Ian's (2) PA, uses for petty cash. Anyway, Ian (3) is always joking about the drugs going missing. One time, he took two of the dogs round the back of the warehouses down near the station to find some Semtex that the sergeant had hidden and they never found it. They reckoned a rat had eaten it or something, and him and Ian (4) were joking about what would happen if the rat got hit by a car or jumped and landed too hard, and when I said, "Shut up, Ian (5), that's sick", Ian (6) said, "Don't be stupid, woman, it's harmless without a detonator." Ian's (7) always calling me Woman. Anyway, Laura says possession of Semtex is not illegal, it's not like possessing drugs or something.'

Lem thought that seven mentions of the man's name would suggest that something was going on. Ameena claimed that no one decides to leave a relationship without another one to go to. She said consumption and possession are based upon the premise that if you can, you upgrade. You don't go into Carphone Warehouse with your old mobile phone that has become a bit of an embarrassment and say, Can I have one a little older and less attractive than this one, please? Ameena's cynicism was inexhaustible. It wearied him, and her absolute certainty about just about everything made him feel stupid. The only person who seemed to rattle Ameena was Devora.

Devora shuffled her bottom closer to his as a large man with shaking hands and a brand new briefcase clambered over the back of the seats and dropped heavily into the space next to Devora. All three froze for a moment so that the embarrassment of the new person who has wandered into the wrong space at work floated between them like a bad smell. She turned in closer to Lem and lowered her voice. The new man wiped the perspiration from his brow.

'I should have known really, because although his emails were sexy, as soon as I heard his voice, my heart sank a little. It was higher-pitched than I'd expected and it sounded strangled, remote. But I needed a holiday so I thought, What the hell. My life had slowed to a crawl and throwing caution to the wind seemed to give it a little momentum.' She sipped her tea, made a face and set the cup on the table. 'How on earth do they get it to taste like that? I suppose the water tank is OK in this place, is it? Try yours.'

Lem, his mind filled with choke chains and mud-spattered paws, felt suddenly tearful, but sipped his coffee as directed. Faint memory of bitter desperation was what it tasted like. And there was something else. He took another sip. Now she came to mention it, there was something of the unmaintained water tank about it.

'Pigeon?' he said. 'Could be pigeon. Or squirrel.'

'Your class were appalling this morning, Devora.' Melanie,

looking terrible with colourless skin and dark circles beneath her eyes, swooped towards them and then swerved away towards Mrs Lusher's hot-cross buns and Mars Bars. 'Completely unteachable,' she shouted over her shoulder.

Lem watched her go in her khaki combat trousers and wondered what the actual physics or chemistry was that caused teachers' faces to droop in the way that they did. It was something very sudden. They would all look quite human on the first day of term, youthful, glowing, energised and eager, and then by lunchtime some sort of vampiric leeching of the soul had occurred and they all looked like that. Sapped.

'Hunger,' said Devora to the space where Melanie had been standing. 'The lesson before lunch is a waste of everyone's time.' She raised her voice, but Melanie was browsing the food counter. 'They need food and water at regular intervals. They're developing organisms, remember.'

He finished off his coffee and started on his hot-cross bun. School served hot-cross buns all year round. Devora's tutor group were notorious. They only behaved for her because she told them secrets and gave them sweets at registration. An unhealthy relationship, Ameena called it.

'So anyway,' said Devora, getting back to Thailand, 'I told myself that judging a person by his voice was just unkind. After all, he was going to have to overlook quite a few imperfections of my own. And anyway, he was paying for the holiday.' Lem looked at Devora's chin, and Devora contemplated her marbled thighs and wedged waist. Over the rim of his coffee cup he allowed his eyes to visit her breasts. 'A person can't help the sort of voice they have, can they?'

Dawn's voice was Welsh and was probably what he missed most about her. My bluff buff boyo, she used to call him in the early days. He loved the wry, downbeat song of it, so different from the flattened monotones he'd grown up with. When she was in a good mood she sounded like she was purring. And when she was purring it was just about the sexiest thing he'd ever heard. Dawn's mum on the other hand had a voice that could get on your nerves, stuck as it was in the riff of her own remorse. Not long before Dawn left, he had been woken up by her voice in the bathroom. Dawn had become obsessively attached to her mobile in those last few months, hunched over the tiny bleeping thing while both thumbs danced over the keypads with what looked to Lem like unnatural speed. That particular night she was having one of her late night calls with Laura, and the tiled walls of the bathroom amplified her voice so that he could hear quite clearly through the half-open door.

'Yeah, so I was in the strongroom, right? And I just froze because it had gone all silent in the office. I was sort of like trembling and everything, and then after a while I heard Lisa again on the phone to her mum saying, "Snood? What's a snood?" so I knew it was safe for a while . . .' He lay still and imagined her standing in front of the washbasin watching herself in the mirror. 'So I lifted the bar up and out and rested it against the cabinet till I was sure it wouldn't drop, right? But when I opened the top drawer, quietly as I could, all I could see was plastic sheeting. Yards of it and bubblewrap too, so I thought maybe Ian had put the stuff away somewhere else after all. I thought, God, bloody Lisa'll be off the phone in a minute, though she talks at least three hours a day about the stupid wedding. Then I saw that in the next drawer down there were metal tubes and tins and inside one was the stuff that Ian had showed me on my first day. It looks like a roll of Cheddar cheese.' The big fish with the orange and white stripes moved slowly left to right in the neon glow of the tank, and Lem thought how the fact that fish have no memory means they don't realise they've just been that way a moment ago. 'He took me in there once because I didn't believe they used the real thing to train the dogs and he'd shown me the Semtex and said, "It's got no smell for us, but to a spaniel it stinks" and he'd shoved it under my nose. "A spaniel's nose has one hundred million olfactory cells," he said, and that's when I knew he was going to kiss me because I got that giggly feeling down in my knickers . . .' Lem heard her laugh. There seemed to be fewer of the other fish in the tank these days. Where were the little black ones with the trailing tails? 'Well, in actual fact, I knew he was going to kiss me the very first time I saw him. He had a mean-looking Alsatian on a long leather lead, its tongue lolling and panting like it was ready to eat me up. Ian snapped the lead so that it cracked like a whip and shouted, "Leave!" and the dog cringed and sat down and just looked at him, trying to keep its mouth closed, then Ian unlocked the cabinet and showed me the stuff. "Only military police are allowed in here," he said, and I could smell the beer on his breath, "but they're too busy to get down here much now, so we keep it safe for them, don't we, Jake?" And the dog's tail's going thump-thump and there's saliva dripping on the floor and that was when he first kissed me . . .' More giggles and snorts, '. . . not soft like Lem's first kiss, but the kind of kiss that leaves nothing to the imagination, tongue straight in there, forcing, pushing . . .'

'Those bloody crows, though,' continued Devora, looking sideways at the man with the briefcase who was rummaging inside it. 'There were no long silences or anything. I suppose I have that to be grateful for. We had plenty to tell each other, after all. But. Well, it was rather as though he'd brought his wife along on the holiday with us. I probably found out more about her than I did about him. We'd only been in Thailand for a few hours when I realised I could not possibly envisage joining my life to his and I thought, Oh, God, Devora, you've gone and done it now.'

Lem thought of Fay, arms wrapped tight around Alan's lean torso, cheek against his back as they rode towards their corrugated love shack in Mersea. He knew how that felt, although he hadn't sat on the back of Alan's bike for more than a decade now. Close physical contact, a bit of danger, clinging onto one another for dear life and conversation rendered quite impossible. It was probably the secret of their happy marriage.

'I had to concentrate in the end, you know, just to remain conscious for the duration of his long rambling soliloquies about Janet's favourite holiday destinations, Janet's favourite restaurant or Janet's favourite flowering succulents.'

Lem looked at Devora and wondered what sex with Don had been like.

She dropped her voice. 'And if you're wondering what the sex was like . . .'

Lem feigned surprise and a wish not to pry, leant down and shuffled a few folders in his bag. Why was everything covered in shredded tissue and black ink? Why didn't that man next to Devora just go and sit somewhere else?

'Well, what do you think it was like?' said Devora, picking a bit of tissue off Lem's sleeve. 'The man's depressed. Not going to be fireworks, is it?'

Lem shook his head, nodded, then shook his head again. Did he want to hear about Devora's sex life in Thailand? Yes, he certainly did. And there were four more minutes to go before the next lesson so they could probably fit it in. If only the man next to them would get up and go.

'Excuse me, but do you have any idea where J09 is?' The large man leant forwards and held a trembling timetable towards them.

'That's the other site. Have you got a car?'

'I came on the Tube.'

'Hang on, Lem, grab Tom, he's usually teaching over there.' She twisted round towards a man exiting the staff-room backwards at speed carrying two cardboard boxes. 'Tom!' The boxes disappeared through the doors. 'Quick. Run!' She helped the man to his feet and turned him in the direction of the doors. 'You'll catch him if you hurry', and she gave him a little push that sent him stumbling towards the doors, hugging his still-open briefcase tight against his body.

Devora glanced at the clock and Lem knew that they weren't going to get to the end of Devora's siesta before Period 5.

'Fortunately, the third day we were in Thailand was when I had the massage with the beautiful man from the Punjab and so during siesta times I'd just let my mind wander down the path to the massage hut. I lay on my face and heard him unstop a bottle, heard the drop drip of liquid into his hands and the earthy scent of bergamot and something else, higher-pitched, lime maybe. And then he stood behind my head and began.'

Lem studied her eyes as she looked out of the window, green flecked with brown and lined from all her holidays in the sun.

'I'd turn over after a while and he'd do the front of me. I was so relaxed by then I couldn't care less what he saw. Ever had a really good massage, Lem?'

Lem nodded, remembering bath time as a boy when sometimes Fay would rub oil into his scabbed scraped limbs. There wasn't room for Alan in the cramped, steamy bathroom as well. It was just the two of them.

'God, the heat and slide of palm on skin. Do you know, he moved his hands over every square inch of me? It was like being sculpted back into myself.'

The bell for afternoon lessons tore through the end of Devora's siesta and Lem wondered who it was who thought bells were necessary in a school. What would happen without them? They had timetables and clocks, for God's sake. What was with the bells?

'Speaking of crows, I had a dream about you last night,' she said, ignoring the bell, and he felt the hairs rise along the tops of his arms.

'Did you?' He felt a modest wave of pride wash over him followed by a chill of uncertainty. 'What was I doing?'

'You were sitting at a table in front of a big picture window which overlooked the sea. It was sort of my kitchen window, only bigger, and I said something like, "Oh, look at that", and you looked up and out at the sea, but you missed it. You were too slow.'

'Missed it?'

'Yes, the crow dropping the peacock into the water.'

She was looking softer, older, all of a sudden. A looseness at her jawline and where her neck joined her collarbone. He put his hand out and touched her there leaving a small dent where his finger met flesh. She felt like heated silk.

She brought her fingers up to the place he had touched.

'What? Have I got a —?' and she stroked away a non-existent crumb. 'Anyway, these two crows were flying out to sea and each was carrying a peacock in its claws. I could see the effort in the lift and beat of the crows' wings.'

'Was it a holiday home we were in then?'

He didn't like the idea of those crows, such fearless birds with heavy dark beaks. They didn't hop like most birds, but walked, strolled about the place like they owned it. Several of them lived in the top of the oaks and chestnuts in the churchyard at home.

'This one crow, the left-hand crow, dropped the peacock and it just fell unceremoniously with a small splash into the sea.'

'Dropped it or let it go?'

A PE whistle blew on the asphalt rectangle outside the window. They could hear the teacher exhorting the students to hurry.

'I think it was a letting go. Fell like a stone. A quiet letting go of that stupid gaudy bird. It wasn't an accident.'

The train braked hard, throwing everyone into a prolonged and impossible-to-ignore lean towards their neighbour. He felt unaccountably tired. The thought of the day ahead filled him with dread. If only he'd trained to be a tree surgeon. Tree surgeon would be good.

Lem checked the people sitting opposite him. A man his age in a suit and tie, who looked like he worked in an office somewhere. That would be even worse, Lem told himself. Static hours at a desk with a phone and a keyboard and paper clips. Systems management. Schedules pending. Customer care. It'd kill him. No, there was at least something human about school and it wasn't so terrible all of the time. 'Don't knock it,' Fay had told Dawn. 'At least teaching tries to make a difference, which is more than can be said for—' And then fortunately Alan had arrived at the table with a freshly baked loaf and the rest of Fay's sentence, which was no doubt related to the training of sniffer dogs, never saw the light of day. He knew Fay would have been proud if she could see those rare times when classes seemed capable of tiny calibrations, so that just as he felt driven to despair by the anarchy and futility of it all, a lesson would occur when a kind of ceasefire prevailed and Simultaneous Equations would reveal a world where incomprehension could be wrestled into coherence by the power of thought. In lessons like these, he felt each person in the room acknowledged the others as sentient beings whose differences and histories were a good thing, were in fact the best thing, and for a short moment he would feel proud, content, and anything seemed possible. The thing was those lessons happened maybe once every half term and he wasn't sure this was enough to keep him going any longer. The main problem was that the buggers kept turning up as if truanting had gone out of fashion. There were just too many of them in the room. Ameena had once said that classroom behaviour was all to do with chemistry and physics and she had a formula for the conditions necessary for positive reactions to occur. She called it $8:1@ < 17°$, claiming that at a room temperature of no more than seventeen degrees a group of eight could deal with one psychotic person. Alter that ratio or temperature or lower the oxygen supply, raise the decibel level of ambient noise for example, and the psychosocial molecular structure would fall apart. If he thought about it, he could see that she was right because on the days that he managed a lesson well, like that time last

Wednesday, Jason and Saskia were always absent, leaving the class with just a couple of psychically damaged individuals to cope with. After a lesson like that one, he would feel a wash of warmth and affection for hormoned, defiant, televisioned, indignant, irrepressible, MTV'd youth; a feeling that could sometimes last as far as the Tube station, where he'd sit feeling almost smug at his good fortune in having fallen into a job that was worthwhile, a job that opened doors for him onto worlds that Dawn and Todd would never know.

He doubted that Fay would ever have bothered with the search for a replacement husband that Devora was on. It was Alan who had found her and, while Lem had held out some hope in the early days, it was clear to him before very long that Alan was not going to disappear. That was eighteen years ago. Now, when he lay in bed, very still and very quiet in the two-up, two-down cottage in Church Path, he would close his eyes and pretend that he was eight again. Eight years old and with another ten long years to rest in this safe, familiar place. Of course, he didn't miss Kinloss Court and he didn't miss Dawn either. He had spent some dazed weeks alone in their flat after she'd moved to Brixton, when he'd often found himself lying on the bed looking up at the light fitting. But apart from feeling more hungry than usual, all he had felt was a growing desire to be back in his room at Walthamstow. The first night he had got into his old bed in the peace and warmth of Fay's home, it was as if he'd never left. Obviously, it was only temporary, while he sorted things out at the flat, sold it, and what have you. It was Alan who had taken pity on him. 'You're bound to feel a bit bruised, lad,' was what he'd said. 'Come and stay for a week or two till you find your feet.'

He was all right, really, Alan. When Lem had first moved back in, it was a bit of a crush with all three of them there together, but lately Fay and Alan didn't seem to be there much. They were nearly always away for long weekends or overnight doing up the beach hut on Mersea Island. It wasn't really a beach hut because it was beyond where the holiday homes and beach huts ended, out towards the eastern tip of the island, and it was made of corrugated iron and so was more of a cabin really. On the nights they were away Lem would stretch and wiggle his toes under the familiar duvet of his childhood and tell himself he couldn't understand the appeal of a windswept cabin out in the middle of nowhere when they had this place.

A couple of years after his dad had moved out, Lem told Devora, Alan came round to start Mum's car and stayed. That had always seemed to him rather a lazy way to acquire a home and a wife, but Devora said it was an excellent method and one that enabled Fay to retain the power. 'Home is where the heart is, after all,' she said, 'which is why lots of women end up with the plumber or the carpenter. If you're going to have a man around the place he might as well be useful.' Yes, but how useful is an AA man? he wanted to ask. He wanted to ridicule and belittle Alan the way it was easy for people to ridicule Todd, but he couldn't. Alan fixed things in a way that Todd didn't. When Alan first moved in, his AA truck had impressed Lem. A six-ton vehicle, Alan called it, not a truck, and he'd shown Lem inside. There was room for five passengers in the cabin and shelves of tools lining the walls in the very back. On the afternoons Alan was due, Lem would wait at the end of Vinegar Lane looking out for him. Those early days, Alan would turn his orange hazard lights on when he saw Lem waiting. He'd get a rush of excitement when he saw the truck swing into view and draw up by the kerb. There'd always be a delay between the parking and the door opening and then he'd see the blue drill trousers and steel-capped boots drop down heavily onto the pavement beside him and he'd hear Alan say, 'All right?', then cup his hand on the back of Lem's head while he walked and Lem pedalled down the lane. At the gate to the front garden, Alan would stride away and in through the front door, which would click shut behind him.

One day, he'd looked down at Lem's bike and said, 'Let's get those gears fixed, shall we?' He had fetched a spanner from the truck and Lem had been filled with a thrill of fear and pride and shuffled forwards on his bike, still astride it, to follow him round to the back. Alan had bent down, his head close to Lem's own, smelling of petrol and cigarettes, small blue eyes in his tanned face, a gold stud in one ear. His dark hair had been long in those days and Lem had marvelled at the softness of it when it tickled his face.

'That should do it,' Alan had said, straightening up and looking at him. Lem closed one eye against the sun and looked back. Alan patted the top of his arm and held it there to help him balance. Held it there and said, 'There you go, Son. Get back on then. Brilliant.'

All at once, Lem was aware of her looking at him. Salma. She was leaning forward and up, her head turned towards the window of the zigzagging connecting door. She had seen him and her face lit up in happy surprise. Her eyes met his, she brought one hand up to tuck her scarf tight below her jaw and her mouth broke into a smile. Lem smiled back and before he could stop himself he lifted his right hand and gave a silly little wave, and suddenly he wanted to talk to Salma, to hear about her life, her mother's work, what contact she had with Helena and why. There was no sinister mystery to Salma, he realised now, sitting up straight in his seat and scratching his head with certainty. She had been with her mother at the Drugs Counselling centre in Finsbury Park or she was doing extra maths lessons up there. Maybe Helena was helping her out; Salma must have met her at the International Women's Day assembly. Or maybe Salma's mum was helping Helena out. Lem half got to his feet so he could cross to the interconnecting door, but the train picked up speed and began a helter-skelter plunge towards Vauxhall.

Trains didn't usually plunge, but this one seemed to be doing so, making everyone lean at an angle. Unsure as he was about structural engineering, it felt as though the tunnel was dug at a steep incline although it was hard to tell with no external clues, just the sensation of velocity. He had in the past suspected that, for this section of the journey, the drivers had their foot flat on the floor or their hand hard on the lever or whatever it was that they used to drive the trains. He even felt that many of the drivers were engaged in a deliberate attempt to intimidate their passengers like bus drivers did. But when he'd mentioned this to Dawn one time she'd said, 'It's the Tube, Lem. What do you want it to do, go slow so you can admire the view?' and then she'd breathed in, raised her eyebrows and made him feel a pillock for even mentioning it. 'And anyway, the quicker you get through the tunnel, the better, surely.' He'd been going to say, Yes, but you never take the Tube, so how do you know what I'm talking about?, but she'd already picked up her mobile and started texting so he didn't bother.

She would know what he meant if she was here now, though, doing what felt like a death-defying seventy miles an hour through the dark. Lem watched the other passengers as they displayed small shy signs of apprehension. It was so hard to tell in these days of sudden and violent death whether what one was experiencing was the prelude to that night's big news story. When the G-force of the thundering Tube train caused the commuters to brace a little harder and to clutch their belongings a little closer, it was the moment at which Lem noticed that they all risked fleeting eye contact with those nearby.

His look kept returning to Salma; his chest felt full of warmth and concern for this girl and he knew that if there was one person he would save on this train, it was her.

14

Vauxhall

'Is he dead?'

'Course not.'

'Why doesn't he get up then?'

Lem recognised their voices: Kakeka, Emily and Jason, but when he opened his eyes, all he saw were furred hoods drawn tightly into a circle around reflective goggles. He raised one mitten and gave a weak smile.

'See? He ain't dead. Here, Sir, get up then.' Emily pulled at his arm.

Lem tried to raise his body, but his legs just slid further down the slope, dragging her with him. Every time he moved, a pain shot up his left leg and he had a nauseous vision of the Little Mermaid, pain like daggers when she danced.

'Lem, you all right, mate?'

Steve's voice, breathless, the crunch of snow and boot as he knelt down beside him.

'His foot looks funny, don't it, Sir?'

'It's facing the wrong way.' And then he heard Kakeka crying, so he opened his eyes and lifted his head and said, 'I'm all right.'

'Let's get those skis off him.'

He heard Steve breathing heavily and from down here Steve's face looked tanned and handsome. He felt strong hands release the ski catches gently on the good foot, hesitate and then do the same on the other one. The pain made his head swim.

'Will there be a lot of blood, Sir?'

'Jason, Kakeka, loosen his hood and undo the top of his jacket.'

Their fingers like moths about his face. He opened his eyes and watched them through iced lashes. Kakeka's lips were sore and cracked and the plug of snot in Jason's nose was frozen and fringed with frost.

Steve had both of Lem's skis off and was releasing the clasps of the left boot. Lem screamed, Kakeka clattered away and Emily said, 'We should get a trauma team up here, Sir.'

It started to snow. Random distribution. Pythagoras knew that the spiral is the key. Water down the plughole, DNA, shells, fingerprints, the Milky Way. Why teach about Nigeria's exports when there were so many more important things to teach them. Like all about Pythagoras or the man who discovered zero.

'You're right, Emily.' Steve pulled off his gloves and pulled out his phone. 'I'm going to go up to that slope over there, so's I can get a signal. Come with me, Kakeka. You speak French, don't you?'

Jason and Emily sank down into the snow next to Lem and gazed anxiously after the stumbling figures disappearing into the white. Lem smiled to himself, glad to be relieved of ski duty for the rest of this school trip.

Lawrence had persuaded him to go because they needed an extra man. The trip had been funded by the City Enterprise Olympic Challenge, which was pumping millions into the UK's chronically unfit youth. This was his first and last day of skiing, and snow seemed to be permanently seeping from his bottom. How it had got there was a mystery, but it probably had something to do with the amount of time he had spent scudding along horizontally on his backside instead of gliding upright on his skis. To make matters worse, all the rules of skiing had changed since he had been that time when he was at school. No more bending at the knees. It was now essential to stand up straight the whole time and bend at the ankles when you turned. Nowadays only idiots bent at the knees and anyway all the kids had moved on to snowboarding.

Having spent the first morning like a disabled child dropped into a snowy waste with badly fitting leg callipers which really hurt, he had then spent the afternoon being rammed up the backside by metal chairs, alcoholic lift operators screaming, 'Assis! Assis!' at him, being thrown back onto icy metal, then lurched forward without a safety bar and juddered up the tourist-devastated alpine slopes above rivers of Youth on boards and monoskis, all addicted to the loop of slow, enervating chair-lifted ascent followed by the swooping neck-breaking plunge back down again.

'Want a Haribo?' Jason was pulling at the packet with his gloves and teeth.

Lem nodded, closing his eyes, the sugar coating rough on his tongue, then the sourness following and making him wince. Kakeka was stroking his face with her mitten so that snow crystals scratched his cheek. That was another thing he should tell them about – the design of the snowflake. I mean what was that all about, for God's sake?

'Don't worry, Sir,' said Jason, lying down, the top of his head against the top of Lem's. 'We won't leave you.'

Out on the platform, the mother was rotating on the spot, head strained upwards above the straggle of passengers plodding towards the exit, her eyes rounded in terror, the ragged hole of her mouth shouting the child's name over and over again. The pushchair that she gripped in her whitened fist swivelled round and round on one wheel behind her, its childless seat spilling crusts and sweet wrappers.

Lem got up and went to the doors. He looked up and down the emptying platform and tried to interrupt the woman's manic face with a 'When . . .?' and a 'Where . . .?'

A uniformed guard walked up the platform towards them, looking over her shoulder and fingering her radio as she did so.

'There he is! He's there!' Salma had stepped out of her carriage and was shouting, running to the entrance tunnel on the centre of the platform. Lem turned and could just see the toddler squatting round the corner, studying his shoes. Lem watched Salma approach him, get down to his level, take his hand and bring him onto the platform, where his mother hurried towards them and grabbed the child without a word to Salma. The doors began their warning tremor and hum and he called out, 'Salma! Quick!', then withdrew his head as the doors shut heavily before his face. She turned to look at him, shrugged and smiled. The little boy looked up at her and the mother sank towards him, pulling him to her roughly, shouting something inaudible and shooting Salma a poisonous look. The train moved away and suddenly Salma was gone. Lem sat back in his seat, smiling at the thought of that clever, fearless girl.

'Obviously, I'm as courageous as the next woman . . .'

Devora had smiled up at Lem as he came over to join them round the department fan heater on the first day of the spring term. She was holding forth to the others about why she had finished with Philip in the Alps at New Year, where she'd been on a skiing holiday with him and some friends. Lem watched the way she slipped one hand down inside her blouse and stroked the place where her armpit joined her breast. He drank from his coffee cup without taking his eyes off her.

'Is it me or is it hot in here?' she said, pulling off her cardigan.

Steve raised himself up in his seat and opened his mouth to quip.

'Keep it in your head, Steve, thank you,' she said. 'Well, you have to be brave if you've reached my age and you're still more or less in one piece,' she continued, 'but poised as I was, at the top of a precipitous black run in a white-out, while Hervé, my predictably handsome instructor, bellowed his repeated refrain of "Relax and don't look down!", I had to ask myself why I was doing this. My friends had long since plummeted with joy and abandon down the mogul-ridden, vertical piste and were probably at the bottom rehearsing their tale of derring-do and near-death experiences with which to regale us all later that evening.'

She leant forward to push the fan heater away with one small leather-booted foot. Lem hoped that Philip was lying head first in a snowdrift at the bottom of the mountain, having sustained an inoperable spinal injury that would render him paralysed from the waist down.

' "What is the point?" I yelled at Hervé above the howling. "Why am I putting myself through this when I'm on holiday?" "Just keep the top ski in front!" Hervé bawled back. But real life is enough of a black piste, I thought. I don't want to do this on holiday too, at which point a forty-something on a snowboard appeared out of the blizzard at head-level and sent me hurtling down the mountain.'

When Marissa opened her mouth to speak, Devora ploughed on and Lem saw that she was a bully. In solidarity he turned his body towards Marissa. Steve started up some ruler wanging, holding one end of it on the table edge in front of him and bending the other end right down with his thumb before letting go.

'During one of the many cartwheels that followed, I realised that probably neither Hervé nor Philip, waiting at the bottom, could understand how I felt. They liked doing this because their real lives weren't a bit like a black run, therefore they craved a challenge. And in a sudden snowy epiphany I saw that Philip was a bore. Nice but boring. And I realised there was no point in yoking myself to that. When I finally stopped falling, I was on my back in deep snow and the sun had come out. I was out of the cloud and at the beginning of a beautiful wide green run fringed with pine trees. And then

I realised. This was it. It came to me in a sudden flush—'

'Flash,' corrected Ameena.

'Flush, actually. I realised I didn't have to do this stuff any more. I had nothing left to prove. The menopause had released me. I was free! Free! Good God almighty, free at last!' Devora spun round in her chair with her arms up in the air.

A profound and terrible silence fell on the room. Ameena straightened up in her seat and began refilling the stapler. Steve's ruler wanged right out of his hands and catapulted towards Marissa, who shrieked, looked terrified, then appalled and stroked the flawless skin at her throat. Lem felt his heart race. He wanted very much to look at Devora, but instead he watched the plastic bags flying outside near the top of the sycamore tree. He thought of Dean, he thought of Dawn, he thought of Todd and Fay and Alan.

Devora hesitated a moment, saw that Marissa was waving her finger round her ear and had an expression on her face that suggested she had a story like that one too. Devora seemed compelled to finish. Ameena, Lem noticed, looked hypnotised.

'Surrendering to the truth was to be my New Year's resolution. As Hervé had explained to me, even ski design has had to change because, let's face it, the old sort just didn't work. Now skis are parabolic, he told me, which means kind of wavy and also means you don't need much skill any more, just nerve, to which I replied, "A bit like love then?"

'He whacked some snow off the top of a spruce tree passing beneath our chair lift and said, "Parabolic means you don't have to try so hard. Just relax."

'Lurking around the mid-points of our lives, as we both were, I like to think we shared a small moment up there as the chair lift swung to yet another inexplicable halt halfway up the mountain, dense cloud occluding what I'm sure was a breathtaking view.' Devora smiled, then added, 'Good holidays everyone?'

'YA PUSSY BOY.'

'YOUR MUM'S GOT SAGGY TITS MAN.'

'FUCK YOU! I'M GONNA BATTER YOUR SISTER BAD BWOY.'

'YOUR SISTER LICK SHIT OFF OF MY ARSE MAN.'

'Ah, the children are back and eager to learn,' said Ameena, striding to the door, glad to have a distraction that demanded immediate action. This she could handle, just watch. 'THEO! JOSHUA! Come back here at once.'

There was a pause before two twelve-year-old boys appeared in the doorway, their pale faces colouring up like chameleons.

Ameena bellowed and paced and gestured in outraged disbelief and the boys shrank and cowered and murmured apologies and agreed with her that no, they couldn't think of a good reason for using such foul language, and yes, the whole sorry episode absolutely did absolutely beggar belief, and no, they didn't know what their parents would say if she phoned them now, this minute, and repeated what the entire maths office had just had to listen to. They studied the floor and swayed a bit, she folded her arms like a force shield and then they scuttled off to sit outside the head of year's office. It amazed Lem how much obedience there actually was in a school. The whole place was more than a little strange.

The train came to a stop in the tunnel. Lem looked at his watch. It was 8.41 and registration would be nearly over. He waited for the creep of anxiety, the band of tension across his forehead and the pressure on his lungs, but he felt none of these things. Devora's ski instructor had a point. It was all about relaxing. Let the gravity of the mountain take you. He sat up straight and took a deep breath in and then out. He could hear the harmonica of *Once Upon a Time in the West*. He need never do marking again or risk life and limb on the Tube twice a day while the whole of his life drifted away before his eyes.

His mind was made up. He wasn't going to go to school.

'I had to fix Devora's cracked inlet nozzle,' Steve had told Lem as he joined him and Devora queuing by the photocopier the other day.

Marissa was making thirty-two copies of an entire textbook.

'To do your washing, more like,' Devora said, reddening and bending down to tug at the strap on one shoe.

Steve laughed and said, 'But I had to mend the bloody thing first.'

His stomach began to knot as he watched them both standing side by side while Marissa said, 'Oh, no' again and again.

'I fixed your inlet nozzle and then I did my washing. Fair dos, Devs.'

'Well, I wasn't calling the engineer out again. Cost a fortune last time.' Devora was giggling and Steve was giving Lem a butter-wouldn't-melt-in-my-mouth look.

'I had to do something,' he said to Lem over Devora's head. 'The poor woman had been waiting years for someone to come and fix her plumbing. You can't leave those things too long, you know. Creates all kinds of problems.'

'Oh, no!' said Marissa tapping at the control pad with one long nail. 'How do I . . .?'

Devora held Lem's arm to stop him walking away, but he wasn't going anywhere, he was going to try and help Marissa.

'Seriously, Lem. You wouldn't believe the trouble I've had with that damn machine.'

Lem stepped forward and stood by Marissa. 'Here. Just press this.'

'Oh, no.'

'Have you ever had one of those days,' said Devora, 'where you wait in all day for the washing machine man and, by the way, washing machine companies, along with all delivery and utility organisations, are still unaware that we have had what I believe is laughingly called a Sexual Revolution, and labour under the illusion that each household contains at all times a little woman in a pinny whose *raison d'être* it is to wait. To wait for engineers and delivery men to call. And then when they arrive, to make tea. To make tea and to hover. Hover in hope. So I take the entire day off school, thus getting myself punished for the rest of the week with an avalanche of cover lessons that consume all of my free periods and, when the man finally arrives at five past three, he says, Your pump's gone, and that he'll have to pop out to get the part.'

'Oh, no, it's . . . I think it's . . . it's doing double-sided.' Marissa flapped her hands like flippers.

'Why do they do that? Why do they drive those great big vans when they're not filled with anything they're going to need? It can't be that difficult, can it? I mean how many spare parts does a washing machine have?'

'Oh, no. How do I stop this thing?' Marissa's index finger hovered over the control panel. Lem dithered next to her and said, 'Er.'

'Anyway, he comes back, puts the pump in, a mere seventy-nine pounds, then goes to leave. But I'm not falling for that one, because I wasn't born yesterday, and so I try the washer while holding one foot against the kitchen door so he can't get out and, sure enough, it doesn't work. Well, now he looks narked because he's got a quota to fill—'

'I know the feeling,' said Steve.

'. . . and so then he says, "Looks like it's your motor."'

'Oh, no! Steve, can you . . . How do I . . .?'

'Then, he stops and stares at the machine and says, "I can't do it, cos I'd have to get at the back of it and you've got your drier on top." I give him a withering look and say, "Well, I'll get the drier off for you", which I do because I've done it before and driers are very light.'

'Oh, no! Call Operator. Oh, it says Call Machine Operator. But I've . . .'

Steve wandered over, opened and shut a few doors, twiddled a knob or two and gave it a kick.

'Well, he has the grace to look a little shamefaced and gets down to putting in the new motor. At the end of that, which was one hundred and ninety pounds or the cost of a return flight to Moscow, he says, "Get your husband to level the legs off for you." "What do you mean?" I say. "They're a bit uneven," he says and I think, You bloody well level them off, mate, they were even before you came.'

Steve pulled away the end of the machine, opened its guts, stuck his hand inside and removed a crumpled, inky sheet of paper. He pushed it all together again and hit the Start button.

'Oh, thanks, Steve . . . oh, is that the . . . oh, right, is that the . . . I need to start again now, don't I?'

' "I don't have a husband," I say and, knock me down with a feather, he levels the legs off for me and he doesn't charge me for the labour, which means I only had to pay two hundred and sixty-nine pounds instead of four hundred and thirty.'

'Oh. Oh . . . I'm in a . . . I'm in a bit of a . . . I'm in a muddle with these pages now . . .'

'And then, after he's gone I notice the vent has come out the back of the drier and I can't for the life of me get it back in again, and, while the first wash is going, I notice an ominous little leak on the floor and it occurs to me that we think our lives are running like well-oiled sophisticated machines and we don't have to think about them, but actually they are on the brink of falling apart the whole time because they've been stuck together with masking tape instead of being properly plumbed in.'

They fell quiet and watched Marissa getting her pages in order. The ozone from the machine was getting to them, a collective headache was settling just behind their foreheads. The bell went.

'Doing anything special this weekend, Lem?' asked Steve.

'Fishing,' he said. 'Last time, Dean caught a tench.' Devora and Steve looked at each other. 'A bit like a carp, only bigger.'

'Now I would love that,' said Devora. 'A day by water as far away from London as I can get.'

15

Stockwell

STOCKWELL. 1294. The tree stump by the spring. The tree stump by the stream. The tree stump by the well. There was probably still an underground spring close to where the train sat right now, this moment, in this deep underground tunnel. Stockwell.

'Well . . .'

Todd's car moved as if on water, effortless and silent. That's what money bought you. It sealed off the outside world so you couldn't hear it or feel it. Protection money, thought Lem. He could do with some of that himself. Todd's car sped them along in a corridor of leather and air-con back to London from Todd's childhood home in Nettlebed.

'Well, the thing was . . .'

The dashboard glowed green in the strafing dark of the motorway and Lem shuffled his body deeper into the leather seat and watched the catseyes zipping beneath the bonnet. He liked this, sitting in the dark, belly full of his grandmother's cooking, listening to Todd's faltering voice.

'. . . when I left Walthamstow . . . well, it was because a kind of space had opened up between your mother and me . . .'

Lem eyed the needle of the speedometer as it crept towards 110 mph and remembered the last time Todd had taken him out on his bike. 'Get back on then,' he had said, picking Lem up and hauling him back onto the red bike. They had struggled to get it going again until Todd had propelled him hard, providing both the momentum and the balance by running just behind, out of sight, holding the back of the saddle all the way down the lane towards the tarmac turning circle at the end, Lem's legs rotating in a frantic effort to keep up with the speed of the wheels. The hard surface juddered up through his fists and arms, the sound of his father's rasping breath behind his head. And then he'd sailed in silence for a few suspended moments, the pitted tarmac speeding beneath his tyres and pumping plimsolls until he heard Todd call his name from what sounded like far, far back. 'You're riding on your own, Lem! You're doing it, Lem!' and he had turned his head, wobbling wildly, seen his father a long way back, panicked and crashed in a heap of aluminium bars, spinning spokes and rubber.

Lem sank deeper into the passenger seat of Todd's car and watched the number plates of the cars in front, adding the digits of each plate as it passed. Twenty-six, seventeen, twelve.

'The truth is, looking back, a kind of hole opened up in me . . .'

Tiredness Kills. Take a Break.

'I think that . . . there was an emptiness inside me that became harder and harder to fill.'

Todd leant across and stabbed the eject button on the CD player, pulling out CDs from the compartment beneath and glancing at them while overtaking a fleet of lorries. 'I woke up one morning when you were about . . .' He pushed Moby into the slot and pressed Play. '. . . and I felt this weight like an anvil on my chest. Felt this weight crushing the life out of me and I thought, I can't do this any longer. I cannot survive another forty years of this.'

M25 London. M6 Birmingham. M4. Last Services for 26 miles.

Lem thought about telling Todd that he couldn't remember him not being there, for the first couple of years at least. All he could remember, in retrospect, was the feeling that Fay was slipping from his reach, avoiding him almost.

'Well, I told myself I wasn't leaving you, I was leaving Fay. And I wasn't leaving you alone, because of course you had Fay and she was so capable. I think it was a relief to her, to be honest.' They were eighteen centimetres away from the rear bumper of the Volvo in front. Todd flashed his lights repeatedly with little jerks of his middle finger. The Volvo slipped away into the middle lane and Todd cruised ahead into the open road.

Lem could still taste the steak-and-kidney pie his grandma had prepared for them, moving in slow motion around her kitchen. They had left her watching *EastEnders*, tucked into her high single bed at the end of the sitting room where he and Todd had carried it down that day from the spare bedroom upstairs. She had asked them to leave the curtains open so she could see the night sky.

'No, the anvil moment came after I'd got back from this TV award thing in LA. I was on the terrace of someone's place in Malibu and for the first time I realised that I had made it. I was a TV phenomenon, the *New York Times* said so, and I felt like a king, a god, a bloody astronaut. Anyway, I remember looking up at this celestial display in the sky and thinking that now I could have whatever I wanted. I wasn't going to end up like Grandpa and Grandma . . . bumbling along in an empty relationship, living in the middle of nowhere, waiting for . . . well, you know.'

It had taken Grandpa seventy-five years to die and now Grandma was waiting for her turn. Her world was shrinking. It used to have a husband, a job, a child and an upstairs, but it didn't any more.

'Yes, I had to put a space between myself and all that. It wasn't that I didn't want you, you know that, don't you?' Lem felt Todd's head do a quick flick towards him and was glad that it was too dark to see or be seen. 'It was just that you were very far away and, well, out of sight really. But you were safe, I knew that. Your mother . . .'

He hated it when they did that. Your mother. Your father. Less than strangers now. What did that make him?

Watch Your Distance. Keep Two Chevrons Apart.

'Your mother, well, she copes, you know? That's what she does. But I remember that night, the sky was enormous, totally clear, a bit like tonight, and I thought of Grandpa and how he used to tell me the names of the constellations and how proud he would have been of me if he could have seen me then up on that terrace in Malibu. I'd made it. I wasn't going to have to slog my guts out in a job I hated for fifty years and then be signed off sick with a pension I could barely live on.'

Lem stared ahead at the catseyes and calculated that they passed three every second, which was one hundred and eighty a minute. He checked his watch. They had been driving for about twenty-three minutes, which meant they had passed four thousand, one hundred and forty catseyes.

'And yes, of course there were women. But you know, Lem, it was only sex. I mean, sex is just sex, isn't it? It's no big deal. And the thing is, women can sniff out success like men can sniff out . . . well, you know . . .' Todd's foot slipped off the accelerator and the car slowed suddenly so that a lorry's lights flooded the rear window. 'Fuck,' Todd said and accelerated hard.

'One of these mornings . . .' The Moby CD warbled on.

'Is this a man or a woman singing this bit?' Todd asked. 'It's hard to tell with some of his tracks. Anyway, then later on, that same night, I couldn't sleep and I'd come out onto the terrace again. It was dark, must have been four, five in the morning and the stars were still visible, but when I looked up at the sky I couldn't get my bearings. Between midnight and dawn the whole thing had shifted, everything looked different. Realigned. And it was that in a way that made me leap . . . the doubt. It sounds strange, I know, but it scared me, the uncertainty of everything. I knew then I was going to take a running jump out of my old life and into a new one. It felt brave, like an escape.'

He decelerated and dropped into the middle lane, his eyes on the rear-view mirror. A police car glided by, lights flashing. 'Trouble was,' he laughed soundlessly, 'I took myself with me.'

In Case of Emergency Stay with Your Vehicle. No Hard Shoulder for 3 miles.

Lem looked at Todd's hands on the wheel. They looked like his own. He sneaked a look at what was left of his father's hair and the way it stood up on end at the back, like a child who had just woken from an afternoon nap.

'I can't deny that I regret what happened. Leaving you, I mean. It's not something I would recommend, living without your child. There were even times, you know, when your mother and I . . . a couple of evenings when we almost . . . It sometimes felt like we might have been able to reach across the bloody great crevasse that had opened up between us. Well, I thought so anyway. I think she did too because our eyes met once or twice and hers were warm, not cold, and I think if one of us had just had the courage to touch the other . . .'

Slow-Moving Vehicles Keep Left. Delays Expected. Apologies for Any Inconvenience.

'But, well, it was just too wide and I suppose there just comes a point of no return. Too much pain. Too much sadness. Too much unsaid. And we were too scared. I was very afraid of your mother's anger. Still am is the truth. It was a lot easier to stay away than to try and bridge that gap. You get used to it, you know?'

Central London 24 miles.

Lem switched on the light above his head and started sorting through the CDs. Apart from 'Extreme Ways', which at least had some energy, there was something draining about the regret and longing of all the other tracks. He pressed Eject.

'Oh. Don't you like this?' Todd looked taken aback. 'He was at this awards thing I was at the other night. Did a couple of numbers. Really cool guy as a matter of fact. I could have got you an autographed napkin, if I'd thought.'

In Case of Breakdown Pull into Coned Area.

There were more and more signs these days, thought Lem, but none that told you what you really needed to know. Up ahead a trail of red lights snaked their way towards the horizon.

'Bloody roadworks in this country. It's a major industry. Show me the bloody invoice, that's what I'd like to see.'

He slowed down to a crawl and Lem smiled into the darkness, not wanting the journey to end.

'If you wanted a change, Lem, you know, from Walthamstow, while you sort out the flat or whatever. Well, there's space at my place now. Too much space really. You know, we could . . . I know it's not as cosy as Church Path, but it's a great location . . . you know, *edgy* . . . but comfortable . . . I was going to offer the spare room to your grandmother but, after today, it's obvious there's no way she's going to leave Nettlebed.'

Bach, White Stripes, Ray Charles . . . Lem stacked the CDs on his lap to form a cuboid.

'And Lem, I've never said this before, but . . . I'm really sorry about your name. It seemed like a good idea at the time, you know, special. Which you were. *Are*.'

Lem put in a disc and pressed Play. Alabama 3 exploded into life. Todd looked over at him, threw himself back in his seat and gripped the wheel tight in mock horror. 'What on earth is this?'

'Ironic hillbilly rock.'

'God almighty.'

Lem turned up the volume. 'You used to watch *The Sopranos*, didn't you?'

Todd shouted, 'Lem, take the wheel!' and took his hands off the wheel to play one stroke of air guitar. ' "Woke up this morning . . ." '

Lem laughed. 'That's more like it, Dad.'

The train slowed to a halt and then rocked its way slowly, reluctantly, a little further along the tunnel. Lem looked at his watch. 8.49. The first lesson had started. He was free.

'You could come with.'

It had been just last week and Dean was slicing chops off a rack of ribs in the empty shop. Lem leant against the cool curve of the chill cabinet and watched a fly settle on the tray of mince.

'What, to Belfast?'

Dean arranged the chops on a tray, lining them up between two rows of plastic parsley, then wiped his hands on his smeared apron.

'Belfast, Londonderry, Lisburn.'

The fly flew lazily over to the chops.

'When are you going?'

He wiped down the block and tossed the cloth in the sink. Then he ran the knife under the cold tap. Lem read the backwards faded letters on the glass of the door. O'Farrell and Son.

'Next Friday, I reckon.'

Lem watched the back of Dean's dark head, the freckles down his forearm, the V of his back. He ought to say, Sorry about your dad, he thought, but instead he said, 'You flying Ryanair?'

Dean nodded, dried the blade and turned round to face him, placing the tip of it on the block and spinning it back and forth between his finger and thumb on the handle.

'Only twenty-nine quid.' He looked down at the floor and kicked the sawdust, then straightened the pile of paper bags by the till. 'Nothing keeping me here now.'

'Friday?' His mouth was dry and the word fell clumsily from him. Taking a step towards the block, Lem could smell Dean's skin, a mixture of sweat and beef.

Outside on the road a fleet of construction lorries thundered by and Lem felt the floor tremble. A woman stopped outside the window, turning in to shelter her face from a gust of grit-filled wind. She scanned the display and hurried on.

· 'Loads of work over there.' He had turned away again so that Lem studied the pores and acne scars on the back of his neck. He let his eyes drop to the copper rivets on the back of Dean's jeans, framed by the white triangles of his apron; saw the lift and pull of the central seam.

'And fishing,' Lem said while Dean placed the blade up on the magnetic bar above the sink.

He wanted to shout it, leap over the block and do some stupid Fred Astaire/Frank Sinatra dance called 'Fishing in the Rain' or 'Butcher Boy'. He needed a drink, a cigarette, a new jacket. He wanted Christmas, an orchestra, a long bungee drop down from the top of a very tall building.

Dean turned round slowly, that grin spreading over his face.

'Fishing like you wouldn't believe.'

16

Brixton

OUTSIDE, THE CLOUD had thinned and the sun had broken through, spilling pools of light onto the damp pavement. He thought of the bag of stupid books sitting on the carriage floor. No one would miss those books except perhaps Ameena, but he wasn't going to think of her now, or her wrath and disdain when she discovered that he had abandoned ship. The air smelt of summer – warm rain and traffic fumes. A seagull swooped at a half eaten bagel in the gutter and pigeons huddled on girders beneath the railway bridge. Lem turned left down Electric Avenue past the stalls of fabric, hair clips, phones, losing the traffic and the sirens as he crossed the road, and slipped into the covered market. He followed the smell of coffee and spices that led past the tattoo artist, the halal butcher, the Hindi video shop and the haberdasher's until he came to Latino, the Colombian café that he and Devora sometimes used to escape to. It was weeks since they had been there.

It was Dawn who spotted the bag. It had made her gag, seeing it like that, a mirror image, a kind of joke bag. She was more than nervous anyway; fear made her limbs leaden and the taste of it filled her mouth. She got to her feet, leaving her own bag on the seat, the bile burning bitter in her throat, and she just made it to the open carriage doors in time. With the surprising violence that emotion and peristalsis can produce, she threw up onto the platform opposite the Danger Deep Excavation sign.

She had been sitting in the empty carriage for several minutes before she did anything about it, her mind stupid with the sleeplessness and the crying. She was late for her meeting with Laura because she nearly hadn't gone at all, and in the end it was the thought that she might bump into Lem coming out of the station that had got her out of the flat. She hadn't seen him though and she was sitting on the almost empty train waiting for it to start its northward journey when she saw the bag. It was all getting a bit out of hand these days. She hadn't minded the graffiti raids or the arson attacks. They were a bit of a rush really. Even the death threats were a laugh because they obviously weren't serious, although she had drawn the line at kidnapping the family's toddler. What had really given her second thoughts, though, was the grave-robbing incident. Not that she had been directly involved, but she thought at the time that was going too far. In fact she had made up her mind then to leave the ALF and Ian, but Laura somehow got wind of it and told her to get hold of the Semtex and she just didn't dare say no.

Anyway, she knew they wouldn't miss it at work. Stealing it was exciting, like shoplifting was exciting when she was at school, and somehow it made her feel better about everything. She had gone into the strongroom one afternoon while Ian was in the field out the back with a new spaniel. Once Lisa had got on the phone to her mother in the office where they sat doing the invoices and the orders, Dawn had got up from her desk like she had forgotten something and said, 'Oh, Ian told me to get the thing from the cabinet. The combination's 1957, isn't it?' and Lisa had nodded and waved her away. Nineteen fifty-seven was his year of birth and she had watched him punch it into the security pad a hundred times. She had pushed the buttons, turned the handle and just gone through. She knew she had time as long as she could hear Ian shouting, 'Steady!' and 'Stay!' at the dog and as long as she could hear Lisa on the phone saying, 'But the ivory makes me look washed out' and 'No, I told you, lilies are bad luck.' Even so, her hands were shaking and it made it even harder to be quick. It was like trying to make your hands work when you wake up after lying on an arm and all the feeling's gone. Except there was too much feeling. In her hands, her chest, her bowels and her head. Her underarms had got wet too, and she had lifted one arm and sniffed the composty scent and bit the inside of her cheek. She was going to be reeking the whole day. Not that Ian would notice. She had got the padlock open and put it carefully on the top of the cabinet, then lifted the long security bar up off its metal hoop at the top and bottom. It was heavy and she had let it slip before she had it gripped properly, so that it dropped back with a clang. Then she realised that Lisa's voice had stopped. She froze for a few seconds and heard the wheeze start in her chest. Lately, her asthma had got worse. The dog hairs probably and the damp in Ian's flat.

Dawn held her own bag close and went to the other door, the one without the sick outside it. Maybe she could just tip out the contents and leave them on the corner seat along with the empty coffee cups and *Metro* newspapers. She wanted to loosen the leather drawstring at the top and slip her hand inside. She thought she could feel the wire cutters and the shape of the Semtex through the leather. She had no idea what they had to do with the Semtex and she wasn't sure that Laura did either. Put a match to it maybe, like a firelighter, and toss it over the perimeter fence. God knows. She looked down the platform to where a guard was standing halfway along near the exit.

'Excuse me.' She felt ridiculous, but raised her voice nevertheless. 'Excuse me.'

To her surprise the guard turned round, smiled politely and took a step towards her. London Transport staff had definitely been on a training course since Ken Livingstone became mayor. All the surliness had gone.

'There's this bag in here.'

The guard stepped onto the carriage, her bright blue London Transport cap perched on top of a pile of black and gold braided coils.

Dawn pointed. 'Over there. It's been there a while.'

A man and a woman got on, his hand leaving the nape of her neck as she stepped in front of him.

'Anybody own this bag?'

Blank looks.

The top flap of the bag was not secured. She went over and lifted it with the tip of her radio antennae. Dawn felt her scalp prickle and looked away, thinking of Laura at Euston. Inside at the top of the bag could be seen several maroon exercise books. The guard twisted her mouth uncertainly, looked back at the passengers and down again at the bag. She spoke into her handset.

'We have a security item on the train on Platform 2.'

Her handset crackled a response. She nodded and turned to the handful of passengers.

'Ladies and Gentlemen. This is a security alert. Please leave the station immediately.'

The man and the woman hopped off and Dawn followed them, thinking this might be the answer to her prayers. The Tannoy burst into life. Passengers trickled from the carriages. Uniformed staff were suddenly everywhere, directing them to the exit.

Dawn hung around at the bottom of the escalators reading the Brixton signs and trying to remember what Lem had told her about it. Some old king's special stone, she seemed to remember. That would be Brixi's stone probably, as in, I'm Brixi and this is my stone and don't forget it, and we hadn't. Here it was a thousand years later. Something else, though, too. Most of Lem's name things had more than one little story attached to them. She unwrapped a piece of chewing gum and put it in her mouth to try to take away the taste of vomit. That was it, Brixton had a house of correction, some sort of prison; well, that was still there and then she thought of Marvin in that too-bright place where everyone was slow-moving, and she wanted to tell Lem she didn't think Marvin would ever get out of there. But God she was tired. That was the biggest problem, she just wanted to crawl into the bed at Kinloss Court and sleep for about a year. She could dump her bag somewhere in the station, go to Kinloss Court and wait for him there. He would be pleased to see her, she was sure of that. Some things never changed, thank God. Going back to him might feel like a step backwards, but from where she was standing, a step backwards was a step towards solid ground.

She could hear sirens, and the Tannoy was still telling everyone to leave. Brixton was something else too, she knew because it had creeped her out a bit when he'd told her. Hadn't it been a gallows that had stood on Brixton Hill sometime back then, God knows when? A deterrent to highwaymen between Brixton and Croydon. She almost smiled remembering Lem's soft voice telling her all that crazy stuff. She joined a crowd of people shuffling along towards the escalators, past the busker hurrying to pick up the scattered coins on his guitar case. She saw three armed police officers taking the escalator two steps at a time.

'The bag is packed and ready,' Laura had said.

Dawn thought she might be sick again and waited by the wall for the feeling to pass. She was almost the last to leave and she moved towards the foot of the escalator thinking how she would get outside on the street, lose herself in the traffic and ring Lem, wait for him until he could come out to meet her, but first she had to get rid of the bag. She couldn't dump it here, the place was swarming with police and besides, she looked up at the camera above her, they were all being watched.

Lem checked that Latino was empty and stepped inside, the smell of coffee and cinnamon filling his nose. The owner, a Colombian woman in a bright red T-shirt, was wiping down the Formica tables. She called out good morning to him as he smiled and sat down next to the window. He watched the queue at the butcher's stall opposite. Chickens with their heads still on hung on hooks from their feet.

The first thing Dean had taught him was how to do the chicken breasts, nicking the skin, peeling it back in one and ripping it off the back end. Then, with the long thin knife, you had to sort of stroke the flesh off the bone, and if you kept going from the throat to the other end, the pale pouch of breast would lift off in one. Once he found he could do it, Lem liked the rhythm of the work, piling the breasts up on the wood, then taking them to the window and placing them in the stainless steel tray. He gave each a little squeeze and pat to plump them up as he arranged them in their frame of plastic parsley. Then there was trussing the whole bird, binding its knees to its tail with the white string, which was kept on a steel pole by the wrapping paper. The last thing Dean showed him about the chickens was chopping their heads and feet off with one sharp blow of the short blade, and then gutting them. Two fingers down the thorax and a twist and a pull and Dean could tug out a bunch of organs all in one go. They didn't do the chopping in the shop in case it upset the customers. Decapitation and gutting took place in the back room, where Patrick O'Farrell sat reading the paper or phoning orders. There was something about preparing the meat that Lem found very calming. He liked it best on the days when it was just him and Dean. Lem would work away trussing chickens with his back to the shop while Dean served the occasional customer. Then they'd be standing side by side while Dean diced someone's neck fillet for them, the slender lambs' necks laced with fat. He'd slice them lengthways with one stroke, then turn them at right angles and slice quickly down the double strips.

'This for a casserole?' he'd ask the customer.

'I thought I'd do a curry tonight.'

'Lovely.'

A Latin American newspaper was propped up on the napkin dispenser. Lem put his phone on the table and tugged his wallet out of the top pocket of his jacket. A folded A4 sheet came out with it and dropped to the ground. He picked it up and flattened it out, curious because it didn't look familiar. His eyes skimmed the torrent of words, racing ahead down the page even as he wanted to tell them to stop. It was a printout of an email to Steve.

'. . . the look of you when you want me the feel of your chest against my face the weight of you between my legs . . .'

The coffee machine shrieked.

The other day, during morning meeting, Steve had leant towards him, arms folded, a smile twitching at his mouth, and murmured, 'Devora said something last night that I never thought I'd hear her say', and Lem had watched his Adam's apple jerk up and down beneath the reddened skin of his throat. 'She said: "Oh God, Steve, don't stop—"'

Lem had felt the blood rush to his head and said, 'Have you still got my denim jacket, Steve?'

Carmen, the café owner, was beside him, leaning across with her cloth so that he had to pick up the sheet of paper. He bent it towards him so that she couldn't read it. She wiped down the table and straightened the salt and pepper before returning to the counter.

'. . . the spread of me beneath you the low wet of your voice on my neck . . .'

He looked at the top of the page for the name of the sender, although he didn't have to. He knew who it was from.

'. . . the rub slip and sweat of you the fetch and fall of me the fucking physics of you.'

Carmen's son came out of the kitchen and saw Lem, raised

a hand in greeting and said, 'What can I get you, my friend? Coffee? *Tostones?*'

He looked up, nodded and folded the paper back up, once, twice, three times, four, five and six, so that it was a very small square. He pressed it hard and held it tight between the fingers and thumbs of both hands. Leaning back in his chair, he tried to monitor his reaction, but all he could think of was the computer screen asking, Do you want to empty the trash?

The last time he had seen them both was at the department meeting the afternoon before. Nothing stayed the same, everything changed. Even the GCSE course, which Ameena had announced the government had decided must be rewritten yet again.

'So basically we have to reinvent the course for the third time in six years,' said Devora, making circles in the air with one foot.

Lem tried to remember her face. Had she looked different? He could see the curve of her belly against the green cotton of her skirt.

'So are we going to complain?' asked Steve.

Steve was the one who seemed different, now he came to think of it. His cynicism had slipped. He was suddenly interested in DfES policies. 'I mean, they're just changing the goalposts again. Must be an election coming.'

'No, we're not going to complain,' Ameena had said. 'We are just going to do it. We're going to do whatever they say, however bizarre. We'll teach maths in bloody Egyptian if they tell us to. The plan is that we let the DfES implode in a black hole of their own making.'

'Cunning plan,' Steve said, reaching across Devora for the biscuit tin. 'Everything turns to entropy as you've always told us.'

'Exactly, Steve. The rationale behind this tactic is that eventually the public will notice that education has become a complete Mad Hatter's tea party and that we're all too shafted to care any more.'

'Are you feeling all right, Ameena?' Devora had asked, moving the biscuits towards Steve.

'Yes, I'm feeling terrible. Never felt better,' and she'd pushed her chair back, smiled wider than they had ever seen her smile before and said, 'I'm pregnant. Let's go home early.'

He wedged Devora's words down behind the metal flange of the napkin holder and imagined telling her where he had left it. An image of her stricken face made him retrieve it and let it fall onto the tabletop. It unfolded a little with a weak, short life of its own and then lay still.

Perhaps she had tried to tell him.

'You're all over the place, Lem. Get a grip,' she had said a few weeks ago. 'You've got to be the author of your own story.' She was putting on her jacket to go home. She was in a hurry and she wasn't offering him a lift to the Tube station. 'The trick is to live your life as if you are in control. Make things happen.'

Lem picked up his phone. It was 8.59 and a secret joy crept over him knowing that someone else would be dealing with Year 10 now. Jason would be sniffing outside the office door, Saskia would be yelling out all the obscenities she had heard yelled the night before, Kakeka would be leaning against the radiator reading Dostoevsky, Salma would be waiting patiently for who knows what or apologising politely for being late, and he wasn't going back there. From behind the counter he heard the crackle of oil in a pan, and the slice and chop of plantains.

He held the phone in his hand and looked at it. Scrolling down the Ds in the contacts list, he studied them – Dad, Dawn, Dean, Devora – feeling the shape of each with his tongue against the roof of his mouth. His coffee arrived, dark and frothless, then a plate of crisp *tostones*. He nodded his thanks up at Carmen, who beamed at him and hurried back to the counter. She returned a minute later with a bowl of sugar and a knife and fork.

She wiped the table again and picked up Devora's folded email. 'Is this yours, darling?'

Lem shook his head and she swept it into her other hand along with some crumbs. He spooned three sugars into his cup and hungrily forked a piece of golden *tostone* into his mouth, barely tasting the butter flood before swallowing a gulp of strong, sweet coffee.

Picking up his phone again, he selected a name, and held the phone to his ear, pressing a grain of sugar onto the tip of one finger. The stalls outside glowed green and yellow and orange. He pulled some coins out of his pocket for the bill and laid them on the table. He felt he should hurry now. He wanted to collect his stuff from Walthamstow and be gone before Fay and Alan got back from work.

'Hello?' The voice he loved, warm and curious. Pleased.

Lem gripped the phone closer to his head, tipping his chair forward and rubbing a pattern with one finger into the film of grease on the table. He looked down at the ageing, familiar front of his jacket. The faded denim cuffs were starting to fray. The jacket was just beginning to look good. Lived in.

Carmen caught his eye, then leant across the counter and gave her son a kiss, holding both cheeks in her hands before slapping him round the shoulders with her tea towel.

He felt their eyes on him as he bent close, inwards towards his mobile. He tried not to laugh. He tried not to shout.

'Hello, Dad,' he said. 'It's me, Lem.'

Acknowledgements

For advice on boys, Fibonacci and stringing a sentence together, many thanks to: Sarah Ballard, Faith Broadbent, John Broadbent, Marcus Broadbent, Dick Chapman, James Crowther, Ben Duncan, Poppy Hampson, Tony Jaffa, Max Metcalfe, Lesley Moors, Alison Samuel, Michael Sheldon, Simon Trewin.

Map of Victoria Line: Reproduced with kind permission of Transport for London © Transport for London Registered User No. 05/4457.

BY SABRINA BROADBENT
ALSO AVAILABLE FROM VINTAGE